THE OUTFIT

John Hansen

*Dedication: to my wife Debi for her never-ending patience
and support and invaluable editing of all my books.*

SUMMIT CREEK PRESS

ISBN: 978-0-578-49997-0

CHAPTER ONE

Cyrus Ellsworth reined his horse to a halt causing those that followed him to do the same. His eyes were fixated on a distant ridge. A weak column of smoke, so light and gray that at times it melted into similar colored clouds on the far horizon, was floating just above the tops of the ponderosa pine that covered the front side of the ridge. It was mid-June and well after noon. For Eastern Montana, or for that matter most anywhere, it was miserably hot. It was a circumstance that only added to Ellsworth and the others' suspicion. Ellsworth sighed deeply. "Seems to me its past bean time. Ain't it?"

Jake Lafarge was to Ellsworth's left. He was of medium build with blue eyes and short dark hair that barely protruded from beneath his black Stetson whose crown had been dimpled on three sides so as to form a peak. He was wearing a dark blue cotton shirt with the paper tabs attached to the draw strings of his Bull Durham tobacco sack dangling out of his left breast pocket. He sat on his horse in silence. Like the others he knew what was coming. A pinto horse beneath a clean shaven man named Silas snorted its fatigue. Ellsworth glanced over at him. He was the antithesis of the young man in appearance and behavior and as such

1

was intimidating. His hat was a gray wide brimmed Stetson with a full crown. Sweat that had soaked through over the years and collected dust radiated out from the base of the crown in a jagged haphazard stain that at a glance gave him credibility with working men. He had short black hair and a full beard. His eyes were green with a piercing look about them. In stature, he was of a medium but muscular build. All told, his demeanor caused the young rider to look away. Ellsworth frowned slightly and then turned back to the smoke. He came again but with more irritation in his voice. "Why would a man have need of a fire at this time of day, especially on my range? There's no good reason for it – not on the Rockin' C there's not."

Jake looked at Ellsworth just briefly so as to pay him the respect he was due as his employer and then shifted his attention back to the smoke. But it was to no avail. Ellsworth drew him in. "Jake, you suppose that smoke is the doings of a Granger up to no good?"

Jake shifted slightly in his saddle causing the leather to creak and spit an arc of tobacco juice off the left side of his horse. With the back of his hand he wiped his thick black moustache before turning back to Ellsworth. "I wouldn't bet against it."

Ellsworth snorted and tossed his head to the side as if Jake's agreeing with him meant more than it really did. "The sons-ah-bitches are everywhere. Building their fences. Plowing up good grazin' land. Running sheep. Fencing off water. They're gonna push us out, Jake."

Jake was reluctant to agitate his boss any more than he already was as he could never distance himself from the fact that Cyrus Ellsworth had been good to him. Nine years ago when he was a green seventeen year old kid Ellsworth had hired him, knowing that he didn't know spit about cattle or horses. His education had begun on the way from Texas to Montana with 3,000 longhorns. Ever since then the Rockin' C had been his home. In a way, Cyrus had filled in for the father that had deserted him and his mother in the deep woods of Louisiana. And so his loyalty caused him to come back with, "I reckon they're sure as hell gonna try." But he took it no further than that.

Ellsworth frowned in a deliberate, angry way. "I don't want to go over that ridge as we've already got our plates heaped full, but I can't let it go. You know that don't you Jake?"

Jake did not turn away but instead locked eyes with Ellsworth. "I 'spect I do."

"You're with me then?"

"Well sir, I'm eatin' yer chuck and sleepin' in yer bunk-house when the situation allows so I reckon I'm in arrears to you."

Disappointment registered in Ellsworth's eyes as he viewed Jake almost like a son. "You know what we're likely to find over that ridge and you know what needs to be done. That goes beyond simple room and board. It speaks to what's right and what's not. It'll test a man. Take his measure. I think you know that."

Jake looked away. He spit in a nervous but yet defiant manner. *Damn him. He's lookin' to me to prop up his back-bone, to tell him it's all right.* Nonetheless, he came back. "It's yer call, Cyrus."

For a moment, a long moment, Ellsworth said nothing and then he sighed. "It is, isn't it? My ranch, my call." He paused and then slowly looked over the three men before him as if their faces had become windows to their con-science. They were young, in their twenties, and short on the kind of life experience that would be needed on the far side of the ridge. After a time, he shook his head. And then he began, looking mostly beyond Jake to Silas McKinney, the baby-faced Texan on the pinto. "Well boys, you know what's been going on of late. I suspect our diligence in this particular matter is going to result in more of the same. So, I'm offering up to you right here and now the opportunity to ride the other way. I'll not speak badly of you if you choose to do so but just know I'll expect you to draw your pay and clear your things out of the bunkhouse."

Jake had to concentrate on not letting his thoughts bleed through to his face. *Well shit, Cyrus. What kinda choice is that? These boys ain't range regulators, they're just simple cowpunchers.*

And so they sat there in the silence, save for a mead-owlark's call and the occasional high pitched chatter of ground squirrels nearby. They searched one another's faces wondering who lacked the guts to ride over the ridge or, more importantly, who had the guts to ride away. It was clear the boys were wrestling hard with Ellsworth's ultima-tum but they had no good choice. On it went, seemingly, the smothering solitude of the grass covered hills punctuated with stands of ponderosa pine and brush filled draws. Any other time its beauty was soothing but not today. And then, just like that, Ellsworth demanded they be men. "So what's it gonna be boys?"

The comeback, apparently having jelled, was quick but it was not from Silas as Ellsworth had expected. "I believe I'm gonna take my leave of this situation."

Ellsworth's eyes widened. He nodded. "I guess I mis-judged you, Billy. You being the bronc stomper that you are."

Billy Hawkins looked out from the shadow cast by his black slouch hat. His voice was quivery but determined. "At the end of the day my only stake in this is thirty and found.

Right now I sleep purty good at night and I have no desire to change that."

Ellsworth's expression went to indifference. It was as if Billy Hawkins was a complete stranger that he'd not known for the past three years and that he and his family had not shared Christmas dinner with Billy and the other Rockin' C hands. Billy no longer existed. Ellsworth came back. "All right, Billy. We may not be back for a few days so you can draw your wages from Mrs. Ellsworth." And then Ellsworth looked at Silas. "And you?"

Silas blurted the words out, almost like he'd been poked with a stick. "I'm ridin' with you, Mr. Ellsworth."

"Fine, let's get underway before we lose the day." And with that Ellsworth reined his horse in the direction of the smoke.

Jake caught Billy's eye and nudged his horse toward him. When they were close enough he extended his hand. "If I ever catch you in Miles City I'll stand you to a drink."

Billy shook Jake's hand and was about to banter with him about doing the town up when he noticed Ellsworth had twisted around in his saddle and was staring at them. He came back simply, "I'll be seein' ya, Jake."

They spurred their horses to a gallop and made straight for the smoke. Ellsworth stayed slightly ahead of Jake and Silas who were riding side by side. The heavy rhythmic pounding of their horses' hooves on the sodded ground seemed loud to Jake. *Good thing these poor fools are on the back side ah this ridge or they'd hear us comin'.* But, on they went taking courage in a way from the strength of their horses as they obediently carried them forward so that they might right the wrong being committed beyond the ridge. Finally, they came to the edge of the trees and the land pitched upward. They slowed their horses to a walk and began meandering through the timber, which wasn't real thick, towards the top of the ridge. The openness of the trees allowed the grass and wildflowers to flourish, especially the lupine. It was in full bloom creating a purple carpet that, when disturbed by the horse's passage, caused the bees to swarm up indignant at being displaced. And the Steller's jays and ravens and pine squirrels chimed in as well creating a cacophony of resentment that these men were there. Jake shook his head and looking over at Silas pointed to the trees and sky overhead, not daring to say aloud what he thought.

Silas nodded his head and whispered so low that you had to read his lips, "I know."

They went on staring at the back of Ellsworth and the butt of his Palomino horse. Jake tried to convince himself that he was no more than a conscript and whatever transpired beyond the ridge would be on Ellsworth's shoulders, but there was little solace in it. And then suddenly the Palomino stopped and Ellsworth stepped down, pulling his Winchester from its scabbard as he did. He turned to face Jake and Silas and put his finger to his lips.

Jake's heartbeat quickened. He took a deep breath and let it out slowly, his thick black moustache partially disguising his nervousness. *Well hell, I guess I'm in it now.* He got down from his horse. His legs were weak. He hadn't felt it until just now, the need to relieve himself. He glanced at Ellsworth. There wasn't a shred of reluctance in his face. In a way he envied him and in another way he feared being like that. And then he looked away and stepped off to some snowberry bushes and stood with his back to Ellsworth. He'd just about finished when he sensed Ellsworth was near.

"Jake, you and Silas bring your lariats."

The words sent an instant sick feeling through Jake. An explosion of resentment went off in his mind. For a moment he was tongue tied but then the words escaped. "You reckon we're gonna need 'em?"

Ellsworth frowned. "Maybe not, but a man has got to protect what's his in a way that others know he means business." He paused as Jake turned to face him. "I hope whoever is down there is just frying up some bacon or some such. But if they ain't – well, God help 'em."

Jake regretted saying anything. He was no match for Cyrus Ellsworth. The man was nearly twice his age and owned over 5,000 head of cattle that he ran on several hundred thousand acres of government land between the Powder and Tongue Rivers. He'd been fighting Indians, rustlers and the elements for the past nine years. He'd proven himself as a man and as a survivor. And what did Jake have to show for himself – his horse, bedroll, a few personal items and a spot in the Rockin' C bunkhouse that was his as long as he did what Cyrus Ellsworth asked of him. It was this montage of facts that suddenly flooded his mind and caused him to be gripped almost by a feeling of humiliation. His brain was spinning for the right words when Ellsworth turned sideways to him and paused. "It ain't gonna be an easy thing, but it's time we got underway. We'll go on foot from here."

Without speaking Silas, baby face Silas, walked up with his Lariat and rifle. His presence, in that way ready to do as Ellsworth, their mutual benefactor asked, only added to Jake's chagrin. And so Jake began walking towards his horse saying over his shoulder, "I'll git my rifle an' rope."

They approached the skyline in single file with Ellsworth in the lead followed by Jake and then Silas. They were as stealthy as if they were sneaking up on a skittish bull elk, having crawled the last few yards on their bellies. It seemed even hotter now as grasshoppers snapped away at their approach. Dirt, pine needles and bits of grass had scratched their bellies and some of it even made it down their pants. But their efforts were rewarded. The ponderosa gave way to sagebrush, grass and scattered juniper trees going down the slope to a flat where two men and the source of the smoke were located. The men had constructed a corral of sorts by stringing multiple strands of barbed wire between about a dozen juniper trees. They'd also made a gate out of barbed wire with several skinny posts embedded in it for dancers. There were, by Ellsworth's count, 18 head of cattle, most all of them yearling heifers in the corral. The men were roping the animals one by one, snugging the head close to a tree and then roping the hind legs so as to be able to throw it easily. One of them would then literally run their branding iron from the fire outside of the corral and hand it over the fence to his partner who would then quickly brand the downed animal before the iron cooled. It appeared they were close to being done.

"Those thievin' sons-ah-bitches."

Jake looked over. Even after all that had transpired this morning he was still a little taken aback by the hatred in Ellsworth's words. And in that very instant, his mind's eye raced ahead in time causing a fluttery sick feeling to well up in his throat. He wished he were somewhere else.

Ellsworth came again. "These fools are too brazen for their own good." He sighed. "There's no justification to take another man's property. These boys should have acquainted themselves with honest labor. They could have avoided what's about to come their way."

And then Silas, baby-face Silas, with a peculiar eagerness jumped in. "It's the wages of sin, Mr. Ellsworth. They'll just be collectin' what's due them."

Ellsworth made eye contact with Silas. He was not a religious man but nonetheless, he nodded, "I suppose they are."

It was obvious to Jake as to how they would likely advance on the unsuspecting sinners from where they were, but that was not his call to make. A shallow coulee ran away from their vantage point. It poured out onto the grassy flat below not more than a hundred yards from where the rustlers were at work. Jake had just finished ground truthing the route with his eyes when Ellsworth pointed to the coulee. "Fellas, I believe we can slip into this ravine and make our way undetected down to where those scoundrels are at if we exercise some degree of common sense and stealth. Are we in agreement on that?"

Silas was quick to offer up, "We'd be well advised to continue crawlin' on our bellies 'til we git well down into the coulee, don't ya suppose?"

Before Ellsworth could respond to Silas' suggestion, Jake countered it. "I've got all the scratches and dirt on my belly that I need for today. My thoughts on this matter is we back off this ridge we're on and walk through the trees about two hundred yards to the east and pick up that stringer of juniper that snakes its way into the coulee about halfway down the slope."

As he spoke, Ellsworth and Silas had visually followed Jake's alternate route. Ellsworth came back. "Might take us a little longer but I agree, Jake. Let's be on our way before these scalawags desert their operation. You lead the way."

Jake nodded. "All right Cyrus." He then pushed back in the dirt from their hiding place and got to his feet. It had not been his intent to become their guide but he took comfort in knowing that when they got to where the cattle thieves were, it would be Ellsworth's call as to what happened then.

They moved silently through the ponderosa and then over the ridge and into the juniper. At one point in the juniper trees they dislodged a flock of pinyon jays. Jake froze in place as through the trees he could clearly see that the noisy birds flushing up into the sky had caught the attention of one of the rustlers. The man, heavy set with a gray shirt and a black felt slouch hat paused to watch the birds. For a moment Jake thought they'd been detected, but then the other rustler shouted something and the big guy turned away. With his eyes Jake followed the man back to the corral. It felt strange watching a man so unaware of how precarious his very existence now was. The man was walking, talking, even laughing at one point – all the things a living person takes for granted. The sick feeling came back to Jake. *He ain't got the slightest idy ah what's about to happen to him.* And then Jake's heart jumped in response to Ellsworth working the lever on his Winchester.

"You boys should ready yourselves, as I suspect these fellas are not ignorant of the consequences of their thievery. We've caught'em red-handed and I have little doubt they know it would be futile to try and talk their way out of what's due them."

Jake studied Ellsworth's face as if he were telling him something that he didn't know. The anger that had been there up on the ridge had evolved into a resignation of what needed to be done. It was, Jake thought, akin to having to do something unpleasant like put down a horse that had broken its leg. No one wanted to be the person shooting the horse, but no one questioned the necessity of it. Jake had never had to put down a horse and he hoped that he never would, but he accepted the fact it could happen. This, however, was different. Nonetheless, he chambered a round in his Henry. He sighed. *For thirty and found I may have to kill a man. What in the hell have I gotten myself into*?

Ellsworth looked out from the coulee and then back at Jake and Silas. "Fellas, keep a sharp eye on these rascals as we'll lose our advantage the moment we leave this draw. Be prepared to shoot. Hesitation could earn you a permanent place in this little piece of paradise." And then abruptly he paused. His eyes fell away. Jake's followed. Silas' right hand was shaking. Instantly, it became awkward between them as the nakedness of Silas' fear grew. "Son, take a deep breath. It'll be all right," said Ellsworth in a tone that none of them believed.

Silas nodded in kind of a jerking motion. He then sucked in a big breath, held it for a few seconds like he was a ten year old kid trying to cure the hiccups, and released it. His right hand still shook, but neither Ellsworth nor Jake looked at it.

Ellsworth came again, his voice seemingly having gone back to when he was a Captain in the Union Army. "All right boys let's go. Three abreast, keep your spacing, on the quick step." And then he was up and out of the coulee heading towards the rustlers holding his rifle waist high leveled in their direction. His departure caught Jake and Silas by surprise causing them to have to run to catch up. They'd no sooner done this when the second rustler, a slender middle-aged man with a full beard spotted them. He did not panic but instantly drew his pistol, a .45 caliber Army Colt and began taking aim. Ellsworth noted it and in similar fashion stopped and brought his 45-60 Winchester to his shoulder. Had the rustler not already committed to shooting Silas he could have saved himself, but he chose wrong. There was maybe one or two seconds between the rustler firing and the roar of Ellsworth's hunting rifle and Silas falling to the ground and the rustler being hit dead center in the chest and thrown violently back into the dirt and cow shit.

Jake had his rifle up to his shoulder searching for the other rustler. From the corner of his eye he could see a faint cloud of smoke trailing away from the barrel of Ellsworth's rifle. Beyond him was Silas lying on the ground whimpering in pain.

"Careful of the other one, Jake," shouted Ellsworth. "I think he means to let us walk in and then ambush us."

Jake shouted back, his voice cracking with a flood of adrenaline. "I know Cyrus, but I'm wary of his tricks."

On they went, their senses painfully acute, visually probing every potential hiding spot. To the south of the corral, by about a hundred yards, was a lone cottonwood tree. It provided good shade and was near a seep with a trickle of open water that wandered a short ways before sinking into the ground. It was beneath this tree that the rustlers had tied their horses. Jake noted the horses and called out to Ellsworth, "This fellow gits to those horses over yonder he'll have the advantage with us being afoot."

Ellsworth glanced in the direction of the horses but then quickly brought his eyes back to the corral and the milling cattle. He said loudly, directing his voice towards the corral, "There's a lot of open ground between here and those horses." He paused and laughed on purpose before adding, "I generally don't have any trouble hittin' a runnin' antelope at this range."

Both Jake and Ellsworth came to a stop about twenty paces from the corral. Each had their rifles raised, finger on the trigger and pointing wherever their eyes went. Jake's heart was pounding so hard his chest was hurting. In his mind's eye he kept visualizing a bullet coming from nothingness. It started as a speck and then came straight for his face at an incredible speed such that he could see it as it got bigger and bigger and then everything went dark as it plowed into his left eye. *Where in the hell can he be*? And then the cattle parted almost as if they were the Red Sea and God had commanded it. There at the very back of the corral was a large rock, big enough to hide a man. It was a revelation that came to Jake and Ellsworth at the same time. They exchanged silent looks. Ellsworth gestured he was going around the right side of the corral and for Jake to stay put. It was like they were playing the shell game and they knew under which shell the pea was hidden. Jake kept his rifle trained on the rock as Ellsworth slowly worked his way around to where he could see behind it. It had only been seconds and doubt screamed at Jake's inner being and, once again, he saw the bullet from nowhere smack him in the eye.

"All right Mister, I've got a bead on you so you had best throw down your weapons."

Jake's heart leapt into his throat as he fully expected to see Ellsworth's big rifle bellow smoke and buck upward, but it did not.

From behind the rock came a voice that was the epitome of fear. "Don't shoot, Mister. Please, have some mercy. Don't kill me. I've got a wife and son"

"Well then, you should hurry yourself along and do as I have asked and throw down your guns. Do you take me for a fool? You've already shot one of my men."

"That wasn't me. It was Roy that done that."

"So you say. Regardless, I'm done quibbling with you so throw out your guns right now or I'm pulling the trigger on this thing."

It was as if the rustler finally accepted the fact he had no hand to play, first came his rifle and then his pistol. They landed in the dirt a good ten feet from the rock. "All right Mister, I'm gonna stand up now."

Jake watched as the big man they'd seen while they were hidden in the juniper, got to his feet. He was obviously no longer at ease or carefree. There were tears in his eyes and his voice trembled as he spoke. His steps coming from behind the rock seemed tentative and unsteady. Jake was close to feeling sorry for the guy. *How could a man be so dumb as to not know the chances were good this day might come if he was to steal another man's cows?*

Ellsworth lowered his rifle to waist level but kept it aimed at the rustler. He looked over at his heifers with a fresh leaning T brand on their left side. He scowled and shook his head. "So you and your friend figured to go into the cattle business did ya?"

"I was just helpin' my friend. They was gonna be his cows."

Ellsworth laughed in a sarcastic tone. "You know Mister, I have no respect for a thief but a thief and a liar -" He paused and shook his head before going on, "At least you could own up to your actions and not blame a dead man."

The rustler went silent, realizing that there was probably nothing he could say or do to alter his fate.

Ellsworth came again, less caustic this time. "What's your name?"

The outlaw's demeanor brightened just slightly. "Nate English. I've got a little place about ten miles south of here on Deer Crik."

Ellsworth scoffed. "Well, Mr. English, that's still part of the Rockin' C."

Nate came back quick, perhaps too quick in light of his situation. "The man at the land office in Miles City said it was government ground. Said I was free to file on it, so I did, 320 acres that runs right up the crik bottom."

Anger came to Ellsworth's eyes causing Nate to grimace. "I'll bet you did and now you'll fence it off so my cattle can't get to the water or the graze there." Ellsworth paused and laughed. "At least that's what you could've done before you decided to steal my cattle."

Fear bordering on panic came back to Nate's face. "You aim to hang me, don't you?"

"What would you do if somebody was stealing your livelihood? It's not enough you damned Grangers plow under the grass and fence off the water, but you steal my cattle as well. No sir, by hell I won't tolerate it."

It was clear to Jake that what he had dreaded was about to happen and he would no doubt be required to play a key role. Regret gripped his mind. *Dammit, I shudda rode out with Billy.*

Ellsworth looked across the corral. "Jake, let these animals out. I suspect it's been awhile since they've been to water."

Jake made eye contact with Ellsworth but said nothing before walking towards the wire gate. As the situation was now in hand he took time to eye the rustlers' handiwork. The corral was about 150 feet across. They'd gone to some lengths to construct it. They had run four strands of barbed wire in a big oval going from tree to tree, even limbing some of the trees to make it easier to staple the wire to it. By the time he'd reached the gate his opinion of the rustlers had gelled a little more. *These boys is purty damned sassy. Maybe they're deservin' of what comes to 'em taday.* The gate was about 15 feet wide. Jake opened it and walked into the corral staying to one side. At first, the cattle stood where they were like they were fearful of being tricked. But then, all of a sudden, two of them bolted through the opening causing the rest of them to snort and buck as they made good their escape.

Nate watched the cattle leave. He turned back to Ellsworth. "Well there, you've got your stock back."

Ellsworth laughed. His tone was cold and wicked. "Mr. English, you must take me for a dimwit."

"No sir, I don't. But I think you're a reasonable and fair man."

"In most cases I am. But the truth of the matter is, if we hadn't stumbled onto your smoke today, you and your friend would have made off with 18 head of my cattle. Where's the reason and fairness in that, Mr. English?"

Nate appeared stymied when suddenly his expression became hopeful. "Why hell, here comes yer man. He ain't but nicked."

Ellsworth looked over to see Silas walking through the gate. It appeared he'd been grazed by a bullet high on his left arm. He called out to him. "How are you faring Silas?"

Silas prefaced his words with a slight grimace, done mostly to justify his laying in the dirt until the situation was in hand. "Believe I'll make it, Mr. Ellsworth."

Nate jumped in. "Ya see there. He's fine. My friend here is stone cold dead. You've got yer pound ah flesh."

It went quiet just then as all of the living looked down at the dead man. The back of his head was resting in a fresh green cow flop. He'd been discovered by the flies and even some big red ants. They were quick to take advantage of feeding opportunities like this. They were crawling in and out of his mouth and nostrils and across the surface of his eyes as they were wide open, extra wide in fact, as if he was totally surprised to be dead. Jake was first among them to look away. He felt a little queasy. He didn't understand it as he'd seen dead men before. Maybe it was because their friends weren't standing there making a case to live. His inner voice shouted out. *Maybe I just ain't got the moxie to do this. Dammit, why didn't I go with Billy?*

And then Ellsworth lifted his eyes from the dead man. His expression was absent the angst that clearly resided in Jake and Silas. He no longer pointed his rifle at Nate, instead he held it down at his side. Looking Nate straight in the eyes, he said, "You say you have family on Deer Creek?" His voice was calm and indifferent but his words hinted at compassion.

Nate immediately took hope. "I do, my wife and boy, Henry, he's just nine years old. They need me."

The reaction that Nate had anticipated was anything but as Ellsworth became enraged. "You disgust me, Mr. English. You say that your family needs you yet you risk your continued presence in that role by rustling, a crime whose punishment is commonly accepted as hanging. And now here you are, playing on my conscience to set you free. To do what – steal from me or some other rancher at some point in the future after sufficient time has passed for you to regain your courage or maybe should I say stupidity?"

Nate cried out. "I'll quit the country. I promise I will. You'll never see me again."

Ellsworth remained quiet staring intently at Nate as he internally debated his fate. Nate too went silent, having the common sense to realize there was nothing more he could say that would help him. And then the silence was punctuated by a sudden gust of wind that picked up dust from the corral causing the living to turn their heads and close their eyes. As the wind subsided, Jake looked over at the dead man foolishly thinking that his eyes would be closed, but they were not. A raven, having no respect for the gravity of the situation, began circling and cackling overhead. Meanwhile, the coin toss within Ellsworth's mind continued giving Nate false hope that he was going to live. For a full minute or two it went on, the raven cawing incessantly above them as Ellsworth, who had turned away from Nate, pondered it all. But then, all of a sudden, Ellsworth turned and just spit it out like he had something bad in his mouth. "I can't do it.

17

Letting you go would send the wrong message to others of your kind."

Immediately, Nate dropped to his knees and began to sob. "Please, I'm begging you for the sake of my family."

But it was as if Ellsworth had gone deaf. He used one of the rustlers' own pigging strings to tie Nate's hands behind his back. It became a pathetic ordeal as Nate did not go quietly or with any semblance of bravery. They sat him on his own horse. Ellsworth offered him a chance to make his peace with God or say goodbye to his family. Nate looked down at Ellsworth with hate boiling in his eyes. He got as far as, *You're a vile sonovabitch and I hope you* before Ellsworth slapped the horse's butt and Nate dropped away.

They went over by the water, the three of them, to have a smoke and not watch Nate quiver and jerk and piss his self. When they'd finished their cigarettes and they were certain Nate was dead they went back to him and lowered his body to the ground. His face was still contorted in a ghastly way suggesting maybe he hadn't gotten a good drop. Ironically, they'd used Nate's own rope to hang him. Fortunately for Jake and Silas, most of the actual hanging had been done by Ellsworth. He'd tied Nate's hands and put the rope around his neck and sent the horse out from under him. But Jake had helped put Nate on his horse and he had tied the rope off to the big cottonwood tree. His conscience would not allow him to tell his self that he had no blood on his hands.

Ellsworth had just removed the rope from around Nate's neck and was coiling it up. He appeared thoughtful and then he said, "I'd like for you boys to cover Nate and his friend over in the corral with rocks so varmits can't get to'em. While you're doing that I'll go fetch our horses."

Jake looked at Ellsworth. He hesitated just long enough to let him know that he wanted no part of dealing with the bodies. *The shit I have ta do for thirty and found*. And then he said aloud,

"All right Cyrus, we'll take care of it."

Ellsworth looked past Silas as if he was a juniper tree or some such and stroked Jake's ego. "You're a good hand, Jake." He then turned and began walking towards the ridge top where their horses were tied. He'd gone about a dozen paces when he shouted over his shoulder, "I won't be long."

Silas allowed Ellsworth to take another four or five steps before issuing a venomous whisper, "You can bet yer ass he won't be back before we got these bodies covered up."

Jake looked over at Silas but said nothing. In spite of his distaste for the hanging and now its aftermath, he still respected Ellsworth. Praise coming from him meant something and he was not so stupid as to jeopardize that by aligning himself with Silas. He moved on. "I'll drag that other fella out of the corral and start coverin' him up there if you wanna work on Nate down here."

Silas frowned further embarrassed that Jake wouldn't pitch in with him in a bitch session about Ellsworth. He scoffed. "Sure Jake, I'll git right to it."

Jake ignored Silas' tone and started for the corral. *One of these days that huckleberry's smart aleck ways are gonna git him ah paddlin'*. But then he went on, not more than eight or ten paces when the thought came to him; *Hell, maybe I'm about on par with a faithful dog. You feed him just enough to git by. Work him hard every day and ever once in a while you pat him on the head and tell him he's a good boy.* Jake sighed. *Damned Silas.*

It was less than an hour when Ellsworth returned with the horses. Jake and Silas had just finished covering the bodies and were sitting near the seep having another smoke. Large sweat stains beneath their arms and in the center of their backs gave proof as to the difficulty they had had in finding enough rocks to cover the rustlers. Whether it was the heat, the incessant deer flies, or just their reason for being there, neither said anything as Ellsworth came to a halt near the rivulet of water before them. He stepped down from his horse and allowed it and the others he'd been leading to drink. The horses were thirsty. They made loud sucking, slurping noises as they struggled to take up enough water from the little trickle that was not more than an inch deep. Ellsworth looked over at Jake and Silas sitting on the bank of the shallow gully where the water ran. It was no more than a foot deep and maybe two feet wide. The grass next to it was bright green and cool to the touch but grazed short. Ellsworth cut right to it, apparently having thought about all that had happened. "Jake, I want you to head on down to Deer Creek. Find Nate's place and give his widow him and his friend's horses and guns. Maybe the sale of those things will enable her to leave the country. Go to where she has family."

Even before Ellsworth had finished speaking Jake's inner voice had gone into a rant. *Oh sure, Cyrus. Let me be the one to go to Nate's widow and boy and tell them that we, that you hung him. Hell yeah, let me be the bearer of that news. After all, I'm gittin' thirty and found.* From the corner of his eye, Jake could see a faint smirk on Silas' face. In the process of hanging Nate he'd not laid a hand on him. Jake glared at Silas. *That spineless shit.* And then he found his voice. "I don't know that it's my place to do that, Cyrus."

For an instant, Ellsworth feigned surprise but then he took ownership, "You can put all the blame on me. She's gonna need someone to hate."

Jake sighed. And then he came back flippantly, "Yeah she will, won't she? I reckon she'll have enough for me too."

Ellsworth looked Jake in the eyes. He shook his head and grimaced. "These ain't the first men I've killed. Carving out this ranch and hanging onto it has come at a price. Every night I'm reminded of that." Ellsworth paused and then said in a tired voice, "I just don't need anymore reminders."

CHAPTER TWO

A horse, being a large warm blooded animal, represents to a horse fly or deer fly sustenance that likely boggles their minds. Add the dead men's horses to Jake's and Jake himself and the resulting caravan became an epicurean beacon that seemed to acquire more and more diners as it went along.

Jake's right hand came up with lightning speed and slapped the back of his neck. "Sonovabitch." He left his hand in place as he could feel the dead fly. Carefully, he pinched it between his fingers so it would not go down his shirt and brought it away. For a moment, he examined its crushed body. It had been gorged with blood that was likely his or the horses' that was now spread, along with mangled fly parts, across three of his fingers. He was in the process of wiping the fly and blood off on his pant leg when another fly sought revenge on his cheek causing him to shout out, "Dammit." But, he was defenseless as his left hand held his horse's reins. Jake took in a deep breath and then blew it out in noisy exasperation. He had been underway for almost two hours keeping Pumpkin Creek, which was about a half mile to the west, in sight. By his recollection Deer Creek, which ran into Pumpkin Creek, was the next drainage. It was slow going leading the dead rustlers' horses, but not all together inconvenient as he had used Nate's rope, the same one he'd been hanged with, to fashion a couple of halters and lead ropes.

He tied the lead rope from one horse to the saddle horn of the other horse and the lead rope from that horse he dallied around his saddle horn but did not tie it off. In the event some jackpot occurred along the way and the rustlers' horses spooked, they would not be jerking his horse off its feet. And too, it freed up his right hand for swatting flies.

The country was all chopped up in endless coulees with little willow lined creeks and buttes with ponderosa pine on the north and east facing slopes and knee high grass most everywhere. Until a few years ago the land had not been despoiled by the Granger's plow but now the Northern Pacific Railroad had made it easy to get there. And in their natural desire to pay for all of the track they'd laid, they advertised in glowing terms the agricultural riches that awaited would-be homesteaders in Montana. Thus, the spigot of settlers had been opened with no sign of it closing anytime soon. They came with little respect for the sacrifices made by the trappers and miners and cowboys and soldiers that had preceded them when the Indians occupied all of it. But all of that was in the past, as it was now 1886 and the Indians were on reservations, at least most of the time they were. The Grangers were simply the next iteration of change to this country. Within the self-proclaimed boundaries of the Rockin' C evidence of this occurred far too frequently to suit Cyrus Ellsworth.

Jake was in the bottom of a shallow no-name coulee with a little spit of a creek running down the middle of it when he spotted a reasonably well formed column of blue smoke coming from behind the ridge in front of him. His mind's eye instantly began to replay the images from earlier that day. For a moment, it was as if he was being held captive and forced to stare into the faces of Nate and his friend. But then he shook free of it and said aloud, "That's probably her supper fire." And then he sighed and nudged his horse, a sorrel colored gelding. "C'mon, Rusty. Let's git this over with."

Jake took a mostly zig-zag route climbing the ridge so as to be easier on the horses. At times he had to meander a bit to avoid pine trees or tall bushes but he soon gained the top of the ridge and a good view of Deer Creek and a small homestead that he hoped belonged to the widow of Nate English. It was a bucolic setting. At the center of it was a cabin with a dirt roof and a privy tucked in behind it amongst towering cottonwood trees. A well-worn foot path led to the privy. To the east of these were a corral and a tiny rectangular chicken coop that was perched about four feet off the ground. A short chicken run enclosed in wire mesh extended from the front of the coop. Close to the creek was a good sized garden plot. It had nice straight green rows of one thing and another that caused Jake to speculate on the bounty that would be harvested later in the summer. He was envious. He shook his head and sighed aloud, "Why in the hell would Nate risk losing all of this?"

For a time, Jake sat on his horse and watched the cabin for any signs of life other than the smoke coming from its tin stovepipe. The door stood open suggesting someone was inside. There were, by Jake's count, five chickens scratching for bugs near the cabin and the empty corral next to it. Off to his left, however, at some distance up the creek he could hear the rhythmic clanking of a cow's bell that was intermingled with an occasional dog bark and the high pitched urging of a child, "Go on home, Daisy. You git." But owing to the dense willows and cottonwood trees along the creek, Jake could not see the source of the voices. He turned his attention back to the cabin. Its logs appeared fresh as they had not yet taken on that weathered gray color that other structures in the area had. *Nate probably built this last fall*, said Jake to himself. And then his eyes shifted up and down the creek. *It don't appear he's done much since.* Jake nudged Rusty' sides and started down off the ridge. He more or less allowed him to pick his way through the scattered juniper trees, sage and grass. Had he just been riding looking for Rockin' C cattle it would've been relaxing, dropping down onto this little creek late in the day, knowing that he'd soon be making camp. But that wasn't the case. His heart had picked up the pace and his stomach was churning as he rehearsed in his mind just what he would say to Nate's widow. He considered too if he would confess to his part in Nate's hanging or if he would take Ellsworth up on his offer and put all of the blame on him. It was at this point his kettle of angst boiled over and he said aloud, "Damned Cyrus ought to be here doin' this his own self."

He'd just reached the toe of the slope and was starting across the bottom of the coulee towards the creek and the cabin beyond it when he caught movement through the window to the left of the door. There were actually two windows on this side of the cabin, one on either side of the door. Each had four glass panes about six inches square that were held in place by narrow pieces of wood that had not been painted. The framing of the windows, or for that matter the entire outer cabin, seemed dull and incongruous to the bright yellow and white checked curtains that hung in them. The curtains had been gathered halfway down and tied back against the window frame so as to allow some light inside. But then, as Jake crossed the creek in front of the cabin, it was like he had ridden into an emotional ambush as off to his left a little boy, a Guernsey milk cow, and a black and white Australian Shepard dog suddenly emerged from the cottonwood trees. The dog began to bark causing a small woman with long dark hair to appear in the doorway of the cabin. She was wearing a blue gingham dress with a white apron tied about her slender waist. Her hands had fallen away to the apron, kneading it as if it were dough. There were pink and blue flowers on the apron that, just like the curtains, didn't belong, at least not today they didn't. Jake could see the look on the woman's face quickly change from surprise to fear when her eyes became fixed on Nate's horse. She started to run toward Jake but stopped after a short ways and shouted out, "That's my husband's horse. How did you come by it?" Before Jake could answer, the little boy and his dog came running up. The boy was shouting over his mother's voice to the dog, "Stop Bella, stop."

A wash of nausea swept over Jake as he absorbed the cries of Nate's family. He felt like throwing up. His inner being screamed, *Damned Ellsworth, he needs to be here. That sonovabitch leaves me to do this.*

Panic gripped the woman's face. "Where's Nate?" she demanded. "Why is it you have his horse? And my brother's horse too? What has happened?"

Jake sat on Rusty, unable to speak as the woman's eyes had locked onto his searching for the answers he was afraid to give. Her scrutiny was intense.

And then to Jake's side the little boy cried out over the barking dog, "Mama where's pa and Uncle Roy? How come this man has Trixie and Jiggs?"

The acknowledgement of her husband and brother's fate swept over the woman like a dam bursting. She began to cry and then still looking at Jake she sobbed, "They're dead aren't they?"

Jake nodded. "I'm afraid they are."

26

Instantly, the woman fell to her knees. The little boy and the dog ran to her and they all huddled together on the ground before Jake. The woman and her son cried and held one another as the dog, sensing something was wrong, pranced nervously back and forth probing with its snout and licking the face of one and then the other.

Jake stepped down from his horse. For a moment he considered asking the obvious but decided against it. Leaving them to their grief he walked on to the corral, leading the dead men's horses. As he walked he could not help but hear their sobbing voices behind him as they rose and fell seemingly mystified as to how or why this was happening to them. Jake knew they were sounds that he would never be able to put out of his mind. They'd be right there with Nate begging for his life and the image of his lifeless body hanging from the big cottonwood tree. Mixed in with all of this would be his own inner voice chiding him for not having ridden out with Billy Hawkins.

He had just finished unsaddling the horses and hanging the saddles on the top rail of the corral fence when he saw the woman send the boy and the dog to the cabin. She then turned and looked at him. She stood still for a moment, as if she was reluctant to hear what had happened to her husband and brother. Finally, she gathered up the apron tied to her waist and wiped her eyes and cheeks and the snot that had run from her nose onto her upper lip. She began walking towards Jake, her green bloodshot eyes staring at him through puddles of tears that continued to overflow and trickle down her face. But there was something different about her now. A moment ago when he'd come riding up she'd been caught off guard. But now her grief had given way to anger. She stopped about ten feet short of Jake and placed her hands on her hips. Her voice was surprisingly steady, "So what happened to Nate and Roy?"

Jake came back quick just wanting to get it out there, one way or another to be free of it. "We caught 'em stealin' Rockin' C cattle. Yer brother shot one of our hands so my boss shot him." Jake paused almost like he was giving the woman nasty medicine that had to be taken in small doses, but this only seemed to agitate her.

"And my husband, what about him? Did you shoot him too?"

Jake shook his head. "No Ma'am." And then as the wheels in his mind were spinning trying to decide how best to say the next part, the part she wanted most to know, Ellsworth's words echoed in Jake's mind, *you can blame it on me.* Like a moth to a lantern, Jake went there. "My boss hung him."

At first it appeared Jake's words would stagger the woman. She went silent for five, maybe ten seconds as she no doubt played in her mind the image of her husband hanging from a tree. But then she recovered. "Who is your boss?"

"Cyrus Ellsworth. He owns the Rockin' C."

"So does that make him God?"

Jake kept quiet even though it flashed in his mind that in his world, Ellsworth was pretty close to God. He was the difference between thirty and found and possibly going hungry and being cold.

"Your boss doesn't believe in the law?"

"The law's clear up in Miles City."

The woman scoffed. "So it was just too inconvenient to take Nate to the Sheriff and a judge and jury."

"Ma'am, its purty well understood by most folks that rustlin' cattle is a hangin' offense. Your kin broke that law."

"Law," shrieked the woman. "Your boss can't make a law."

28

"It's the law of the land. Been that way since before they had any real law presence here."

"Well, I intend to take this matter to the *real law*. And you can tell your boss that."

Jake came back. "I don't blame you for being upset but my boss coulda just kept your kin's possessions but he didn't. I've ridden close to ten miles to return these horses and guns and money too." Jake paused and dug in his shirt pocket. "There's close to four dollars here," he said as he pulled out a few bills and coins. "And your husband's pistol," he said as he turned to Nate's saddle on the fence and pulled it from the saddlebag. "This ought to be worth something."

The woman took the gun and its holster from Jake's outstretched hand. She started to say thank you but caught herself. Instead she came at Jake in a bitter tone. "I can't believe this Ellsworth fellow did this alone. Who helped him? You can tell me or the Sheriff because I promise you, he will come."

The uneasy, scared feeling within Jake flared up like kerosene being poured on a fire. He'd never in his life been one to not own up to things that he regretted doing, but this was different. His silence, however, was as telltale as if he'd shouted at her, *Yes Ma'am, I helped my boss hang your husband.*

At first, she began to sob as the realization took hold that she was standing before one of her husband's executioner's. And then she seethed, "What kind of a man are you to just take it upon yourself that another person should die?" She scoffed. "You've come here no doubt to ease your conscience. Well, I'll not give you that satisfaction."

It happened real quick but, truth be told, Jake didn't have the slightest suspicion that she would pull her dead husband's pistol from its holster and cock it. Her hands were shaking as bad as Silas' had been at the corral, but she had a two handed grip on the gun and they were within spitting distance of one another. And too, Jake could see that her finger was inside the trigger guard. As he stood there staring at the opening of the pistol's barrel his earlier fear of a bullet coming from nothingness and striking him in the eye came back to him, except this time it was more real. Just as Nate had been, he was frantic in his search for words that would save his life. But none came to mind, at least not any that would excuse what he had done. And then the pistol roared like a thunderclap that catches a person by surprise. Contrary to his premonition the bullet emerged from the black powder smoke quicker than the blink of an eye, so quick that he could not see it but he felt it as it plowed through the muscle beneath his left arm. It was like he'd been kicked by a horse and spun part way around before falling to the ground. His flow of adrenaline was immense which was good for two reasons. One, it held the burning pain at bay and two it sharpened his reflexes such that he now had his pistol in hand with the hammer back and aimed squarely at the woman's chest. He might have pulled the trigger had she not been crying uncontrollably. Nonetheless, he called out to her. "Drop that six-shooter, Ma'am, or I'll be obliged to shoot you."

The gun shot had given the boy and his dog sufficient justification for the boy to break his promise to stay in the cabin until his mother came for him. He and the dog were now running towards her, the boy alternately crying and shrieking, "Mama, Mama" and the dog barking excitedly. Shortly, the boy reached his mother, who was still holding the gun, and threw his arms around her waist crying hysterically, as was his mother. The dog, on the other hand, came straight at Jake stopping only a few feet from where he lay on the ground. She began growling and snarling in between barks.

Although it was likely inaudible above all of the emotional racket, Jake said aloud, "Oh, for hell sakes." And then he said to himself, *What am I doing here. Here I am on the verge of shootin' a woman or maybe her dog.* He called out again. "Ma'am throw down your gun. And call off yer dog."

For a little while longer it appeared the woman had not heard Jake. He was becoming fearful that if and when the dog allowed him a shot, he would have to take it before she did the same to him. And then abruptly, like she was physically spent, she lowered the pistol to her side and let it fall to the ground. She called out, "Bella, that's enough." The dog stopped barking but stood its ground, offering an occasional low growl. "Come Bella, come." But it seemed to want assurances that it was ok to leave its assumed post. Suddenly, it occurred to Jake that he was holding a cocked pistol on a mother and son and their pet dog. He felt sheepish and lowered his gun whereupon the dog turned and trotted back to where the woman and her son were standing. Jake got to his feet and faced her, the left side of his shirt now soaked with blood.

The woman had composed herself somewhat. Her eyes hinted at being regretful that she had shot Jake but she did not go there. Instead, she said, "My husband and brother deserve a Christian burial. Can you draw me a map of how to get to where they are?"

Jake instantly recalled the looks on the dead men's faces, the blood on Roy's upper torso and the fact Nate smelled of urine, and the flies, and the likelihood they would be bloated and ripe by the time she could get to them. And so he tried to dissuade her from going, at least not now. "Ma'am, we covered 'em real good with rocks. It'd take a purty determined critter ta git to'em."

"Rocks. No, they need to come home, here where we can tend to their graves and visit them. It's all we've got now, thanks to you and your boss."

For a split second Jake considered not saying it but then pain from where she'd shot him pulsed through his left side and he let go of the words. "Ma'am, your kin brought this on themselves."

The woman scowled at Jake. "That doesn't mean you had the right to kill them."

Jake was incredulous and allowed his face to show it. He came back, his words quick and edgy. "Your brother shot one of our hands. He fired first. It was him that caused my boss to shoot 'im."

The woman closed her eyes and shook her head. She whispered, as if she'd been there and saw it happen, "I know. Roy's that way." She paused and then said, like she knew how things had gone, "Nate didn't give you any trouble, did he? That's not how he was."

Jake searched his memory for how Nate had been, cowering behind the big rock, waiting for him and Cyrus to walk up so, Jake supposed, he could shoot them point blank. And then Jake, without thinking, surrendered his advantage. "No, not really."

"And so you hung him anyway."

Jake instantly regretted showing the woman any compassion. He moved on. "If you'll git me paper and pencil I'll draw you that map you wanted."

The woman seemed taken aback that Jake could so easily distance himself from blame and the guilt that went with having killed her husband. She looked at him as if to shame him into saying he was sorry, but Jake had had enough. Finally, she said, "Come to the cabin."

Jake followed Nate's family to their cabin. At the door, the woman stopped and looked at him. "Wait here."

Jake stood back a few feet from the open doorway. There were good smells coming from inside. His senses put it at stew, fresh biscuits and for sure an apple pie that he could see sitting on the table that was directly through the door in the middle of the room. He was fantasizing how it would all taste when the woman returned with a single piece of paper and a pencil. Jake looked at the paper in an awkward way and then to the table, but she was unmoved. He sighed and took a seat on a stump sized piece of firewood that was sitting on end not far from the door. Placing the paper on his thigh he began to draw. He put an X where they were and then ran a line down Deer Creek to Pumpkin Creek and then another line north for what he thought was about ten miles and then another squiggly line off to the east for what he figured was about a mile and put another X. He held the paper for the woman to see and pointed to the second X. "Your kin are right here at Jawbone Springs."

Her face was blank if not fearful. "How will I know when I'm there? This country all looks the same to me."

A grin started to develop on Jake's face but he squashed it before it could be taken for such. "Well Ma'am that'd be the heck of it. The little coulee where Jawbone Springs is located is not especially peculiar in any way that I recall. I guess a person just needs to know the lay of the land."

She shot Jake a dirty look. "You think because I'm a woman I can't find this place."

"Well Ma'am, in this country it don't matter if a person wears a dress or trousers if you ain't real familiar with it you can git turned around purty easy."

Jake could see the woman was perplexed. There was an obvious solution to her problem but she was too proud, too resentful to ask. His inner voice was telling him, *You've done what you was told to do. Just ride out. This can't go anyplace good.* But then from deeper in his mind came the voice of his conscience. *Take her there. Offer it up.* The thought of it, just the thought of it eased a tiny bit the shame he felt for his role in hanging Nate. And so like a thirsty animal with water in sight he went to it, "I'd be willin' Ma'am to show you the way"

A flicker of relief came to the woman's eyes but then as quick as it had come, it was gone. She came back with indifference in her voice. "I believe I can find my way. Nate talked of other homesteaders in the area. If need be, I'll inquire of them."

Jake looked at the woman and shrugged his shoulders. It was apparent to him that he might not ever get beyond her hatred. His voice was tired. "All right then. I'll be camped down the creek ah ways. Probably head back north about sunup if you change yer mind."

The woman seemed to be staring through Jake. She shook her head slightly. "I've no need of you." And then she turned away putting her arm around her son and started towards their cabin.

Jake gathered Rusty' reins and started to reach for his saddle horn with his left hand. Instantly, the pain shot through his left side causing him to drop his arm down. "Oh dam," he seethed as the pain took his breath away. For a few seconds he stood frozen next to Rusty. And then his pride forced him to take the reins in his right hand and lead Rusty past the cabin and the good smells of supper and go on down the creek. It was not lost on him that had things been different, being a weary traveler, he would've been invited to eat.

CHAPTER THREE

It had not been their intent when they set out yesterday morning from the Rockin' C line shack on Beaver Creek to be gone overnight. As a consequence, Jake had only his rain slicker and saddle blanket for a bedroll and two pieces of jerky for supper. But, this was by no means the first time he'd spent the night in the hills without a bedroll or grub. It was, however, the first time that he'd had to do it with a bullet wound. The night had been fitful. He'd been mostly awake for the past couple of hours and, although the sun was still hidden beyond the far end of Deer Creek, there was enough light to saddle a horse. Jake's first attempt at putting the saddle on Rusty ended with it coming back on him and landing on the ground. Like a wounded animal, he'd stiffened up during the night. Even though he'd soaked his shirt in the cold creek water and cleaned the furrow that the Widow English had plowed in his side, it throbbed with pain. He felt weak from the loss of blood and having had so little to eat but he had no choice, he had to make it back to the line shack. He'd just reached down for the saddle when he heard a horse nicker behind him. He turned quickly and looked up the creek. Coming through the cottonwood trees were two riders. For a moment, he watched their approach. It caused him to grimace. *Ah hell, I don't need this.* And then his pride kicked in. He turned back to the saddle lying on the ground and picked it up. He took a deep breath and braced himself for the pain to follow and then lifted the saddle onto Rusty' back. It was all he could do to not cry out. He hoped she was not close enough to see how he truly was as he leaned into Rusty and held on waiting for the wave of weakness and nausea that had come with lifting the saddle to pass.

The horses came to a stop behind him. "I've decided to accept your offer."

Jake pushed away from Rusty. As he did he scoured, as best he could, the look of discomfort from his face before facing the Widow English and her son. He said simply, "That's probably best." He paused and then came back in a tone that was mindful of her contempt for him, "I'm about ready to go." He then turned away and began doing up his cinch.

Silence, save for the singing of the birds, descended upon them. It was mostly bluebirds, chickadees and meadowlarks all intertwined with one another as none respected the other's time to sing. And then Jake could feel it before she spoke to his back, "You don't look well."

He turned halfway around so she could see his face. "That kinda comes with gittin' shot."

She came back quick, her face absent any remorse. "Tell me you wouldn't have done the same thing had you been in my shoes."

Jake smiled slightly and tossed his head. "I reckon I wudda been tempted."

The woman, still stern in her demeanor, "I know you would."

And then, out of the blue, Jake paused and looked the Widow English hard in the eyes. He'd had enough. "Ma'am,

36

I think you've made it purty clear what you think of my moral character. So, since it appears we're gonna be spendin' the day together, I suggest you let that dead horse alone."

The woman appeared angry that Jake had called her on her criticism of him. She was about to come back at him when Jake cut her off. "I'm not of the temperament for it, Ma'am. Either we put it to rest or we go our separate ways."

The woman began to tear up as did her boy. She said defiantly, "Well, are you sorry for what did?"

"Well, hell yeah I'm sorry. I truly am. I didn't want any part of it. But – it's just a lot more complicated than that."

She studied his face and then said in a quiet, somber tone, "I believe you are sorry. It'd be a terrible burden."

Jake frowned in response to what he felt was another guilt ridden arrow that she had flung at him. Nonetheless, he moved on. "My name's Jake LaFarge."

At first, the woman hesitated and then the realization that they were both seemingly without choices and locked in to what they had to do today apparently come to her. "I'm Ellie English and this is my son Henry."

Jake nodded. "It's unfortunate we're not meetin' under better circumstances."

Ellie's eyes were uncertain. "Yes, it is," she said almost stumbling over the words.

Jake went away from her uneasiness to the task at hand. "I see you brought a shovel."

Ellie glanced back at the shovel. She had tied a burlap sack around the head of it so as to prevent it from accidentally cutting Nate's horse and inserted the handle into the center of two wool blankets that she had rolled up and tied on behind her saddle. She came back. "I thought about what you said. It's probably best Nate and Roy stay where they are as I don't have the means to bring them home nor the funds for even a simple pine box."

Jake felt weak at the surge of guilt that came over him. He wanted to offer up that he would go to the Rockin' C's headquarters and get a wagon and team and lumber to build the coffins but it was close to 50 miles there. In his mind's eye he set off on that journey and him having to play on Ellsworth's conscience and ask for these things. And then he would come back cross country where there were no roads and uncover Nate and Roy who, by then, would be bloated to the point they would have burst and in the stench load their maggot ridden bodies into the coffins and drive them back to Deer Creek. He came back, not fully looking her in the eyes lest she see within him, "It's probably for the best."

And so they set out for Jawbone Springs riding single file, each with their own thoughts. They were filled with anticipation, imagining how it would be and none of it was good. For close to an hour and a half there'd not been more than a half dozen words spoken between them. It was a somber procession that talking most likely wouldn't have helped. But then all of a sudden, Jake, who was in the lead, abruptly stopped just as he reached the crest of a small ridge. Since he'd already been spotted he didn't wave Ellie off and allowed her to ride up beside him. "What is it?" she asked.

Jake gestured with an outward head tilt in the direction of Pumpkin Creek. "Indians. Up to no good I suspect."

Fear came to Ellie's face as she followed Jake's eyes to a place down on the creek about 400 yards away. There were five saddle horses and two pack mules. The riders of the horses were all on the ground, some kneeling, some standing, and occasionally one or two of them would carry what was clearly a large portion of a cow to the mules and load it into a pannier. They wore a mix of white man's clothing and buckskin. Several had a feather sticking up from their hat. Since game in the area was scarce and there were more cows just beyond the Indians, Ellie asked the obvious, "Is that one of your cows they're butchering?"

"More 'an likely."

Ellie's voice quivered as she spoke. "What are you going to do?"

Jake continued to stare hard at the Indians who were now looking back at him. They were waving their arms and pointing and talking loudly. Jake shook his head and sighed. "I can't let it go. If I do, there'll be no end to it."

Fear bordering on panic took hold of Ellie's face. "But there are five of them. If they kill you what will become of me and Henry?"

Jake laughed sarcastically. "I suspect it will not be good. But if they succeed in killing me you'd better skedaddle for the nearest Granger's place."

Ellie scowled at Jake. "You can't do this. Where's your sense of responsibility?"

Jake said nothing and turned away. He nudged Rusty' sides and started at a trot towards the Indians. Several of them took up their rifles which had been leaning against either willows or sagebrush. They didn't draw a bead on him but they had their guns pointed in his direction. Jake's heart was pounding hard. He struggled to suppress his fear. He took a deep breath and let it out slowly. *I can't let 'em see that I'm afraid.* And then he brought Rusty to a halt in front of them. He was no expert on Indians but he suspected they were Cheyenne that had come off of their reservation in search of game or plunder. One of them stepped forward. He was a large man and muscular from what Jake could tell. His hands were both bloody but the right one held a knife. He had on a red shirt, buckskin pants, moccasins and a black derby type hat with a single feather protruding from it. His hair was long in a ponytail. Jake placed both of his hands on his saddle horn and looked at the big Indian. "Do you know the white man's talk?"

The Indian nodded. He said clearly. "Yes, I learned it from the missionaries." And then he paused just briefly before laughing. "But I know a little Cheyenne too if you want to talk Indian." He laughed some more as did several of the others.

Jake laughed politely lest he insult them, but before the laugh lines were gone from their faces he came back, "It appears you've killed my boss' cow. He will not be happy."

The big Indian became more serious but not outwardly angry. He pointed to other cows off in the distance. "Your boss has lots of cows. We have none and we are hungry."

Jake countered. "How can that be when the Army gives you cows so long as you stay on the reservation? Maybe that's why you are hungry, you are not on the reservation."

The Indian scoffed. "I do not come and go because the white man has put a line on a map and says that I am no longer welcome beyond it."

"It is what your leaders agreed to."

"They do not speak for me. They don't feed my family. I am not an agency Indian who lives like a dog that begs for scraps."

"Times are different now. If you take up the plow and work the land you could grow your own food. You wouldn't need agency scraps."

The big Indian came back indignantly. "It is not our way to follow behind the horse. Besides, we need meat."

"In the past I have brought cattle to the agency, thousands of them from a place called Texas. Some of those were mother cows. You could raise your own beef. What about those?"

"They are no more and our hunger is still with us."

Jake went silent, allowing the Indian's words to hang in the air between them. He sighed in a subtle way so as to not let on his frustration with them. *I'm swimmin' upstream against a fast current here,* he said to himself. From the corner of his eye he could see the dried blood on the Indian's hands and the knife he still held. It caused an involuntary shiver within him. As a group, they were becoming impatient. Jake came back. "I'm sorry yer still hungry but you can't be killin' other people's cattle. That's just the long and the short of it."

The big Indian smirked. "Your cow ate our grass. It wouldn't be fat like it is if it didn't have our grass."

Jake wanted to scream at him, *it's not your grass,* but he knew better as it would only invite more debate, more talking in circles. It was clear to him that this Indian, right or wrong, viewed things the way they were before the white man had come. Jake, on the other hand, was left with defending the present. No amount of talking was going to change either of their positions. The silence between them had grown to the point that the Indians were now talking to one another in their native tongue. Jake's heart surged. *Oh shit, this ain't good. These boys could be conspirin' ta lift my hair right here in front of me. Thirty and found ain't worth it.* Jake caught the eye of the big Indian. "I'll tell ya what. I'm a reasonable person. Since you boys purty much got this beef done up I'd be willin' ta say you can just take it and be on yer way, but just know that my boss will likely take a dim view of you killin' anymore of his cattle."

The big Indian looked at Jake like his fear was a coat that he had just put on, and it was plain to see for all of the Indians as they were grinning and mumbling to one another in Cheyenne. And then the Indian with the bloody hands waved the knife at Jake and said, "And if we are still hungry and kill another of your boss's cows, will he pile rocks on us like those white men?"

Jake felt like he was the proverbial mouse and the big Indian was the cat, playing with him until he was bored at which point he would end the game. Jake came back, trying to keep his voice steady, "They tried to take a lot of his cows. It made him purty mad."

The Indian smiled in a sinister way. "Well maybe we'll just take them one at a time. That way he won't need to get mad." And then all of the Indians laughed.

Jake thought to tell them that might bring the Army down on them, but then it occurred to him that ten years ago, at about this time, some or all of these men could have been helping to kill Custer and his men. He quickly abandoned that idea. Nonetheless, he wanted to be free of the situation he was in. So he put it out there, like he'd finally worked up the courage to jump off the cliff above the swimming hole. "Fellas, I've said what I come to say. So you can do with it what you think best, but I'm gonna take my leave of you now." Jake reined Rusty around, not waiting for any response that might continue the game of cat and mouse. He started at a walk so as to not show fear. The muscles in his back had become rigid as if they could deflect the bullet that was sure to come. But after about 50 yards, when he still hadn't been shot, he urged Rusty into a trot back toward Elle and Henry. As he neared them he watched their faces as if they were a mirror to what was happening behind him. They appeared relieved he had returned.

"What did they say?" asked Ellie before he had come to a complete stop.

"Kind of what you'd expect them to say, I reckon."

Ellie's look suggested she was not satisfied with Jake's cryptic answer, but she did not press him on it. She came back, "You're going to let them keep the cow?"

Jake snorted. "You wanna take it away from'em?"

"You took back the ones Nate and Roy had."

For an instant, Jake considered explaining to her why Nate's situation was different but then it came to him, *She knows damn good and well why I did what I did.* He said as if he hadn't heard her, "We need to move on 'fore those boys come closer and see that yer a woman in man's clothes."

The blood instantly drained from Ellie's face. She looked down at her brown shirt. It was drab and loose fitting and hid her breasts well. She was wearing Levis that had belonged to Nate. They were too big but she had cut a new notch in her belt and gathered them in. And she had on boots, scuffed and dirty looking. But then it came to her like an apparition that had suddenly been revealed. "Oh no," she said in a fearful tone as her hands shot up to her long black ponytail and the conspicuous yellow bow that she had tied in it. Frantically, she started to lift her hair and stuff it under her black slouch hat.

"Leave it," said Jake. "It's likely too late."

Ellie stopped as if Jake's words had frozen her hands behind her head. In the distance she could see that the Indians, all of them, were looking toward her. The fear that she had been struggling to keep at bay ever since they had come upon the Indians now took hold of her. She let her ponytail and the yellow ribbon around it fall away from her trembling fingers. Her voice quivered. "What do you think their intentions are, Mr. Lafarge?"

Inwardly, Jake smiled to himself at the sudden respect he now commanded. He shook his head. "I don't know Ma'am. They can be unpredictable. They've got a lot of fresh beef so that might satisfy 'em. But we've got three horses for the taking and –"Jake suddenly went quiet, allowing the words he was going to say play out in his mind, *and in days gone by you and the boy would've been a prize to them.*

Panic took hold of Ellie's face as she interpreted the silence. "I know what they do to women."

Jake moved on. "We should go, Ma'am. Ain't no point sittin' here temptin' 'em"

And with that he started out at a slow trot looking back periodically to see if the Cheyenne were following them. As best he could tell they were not, but he supposed he wouldn't be the first white man to think that only to meet his fate on up the trail. They maintained this pace, except for when they crossed a couple of little creeks coming into Pumpkin Creek from side drainages. In about a half hour they came to the mouth of a dry looking coulee that ran off to the east. Jake brought Rusty to a halt. He looked at Ellie and nodded up the coulee. "It's just a few minutes ride from here. You won't have any trouble findin' it."

Ellie's eyes grew big, and then anger started to well up in them until suddenly her bold words of yesterday echoed back to her as humility and fear consumed her. She was still struggling for the right words when Jake came to her rescue.

"I ain't sayin' you couldn't find the place, Ma'am, but I'd be willin' to take ya right to it if you like."

And then Henry, who had said little all morning but had been like a sponge soaking up the fear and tension created by the Indians, blurted out what his mother was slow to say. "We'd like that a lot, Mr. Lafarge. We surely would."

Ellie nodded. "Yes, we would."

What had been a lingering possibility in Jake's mind suddenly became a reality, at least to him it was. He looked at the images playing there on the stage that foretold the future and right off he saw that it would be a tearful scene if he was to abandon them once they got to the rock graves. But in his defense, he was bleeding again and he felt weak. He came back at his conscience, who was sitting in the front row watching all of this unfold, *I won't be worth a dam diggin' in this hard ground.* His conscience, however, was unmoved. *The sight of those Indians has got 'em boogered. You and Ellsworth have left 'em no better off than a couple of orphan buffalo calves with wolves lurking about. You'd be ah sorry shit ta just ride out.* Jake thought to inject his voice with some strength and optimism that would suggest everything was going to be alright, instead he sighed. "Well, I guess we better git to it then."

Jake could see in Ellie's eyes that she had heard him, but when she said nothing in the time one would expect her to respond, he turned away. He looked down at the boy. There was desperation in his eyes, but he was not in control of his fate.

And then it came, "We're grateful for your help, Mr. Lafarge."

As he touched Rusty' sides, Jake hollered over his shoulder. "Not a problem, Ma'am." But it was; he was doing good to just sit in his saddle, let alone deal with Indians and re-burying the dead. Regardless, for thirty and found, he'd had a hand in killing her kin and now his conscience was requiring him to make amends. So far, it had won out.

Jake had not said anything in the event he was wrong, but he'd gotten a bad feeling when the big Indian had mentioned the rock graves. And now, although they were about a hundred yards from them, he could see that the graves had been disturbed. It wasn't because he could see that the rocks had been moved, but rather it was the flock of ravens jousting with several turkey vultures right where the graves were located. He felt the anger well up within him. *Ain't no way those birds could've moved those rocks.* It came to him that in the old days emmigrants and soldiers quite often didn't mark their graves if it was an unsettled area and there were Indians about. But that was before the Indians had been placed on reservations. Jake paused and waited for Ellie to come along side of him. He didn't allow for a discussion, he said simply, "Wait here."

Reluctantly, Jake rode toward the birds. He'd seen their handiwork on lots of dead animals. On a couple of occasions when he was driving cattle up from Texas he'd observed how clean they can pick a man's bones. One of their hands had drowned while pushing cattle across the

Platte River when it was at flood stage. They didn't find him for three days. The vultures, however, had found him not long after he washed up on shore. Jake had no respect for these birds as they were not particular about who or what they ate, just so long as it had meat and blood. He rode on, the smell causing him to gag. In their arrogance, the birds were slow to fly off and then it was more like they had no fear of him as they landed a short distance away. And then Jake caught sight of Nate. His eyes had been pecked out and most of the flesh from his head was gone. And it appeared that coyotes or maybe wolves had lent a hand in ripping most all of his clothes off so as to better get at the meat. The gruesomeness of it coupled with the overpowering stench stopped Jake where he stood. He raised the red bandana that was tied around his neck up over his nose, but it did little to fend off the horrible odor. And then he sensed he was getting sick to his stomach. He turned away from Nate only to somehow lock on to Roy's severed head and its empty eye sockets. It was an image that exceeded his tolerance for morbidity. He turned once more, this time facing back towards Ellie and Henry and dropped to his knees barely jerking the bandana down in time to expel what little he had in his stomach. He retched loudly, moaning as if it was his penance for having helped to subject these men to such a terrible fate. His grief, his regret was made all the worse when he saw that Ellie and Henry were once again crying and holding one another. He remained on his hands and knees, feeling like he was drunk. And then slowly he started to take control of himself. He brought his right hand up and swept away a stringer of spit from his mouth like it was a sticky cobweb, as he did he could see it, the reason for the birds having their way. Roy's feet were bare. Jake went back to the smirk on the big Indian's face. *Those sonsabitches stole their boots. Dug 'em outta the rocks and stole their boots. Those sorry bastards.*

"Mr. Lafarge, are you alright?"

Jake looked up. Ellie and Henry were walking towards him. Instantly, he came up to his knees. He yelled as loud as he could. "Stop. Go back to the horses." Ellie paused momentarily but then on she came, Henry too.

Jake got to his feet and took a step towards her. "Dammit woman, did you not here me? I said go back."

A confused look came to Ellie's face but she stopped and stared at Jake.

Jake called out as if all of this was his fault. "I'm sorry Ma'am. I'm sorry." He began walking towards her and the boy. He knew what had to be done. It was the right thing to do, but he didn't know if he was capable. His mind was like a raging river of thoughts that were being pulled under and then would suddenly bob to the surface. But one of them was akin to a big old cottonwood tree that just wouldn't ever go down. *That damned Ellsworth. He didn't have to do this. Look at the mess he's created, the heartbreak. Sure Jake, you go ahead on and take care of that.* And then he came to them. The smell of their kin had preceded him.

Ellie stepped close to Jake. Through her tears he could see that she had contorted her face into disbelief and anger. Suddenly, she lashed out at him with both of her fists. She pounded his chest as she sobbed, "You bastard. No one deserves this." And then she cried and sobbed unintelligibly as she repeatedly struck Jake until finally her emotions began to ebb and her hands fell away. She was spent, both emotionally and physically. She stood there before him with little Henry leaning into her side and quietly crying. It was like she expected him to right this wrong, to fix it.

Jake had droplets of spittle clinging to his moustache and his breath smelled of vomit. But, he was oblivious to it as he gently touched her shoulder so as to guide her. He said in a somber voice, "Let's go back."

They went to the horses, away from the stench of their kin and to where Jawbone Spring originated. It was the same place that Jake and the others had gone while they waited for Nate to die. There was something soothing, innocent almost, about green grass and a small amount of cold clear water. It represented life, at least to Jake it did.

In Montana, in late June the days are long. Still, by the time Jake was done burying Nate and Roy in more proper graves the sun had perched itself on the very top of the timber covered mountains to the west. It was as if it was serving notice that it was about to move on and the stars and the moon would soon be taking over.

Jake pointed up the slope. "They're just this side of that juniper."

Ellie's eyes followed Jake's outstretched arm to where the ground was disturbed. There were two crosses, side by side, that he had made out of juniper branches. She shifted her eyes back to Jake. His entire upper torso was heavily stained with sweat and dirt and blood from where she'd shot him on his left side. The graves were simple and crude but she said, "They look real nice, Mr. Lafarge."

Jake nodded. "You wanna go on up, maybe say some words over 'em."

"Yes, I'd like that."

It was about a hundred yards up a gentle slope to the graves. The smell of death lingered in the air but it was no longer overwhelming. The vultures and ravens had lost interest and moved on. They had been replaced by decent birds whose songs were pleasant to the ear.

"Nate's on the left," said Jake.

Ellie glanced at him and then went to where she and Henry were standing directly above the crosses leaving Jake by himself at the opposite end of the graves. Henry began to cry more openly. Ellie pulled him close to her waist. "Your pa and Uncle Roy have gone to a better place," she whispered.

It suddenly occurred to Jake that he, of all people, should not be there. He said quietly, "I'll wait for you at the spring."

Ellie looked up. "You're welcome to stay."

"Only if you want me to."

"You're not a religious man?"

"Sundays usually find me on a horse somewhere out in the mountains."

"You believe in the Lord though, don't you"

"Yes, I reckon I do."

"Then stay."

Jake nodded. "Alright Ma'am, I will."

And then Ellie bowed her head, looking straight down at Nate and Roy. She began, "Lord, these men have sinned. I cannot deny that, but I believe in their hearts they were good men temporarily gone astray. Unfortunately, that indiscretion has caused them to now make application for entry into your kingdom. It is Lord, my utmost hope that you will show them mercy. I ask Lord that you show mercy as well on the men who took their lives for they are ignorant in your ways. The fact that one of them is here today, Lord, I believe is ample proof as to his true character. These things Lord, I humbly ask in the name of thy son Jesus Christ. Amen."

"Amen," whispered Jake. He looked up. Ellie and Henry were staring down at the crosses, weeping quietly. He felt awkward being there. It was their kin, their time to grieve. He thought about just slipping away and giving them this time, but he didn't. He was sorry that Nate and Roy were dead, but mostly for selfish reasons. And then he noticed it, the bottom edge of the sun had sunk below the tops of the mountains. *Three hours and it'll be dark. If I leave now I can make it to the line shack while it's light and they can make it home.*

"We'll come again," said Ellie in a reassuring voice.

Henry reached out and touched his father's cross. "When Ma? When will that be?"

"I don't know. Things are different now, we'll have to see."

The tone of Ellie's words took hold of Jake's conscience in a foreboding way. He'd not yet deciphered this feeling when she suddenly made it clear to him. "I'm afraid, Mr. Lafarge. These are wicked times. A widow woman is vulnerable. She is easy prey."

The implication of Ellie's words caused Jake a sense of just having been ambushed. For the past two days he felt as if he was mired down in a black bog and now, when he was about to be free of it, she was poised to shove him back in, but only if he allowed it. Her eyes were expectant, pleading almost, but he did not go there. He said, like he had not grasped the true intent of her words, "These can be dangerous times for man or woman. A person needs to keep a sharp eye out."

Ellie laughed disbelievingly. "To what end, Mr. Lafarge? I've fired a rifle twice in my life."

Jake knew that she was right but, at the same time, where did the obligation to the widow of the man he'd help hang end? And then it was like his conscience had queued up images of the big Indian, his friends, their bloody hands, their defiant laughter and Nate with his bulging eyes hanging at the end of a rope. The images began to play in his mind. At first his extreme fatigue and hunger were fending them off but then Ellie seemed to sense it, and she came back, "I need your help, Mr. Lafarge."

Jake sighed. "I've got a job, Ma'am. They'll be wonderin' where I'm at."

"Please, just escort us home." And then she added, "If we were your family you know that you wouldn't let us travel alone – not with Indians in the area."

Jake laughed. "Well, if we were kin I'd hope that you wouldn't have shot me."

"I'm sorry. It was an impetuous thing to do."

Jake grinned and nodded his head in agreement. "Ain't no doubt about that, at least to my way ah thinkin' there ain't." Their exchange melted a little of the tension in the air and caused Ellie to appear hopeful as Jake went silent for a moment to consider what it might lead to if he was to escort them back to Deer Creek. He could see her playing on his emotions come tomorrow morning. He came back, like it was his last word on the matter, "Come sunup, I'm going back to the Rockin' C."

Ellie looked relieved, but not entirely. "I understand, Mr. Lafarge."

They headed south, the three of them, marking time with the setting of the sun and the lengthening of the shadows. It was getting difficult to see far away due to the poor light, but Jake was certain he'd seen four riders up ahead down by the creek. He pulled up all of a sudden and studied the movement to confirm his belief that they were white men. The man in the lead was riding a gray horse.

"I know that horse," said Ellie. "It belongs to our neighbor."

Jake recalled that a short while ago they'd passed a cabin that was on the other side of Pumpkin Creek. Smoke was coming from the chimney and there was pale light showing in the windows. He'd commented on it at the time, thinking it would be of some comfort to Ellie having neighbors that close. Her response was, *that neighbor would have expectations if he were ever to do anything for me.*

Jake urged Rusty on. He could see that the riders had spotted them and were coming towards them at a faster pace now. It wasn't long before they poured onto the trail in front of Jake, their horses' nostrils pulsating as they noisily drew in the evening air. All of them wore pistols and at least two of them had rifles in forward pointing scabbards. The man on the gray horse was still in the lead. He was middle aged and much older than those who followed him. He was heavy set with short red hair, blue eyes and an unkempt moustache that hid his top lip. His hat was charcoal colored. It had a large wide brim that radiated out from a crown which was round and bulbous looking. There wasn't a hint of a crease or dimple anywhere in it. From Jake's perspective, it complimented the man's size but not in a good way. For a brief moment, the man's horse pranced nervously in front of Rusty before settling itself. The man looked at Jake's disheveled appearance with bewilderment that bordered on disdain and then he locked eyes with Ellie and said quickly, "Is everything alright, Mrs. English? Where's Nate?"

Whether it was verbalizing for the first time to an outsider that Nate was dead or it was the shame she felt for what he and Roy had done, Ellie began to cry. The man sat on his horse staring at her like he was in a bad dream that didn't make sense.

"Nate's dead, so is Roy," said Jake abruptly.

The man, seemingly reluctant to look at Jake, finally did so. "Dead? How is it that came to be?"

A voice in the deeper part of Jake's mind was now shouting out a warning. It had not occurred to him until a few seconds ago that this man, being a Granger and, he suspected, sweet on Ellie if she'd have him, might take it upon himself to finish what she had bungled when she shot him yesterday. His mind was frantically spinning the right words, the right lie to say when Ellie spoke up.

"They were murdered, Mr. McDonald."

Shocked, McDonald cried out. "Murdered, by whom?"

Jake's heart was near exploding. He didn't know if he should look at Ellie or not. *Dammit, I shudda rode north. If these Grangers want revenge, I'm done for.* He felt like his life was grains of sand in an hour glass and it was about to run out, just as soon as Ellie tells McDonald what happened.

And then Ellie cleared her throat as she wiped at the tears on her cheek. She said clearly, almost emphatically, "I don't know."

Jake felt instantaneous elation. He'd been prepared to ride for his life or shoot it out.

Ellie looked toward him before going on, "Mr. Lafarge was kind enough to bring me word of Nate and Roy's demise."

McDonald turned his attention to Jake. "I'd wager it was Indians that killed poor Nate and Roy. That's what has got me and my son's out at this hour. Those thieving red devils stole three of my horses that I was pasturing on the creek by my place. They butchered a beef too. We found the gut pile not far from here, but that's of no concern to me. It'll just be one less cow that gets in my grain field." And then McDonald and his boys laughed even though it was fairly apparent that Jake was a cow hand and they might be insulting him.

Jake eyed the four of them. *What sons ah bucks you are*, he said to himself. And then he said to McDonald in a firm tone lest he start unnecessary trouble with the Cheyenne. "I'm confident Sir, that Indians had no hand in killin' these poor fellows."

"How can you be so sure?

"" They wasn't scalped."

McDonald nodded. "Oh yes, I hadn't thought about that." He shook his head. "Despicable practice that is." But then in the next instant his eyes fell upon Jake's bloody shirt and the bullet hole, which fortunately had torn and no longer resembled its original shape. "What happened to you?"

From the corner of his eye he could see the apprehension in Ellie's face. It wasn't, he suspected, that she feared what McDonald would think of her for shooting a man who'd had a hand in hanging her husband as much as they'd lied to the man which would likely insult him if he ever found out. Jake came back, the words rolling of his tongue like warm honey, "I stumbled and fell on a downed cottonwood. There was a broke off branch that laid my side open purty good."

McDonald grimaced and tossed his head to the side. "Well, that's a helluva note."

"Yes sir, it is."

And then Ellie interrupted McDonald's attempt to satiate his curiosity, lest he trip them up in a lie. She said, "I appreciate your concern, Mr. McDonald, but we have just returned from burying Nate and Roy and we are exhausted. We are in need of food and rest, especially Mr. Lafarge."

"I understand Ma'am." But then in the next instant Mc-Donald shot Jake a look of indifference and probed, "Where do you hail from, Mr. Lafarge?"

Jake sighed. *This sonovabuck is bullin' over Ellie and he thinks I got eyes for her.* Jake came back abruptly. "The Rockin' C."

It was like McDonald and his boys had been prodded with a hot poker. Their faces took on an unfriendly, hostile look. Old man McDonald came back sharply. "You're the man I need to talk to."

"Why's that?"

"Your' damned cows are destroying my crops."

"You need to take that up with my boss. I'm just a hired hand."

McDonald scoffed. "How about you do that for me? You tell your boss the next time his cattle knock down my fence and get in my grain that me and my boys are going to be eating beef. Maybe quite a bit of it."

Had he not been tired, hungry and in pain Jake might have chosen his words more carefully, but that was not the case. He came back with an edge to his voice. "There could be hell to pay if a man was to do something like that."

McDonald became enraged and then he laughed in a sinister way. "You sir are lucky that we are in the presence of a lady. Had that not been the case me and my boys would have changed your opinion on this matter."

And then, even though his voice of common sense was screaming at him, the fact that he was exhausted and hurting took over. He purposely looked at Ellie, as if he was on better terms with her than he was, and then turned to McDonald, "Well, I reckon it's my good fortune that, *Ellie,* is here. But maybe we'll meet another day when *Ellie's* not with us and we can discuss this, assuming that you got yer boys with you."

McDonald exploded. "Why you insolent sonovabitch –"

Ellie cried out. "Mr. McDonald, please. Let us be on our way."

And then from behind old man McDonald, one of his sons who was a dead ringer for him minus twenty years, hollered out, "Let's give 'im ah thrashin', Pa."

It appeared to Jake that things were about to go that way when all of a sudden Ellie and Henry began to cry. She looked at McDonald and sobbed loudly, "Please *George*, I just want to go home. I've had enough violence for one day."

McDonald's anger was like a runaway team. He had gotten off his horse and was walking towards Rusty intending, it appeared, to pull Jake to the ground under the watchful eyes of his boys who had drawn their guns. But then it finally registered with him that Ellie had personalized her renewed plea. She had not, in the year that they had been neighbors, ever called him by his first name. Between that and her tears and the fact that Jake seemed un-phased by his approach, he stopped just short of Rusty. He stared up at Jake in a menacing way and then scowled, "You win today, Mr. Lafarge." He then looked beyond Jake to where Ellie sat on her horse. "I'm sorry for your loss, Ellie."

She nodded. "Thank you."

McDonald maintained eye contact with her as he touched his hand to his hat. He then turned and started for his horse. He called out, "Holster your guns, boys."

The McDonald boys did as their father ordered. And then after mounting his horse, George doffed his hat to Ellie before heading on up Pumpkin Creek in the direction of his cabin. He was hopeful that he had curried favor with Ellie who was now truly eligible.

CHAPTER FOUR

Not counting the days when he had gotten drunk the night before Jake could not recall since becoming a cowboy, a single day, even including Christmas, that he had not been up before the sun. But today was different. Ellie had cooked him a big steak with all the fixings for supper last night. As he ate it, he tried to put out of mind the possibility that it might have come from a Rockin' C steer. Regardless, he took the blankets she had given him and his saddle and made up a good bed down by the creek. He'd slept hard and was only now being nudged awake by the awareness of daylight and meadow larks singing. For a time he laid there savoring the effects of last night. He looked out from his bed up the grassy slope towards the cabin. Smoke was coming from the stovepipe and the door stood open allowing him to see the effects of the lantern inside. *She musta got up 'fore the chickens. Said she'd make me breakfast.* He sat up and yawned, reluctant to throw the blankets back. And then he saw movement within the corral followed by the gate swinging open and Daisy trotting through it after having given up her burden of milk. Bella came behind the cow with Henry trailing after her. His upper body was badly tilted on the right side as he struggled under the weight of the full bucket. But it did not prevent him, as he caught sight of Jake, in attempting to wave with his left arm. Jake waved back. *He's a good kid.* Suddenly, he became aware of how comfortable he was in these surroundings and with Nate English's family. Guilt flooded his mind. Angrily, he tossed back the blankets and reached for his boots. *I need ta git the hell outta here.* Each boot caused pain in his left side that was reflected in his face as he labored to pull it on. But the worst was yet to come. Ellie had given him one of Nate's shirts to replace his torn and bloody one. He'd tried to refuse it but she was insistent, he supposed, because of her Christian beliefs. *Love thy enemy or some such,* he'd told himself. And so he put it on, it was dark green made of cotton and fit just about right. He started up the slope. The shirt gave him a queer feeling like Nate was there with him and watching his every move. He wanted to be shed of it, but she had given it to him and that he recognized was a far cry from two days ago when she had shot him. Still, he thought, *When I git back I'm gonna burn this thing.* He was just short of the door when the smell of bacon frying drifted out to him. Inside, standing in the light from the lantern that was sitting on the table in the center of the room, was Henry. He again waved but said nothing. Bella, on the other hand, began barking. Ellie turned away from the bacon she was tending on the stove across the room. She struck Jake as somber, almost sullen. He almost took offense to her demeanor until his inner voice reminded him, *Well hell, she's a widow and you had a hand in making her that way.*

She managed, "Good morning, Mr. Lafarge. Have a seat. Breakfast is about ready."

Jake moved across the pine wood floor to the table which was covered with a blue and white oilcloth that had little yellow flowers on it, and sat down. His chair appeared to be made from Aspen. It was blonde and smooth and knotty all over. He suspected Nate or Roy had made it but he dared not ask.

"Coffee, Mr. Lafarge?"

"Yes Ma'am, that'd be nice."

Ellie took a heavy white porcelain cup from a shelf on the wall to the right of the stove and poured the coffee. She set it on the table in front of Jake not far from the coal oil lantern. Steam from the cup flowed up into the light as if it were smoke before disappearing. "Cream, sugar?"

"Black's fine, Ma'am."

"And your eggs. You do like eggs, I hope?"

"Oh yes Ma'am. Cook'em however ya like."

"All right, over easy it is then."

Silence fell upon the room as Ellie went about cooking the eggs. Each of them knew he was leaving right after breakfast. That's what he'd told them last night. It was all decided. An hour from now he'd be gone and they'd be left to fend for themselves unless, of course, Ellie would accept George McDonald's help. Henry had been privy to the discussion. He now sat on the edge of his folks' bed against the back wall of the cabin. The light from the lantern didn't quite reach that far. It allowed him to quietly pet Bella, who sat in front of him, and not look in Jake's direction. It was a strange mix of emotions.

Jake picked up his cup and took a noisy sip. He thought to compliment Ellie on how good the coffee was and strike up a conversation like they had last night, but couldn't bring his self to do it. There was something about the mood of the room that held him back. It was like there was an air of obligation that he was expected to fill. She'd said in passing last night, or at least that's the way she'd offered it up, that she needed to build a shed for Daisy and the horses before

59

winter and put up some grass hay and dig a root cellar. *Oh my, I'll be busy,* she'd said. *But maybe that will be good. I know that I can't just sit here and pine over what's done.* And then, as if there was any room for more guilt on his plate, she added, *I expect I'll have to hire somebody if I can find the money.* At that point he had excused himself to go outside and have a smoke. But now, this morning, it was like they'd all seen that white elephant in the room last night and nobody wanted to let it back in. Jake sighed and said to himself, *if her damned kin had tended to business instead of rustling cattle she wouldn't be in this fix. No sir, ain't my problem. I need to just git on outta here.*

From behind him, she announced, "Its ready Henry. Come sit up to the table."

The table had been set for three with tin plates and knives and forks. They looked cheap and reminded Jake of what they used on cattle drives and spring roundups. He suspected Ellie had not known many nice things in her life. There was nothing, absolutely nothing, in the cabin that would suggest otherwise. Straight across the room from him along the wall opposite where the stove sat was Henry's bed. It was homemade from rough pine boards with a straw tick for a mattress. A pillow with a dark blue covering and a patchwork quilt with little red yarn ties sticking out of it lay in disarray on it. Just to the right of it, near his folks' bed was a dresser, two drawers wide by four high. But it too looked cheap. It appeared to be made from yellow pine with tin drawer pulls. Jake had seen one like it for sale at the Mercantile in Miles City. It went for a song. Still, the top of it was where Ellie displayed on a white doily, with some pride Jake supposed, a picture of her and Nate on their wedding day. A hand mirror, brush and bible lay near it. Above Henry's bed two sets of large nails had been driven part way into the wall. Nate and Roy's rifles rested on these. To the left of these were more pine board shelves with food items resting on them. Just right of the door, sitting beneath the window, was a cream separator. Like the stove, it was an implement of some value.

Henry emerged from the shadows and pulled his chair out from the table, scraping its legs across the uneven wood floor. He looked at Jake and then sat down without speaking. It occurred to Jake that he was wearing Nate's shirt and maybe sitting in his chair. He said, doing his best to sound jovial, "So yer the cow milker?"

"Yes sir."

"That's quite a chore for a young fella like you."

Henry looked embarrassed and shrugged his shoulders. "It's what Pa put me to."

"Henry's my little helper," said Ellie as she set a platter with the bacon and eggs on the table. "He feeds the chickens, collects the eggs, helps me in the garden, oh, land sakes I don't know what I'd do without him."

There was something in Ellie's almost gleeful tone that didn't ring true for Jake. In his mind he asked, *what the hell did Nate do around here*? But he said aloud, "That's real nice, Ma'am. It's not every mother that has a hard workin' boy." And then the moment became awkward as the white elephant passed through the room. Ellie turned quickly toward the stove. "I've got sourdough bread in the oven. Do you like sourdough, Mr. Lafarge?"

"Oh, yes Ma'am."

"There's fresh churned butter and chokecherry jam to go with it," said Ellie as she removed the hot bread from its pan.

And then Jake, caught up in the moment, said with a laugh, "Goodness Ma'am. With temptation like that you'll have me ridin' back over the mountain." He'd no sooner said the words than he regretted it, as he did not want to give them false hope that he would return to do what Nate should have been doing instead of stealing Rockin' C cattle.

Momentarily, Ellie returned with slices of bread on a plate. She sat down. "Shall we say grace?" And unlike last night, when only she and Henry held hands, she extended her other hand toward Jake.

Jake looked at her hand almost like he lacked the coordination to take hold of it. With the exception of an occasional dance where men usually outnumbered the women five to one, or a drunken trip to a bawdy house, he seldom touched a lady. He was still locked in that moment of indecision when he felt her take hold of his hand. He looked over at her, but she had already bowed her head.

She began. "Lord, we thank thee for this food we are about to receive and we ask that it might strengthen and nourish our bodies so that we might perform the tasks that lie ahead of us. We ask too, Lord, that you watch over Mr. Lafarge on his return trip. These things, Lord, we ask in the name of thy son, Jesus Christ. Amen."

Jake thought, or maybe he just wanted to believe, that she had allowed her hand to linger a second or two longer than necessary after the prayer was over. He was distracted in recalling the size and feel of her hand when she said, nodding towards the platter in front of him, "Go ahead and help yourself to some bacon and eggs, Mr. Lafarge."

Embarrassed that she may have read his face, he quickly picked up the platter and slid a couple of eggs and pieces of bacon off onto his plate. He then passed it on. At that very instant, he felt like a foolish school boy.

Ellie, who appeared unaware of her effect upon him, continued on. "So what will be your destination today?"

"Fer sure our line camp on Beaver Creek. That's about 20 miles," replied Jake as he reached for a slice of bread. "If I make good time I may go on to the ranch headquarters which is about another ten miles, but these days with the way the country is getting all chopped up with fences a fella can't always take the most direct route."

"Times are changing, Mr. Lafarge. The land can't stay wide open forever."

Knowing they were in different camps on this matter, Jake chose his words carefully. He said simply, "I suppose they are."

"Someday, everybody will have to build fences to protect what's theirs."

Jake was reluctant to go where Ellie, for some reason, was going. He took in a fork full of eggs and chewed a couple of times. He came back. "Yes Ma'am."

Ellie smiled. "I sense you don't agree."

Jake paused from eating and looked up from his plate. He said, "Oh, I reckon fences are like the wind. I don't like it when it blows but there ain't a lot I kin do about it."

"What about Grangers, Mr. Lafarge?"

"Grangers?"

"Yes, can you abide them? Is there room for them here?"

Jake was becoming leery of where the conversation was going. He shrugged. "I suppose they're like the wind and fences as well, I ain't got any choice."

"But you don't like it?"

"Well Ma'am, it was trappers and miners and cattlemen that opened this country up. They fought the Indians and the elements to carve out a place for themselves. Purty much they tamed this country and now the government has gave free rein to outsiders to come and take what they want. It don't seem right to me."

Ellie appeared a little surprised at Jake's response, but mostly disappointed. Her voice was sad. "Oh, I guess I misjudged you."

"Whaddaya mean?"

"It was just a foolish thought."

"Well, I'll give ya my two cents on the matter if you tell me what it was."

Ellie sighed. "I was trying to gauge, Mr. Lafarge, if you would be interested in working for me building fence, planting crops and the like. I couldn't pay you until we harvest the crops but I'd be willing to give you half."

Jake knew what his response would be but he didn't fire it back at her. He acted like he was pondering her offer and in a way he was, as at that moment his inner voice reminded him of what Cyrus Ellsworth had required of him for thirty dollars a month and board. But the temptation to now act upon his regret of not having ridden out with Billy Hawkins was short-lived. Ellsworth had taken him in and given him a job when he really needed it. He couldn't turn his back on that fact. But then his inner self came at him from a different angle, one that he noted the first time he'd seen Ellie up close. She was a pretty woman with her long black hair and green eyes. She was buxom and shapely as well, attributes that no man could ignore. But, he'd had a hand in killing her husband and his shame would not allow him to go there. He said to her, "I'm a cowboy Ma'am. It's all I've ever known."

Ellie's confidence suddenly took on a look of embarrassment. "Well, if you should change your mind you know where we're at – at least for now anyway."

CHAPTER FIVE

The quickest way to the line shack would have been to take the trail that paralleled Pumpkin Creek and go north to where Beaver Creek came in and then go east about a mile to the cabin. But starting out, Jake stayed well back from Pumpkin Creek going cross country climbing in and out of coulees and crossing little creeks until he figured he was well beyond George McDonald's place and the bird's eye view it had of the main trail. At that point he cut over to Pumpkin Creek. It wasn't that he was afraid of McDonald and the fight that was sure to happen if he ran into him, but rather his moral compass just didn't point in that direction. He'd thought about it during the night, how it would likely go if he went parading past McDonald's house. *I ain't takin' no ass whippin' from that bunch,* he'd told himself. *It'll come to gun play, no doubt about it. Just need to let that fire burn its self out.*

It was late afternoon when Jake came into view of the line shack. Nothing about it suggested that anyone was there. The corral next to it was empty and at first glance he could not see any horses hobbled amongst the aspens and willows over by the creek, which was no more than a good rock throw away. The door was closed and as best he could tell through the dirty fly specked window to the right of it, there was no movement inside. He got down from Rusty and tied him to the corral, uncertain if he was staying or going. There were fresh horse tracks but there was no way of knowing if whoever made them was coming back tonight. He started toward the cabin. Unlike Ellie's, its logs had turned gray over time and the dirt on its roof supported a number of weeds that had sprung up almost two months ago but were now badly wilted on account of no moisture having come during that time. Jake was about to open the door when he heard a horse behind him clear its nose of the fatigue it was feeling in that staccato way they have. This was followed by, "You might as well git back on yer horse."

Jake turned around to see Silas coming slowly toward him atop his big bay horse. He allowed him to get close enough so they could speak in a normal tone before asking, "What are you talking about?"

Silas had a smug look on his face like he couldn't wait to say what it was he had to say. "The law's wantin' to talk to you. Cyrus too."

Jake played dumb like this would all go away if he didn't acknowledge what he knew this was undoubtedly about. "The law, what for?"

"What the hell do you think?"

"That ain't been but three days ago and I know for a fact that widow woman didn't go to the sheriff."

Silas laughed as he wasn't on the hook for hanging Nate. "No, but your friend Billy went straight to town and got all liquored up in the Yellowstone Saloon and proceeded to tell everyone how we hung some Grangers."

"The hell you say."

66

Silas shook his head. "I'm tellin' ya like it is, Jake. They fetched me in to the home place 'fore noon today. The sheriff was there brow beatin' Ellsworth. And then when I show up he makes Cyrus be quiet while I tell him what happened."

Jake suddenly felt sick to his stomach. "So what did you tell them?"

Silas' voice began to shake. "I didn't have no choice, Jake."

"You told the sheriff I helped hang Nate?"

Silas appeared like he could cry. "I'm sorry, Jake. I'm an idiot. I fouled up. Ellsworth tried to tell him he did it by his self but the sheriff didn't believe him."

Jake scoffed. "So I suppose the sheriff wants to talk to me now."

"Yeah, he told me that when you showed up out here that you was to come into town and see him. He said if you didn't he'd come lookin' for ya."

"Well, what about Cyrus? They throw him in the hoosegow?"

"I don't know. Him and the sheriff were still arguing that point in front of the barn when I left but if I was to put money on it, I'd bet the sheriff took him back to town." Silas paused and laughed so as to give proper introduction to what he had to say next. "I'll tell ya, if the sheriff does take Ellsworth back he better stuff some cotton in his ears. I'll bet you the air where they was standin' by the barn is still blue." Silas laughed again. "Ole Cyrus was purty much tellin' that lawman how the cow eats the cabbage."

As Jake listened to Silas all carefree and unconcerned relating what had happened with the sheriff, it occurred to him that it'd be a long night if he were to stay at the line shack and go on tomorrow. This telling of the morning's events would undoubtedly not be the last time he would hear it if he stayed. To him, Silas' attitude was akin to the man who sees that his friend is mired down in quicksand and does nothing but yell from solid ground, *Yes sir, yer in a helluva fix*. Jake came back. "Ya know, Silas, I believe I'll push on to the home place. No offense, but they got better chuck there." And then, even though he didn't much care for Silas, he laughed briefly just to keep things on a friendly note.

But Silas, being who he was and in no apparent danger of going to jail, tried to top Jake. "That's probably a smart idea as I suspect the chow at the jail won't be anything a decent cook would lay claim to." And then he laughed as well.

Jake looked at Silas and frowned. He said to himself, not really caring if his eyes spoke it too,

You stupid shit. He said aloud, "Be seeing ya, Silas."

Jake started to walk away, as he did it suddenly occurred to Silas that Jake had been on a mission for Ellsworth that might shed more light on this whole affair. He called out, "Did ya find that fella's widow?"

Jake untied Rusty. He glanced over the top of his saddle at Silas and hollered, "I did."

"What did she say?"

He thought to not provide Silas, baby face Silas, with anymore gossip but instead he looked hard at him for just an instant and said, simply, "She shot me." He then stepped up onto his saddle and started Rusty off at a trot, not caring that Silas was shouting questions at him.

It was another three hours of steady riding to Dead Horse Creek and the home place where Cyrus Ellsworth and his wife Agnes and sons Ben and Walter and his daughter, Hope, when she was not off to college back east, lived. From the perspective of the homesteader living in a one room shack the Ellsworth's lived in opulence. Their house sat amongst big cottonwood trees along the creek. It was constructed of logs cut from stands of ponderosa pine not far away. If a person studied the house for very long it became apparent that it had been built piecemeal. It started out as a one room cabin back when Cyrus first came to the Powder River country in 1878 with a herd of Longhorn cattle from Texas. For several years nothing more was done to the cabin as the times were too dangerous for Agnes and the kids to come north. They stayed in Texas while Cyrus and his men struggled in Montana to lay claim to as much open range as they could. It was not an easy thing to do as the Sioux and Cheyenne were not going quietly and there were other white men with similar notions of getting rich off of cattle, or some who just wanted a little place of their own where they could till the land. Nonetheless, it was not without reward for Cyrus as the Army and the railroad needed beef. Finally, in 1881 the Northern Pacific Railroad reached Miles City and with it came Agnes and the kids. They were greeted by a newly renovated cabin that had three bedrooms, a kitchen with a hand pump for water and dining area, a living room with a leather couch, big padded chairs and a tall cobble rock fireplace that had a study off of it where Cyrus could do paperwork. It was a quaint setting. To get to the house, a person had to walk across a boardwalk bridge that was about four feet wide and spanned Dead Horse Creek, which was only ten feet across at that point. On the wooded side of the bridge, where the house was at, it was like another world, peaceful and safe and secure from all of the discord and, at times, violence of the open range. There had been times during the summer when Jake had gone there to see Cyrus and they'd sat on the screened in porch that Agnes had insisted on and drank cold lemonade. Jake recalled the birds, lots of them in the trees surrounding the house, singing all at once.

69

But it was the other side of the bridge, the real world, that made all this possible.

Jake started down the ridge overlooking the home place. The slope was steep, such that there were two switchbacks in the trail which wound its way through scattered ponderosa pine trees. At the second or lower switchback, he had a clear view of the cook shack. Smoke, wispy and unorganized, gently spewed up from its chimney suggesting to him that supper was still being cooked or it was over and water was being heated to do the dishes. He hoped that it was the latter as he had no desire to speculate with the other hands on his prospects for remaining a free man, at least not while he was eating.

Jake had been with Cyrus years ago when he decided to settle on Dead Horse Creek. As a result, he'd had a hand in building most everything on the place. The house, cook shack and ice house had required him to be a logger as well as a carpenter. However, when the barn, bunkhouse and chicken coop were built, a saw mill that offered heavy beams, studs and rough pine boards had started up nearby. And so ended Jake's career as a logger, which pleased him greatly.

Jake rode straight to the barn and through its big open doors. He unsaddled Rusty near the entrance to the tack room before giving him some oats and leading him past the empty stalls to either side of him and out the far end of the barn. He released Rusty in a pasture enclosed by a pole fence that started at the north wall of the barn and ran down to a water gap on the creek and then downstream along it for about a half mile before looping around on the bottom of the canyon and back to the barn. It was where horses that were used regularly and Matilda the milk cow were kept. He was walking back through the heavy shadows and odor of manure inside the barn when he saw the outline of Elmer, the chore boy, appear in the doorway. Elmer was far from being a boy as he was twice Jake's age. At one time he'd been a top hand, but a couple of Indian arrows and some nasty horse wrecks on top of his years had saddled him with his current title. As the chore boy, he milked the cow, gathered eggs, fed the chickens, cut fire wood, hoed weeds in the garden and anything else that Mrs. Ellsworth or the cook wanted done. He was especially at the beck and call of the cook as he occupied a small room at the end of the cook shack. It had an outside entrance but it could also be accessed by a door right off the eating area inside. It wasn't often but sometimes she just barged in on him. Elmer hollered out to Jake. "Greta's got a plate for you in the oven."

"Much obliged," said Jake as he continued walking. "Headed that way now."

"Heard you had a run in with some rustlers."

And so it began. Jake sighed and stopped. "We did, down by Jawbone Springs," he said knowing that Elmer and likely everyone else at the home place already knew the particulars of what had happened.

Elmer was a little skinny guy with a big gray moustache and green eyes. He'd chewed plug tobacco since he was a kid and his teeth had paid the price. Several of them in the front were missing; those that remained were badly stained. By his own admission he was five foot five. He was the only cowboy that Jake had personally known who wore a flat cap, a worthless hat in Jake's opinion. Beneath his cap Elmer was as bald as a copper pot. He looked at Jake straight on. "Well, I'll tell ya, to my way ah thinkin' that Melvin Nye has got some moxie haulin' Cyrus off to town after he caught those fellas red handed and they shot Silas ta boot. The sons ah bitches deserved what they got."

"The Sheriff took Cyrus, did he?"

Elmer slowly rotated his head to the side as he drawled, "Yeah he did. He didn't put no handcuffs on him, likely because he didn't want to have to fistfight Cyrus and probably Ben too."

"Ben? I thought he was up north on that roundup."

"Well, he come back two days ago. I guess when yer the boss' kid you can do as you please." Elmer laughed and spit a stream of tobacco juice to the side. "I think the boy has got woman trouble."

Jake grinned. "I reckon that just goes with being 20 years old. It keeps a fella in the rut most all the time."

Elmer laughed. "Hell, you ain't much older than that and I don't see you chasing skirts all over the country."

Jake started to turn red but, before his face got to peak color, Elmer came back.

"I hear Ben's sweet on some Granger girl down south ah here. Somewhere down there in that Jawbone Springs country. Cyrus ain't too happy about it. I heard him giving Ben hell over it one day, but Agnes, she don't seem to care."

Even though he suspected that Elmer, being Mrs. Ellsworth's gardener and go fetch it person would likely know these things, Jake's inner voice shouted out to him, *it's probably not smart to be analyzing Cyrus' family matters.* He came back like they'd never been talking about Ben. "There ain't but two sacks of oats left in the tack room, Elmer."

Elmer's expression abruptly changed from what appeared to have been entertainment to business. "I know. None of these sodbusters close by has got any for sale. Not at this time of the year anyway. I told Cyrus about it. The hayloft is empty too."

"What'd he say?"

"Said we'd have to go into Miles City and git enough to tide us over until folks out here thrash."

Jake nodded and moved on. "What kind ah mood is Greta in?"

Elmer tossed his head slightly and snorted. "Kinda like she always is, pleasant as a grizzly comin' outta winter."

"I guess a smart man wouldn't keep her waiting."

"No, not if he don't want his supper goin' to the dog he won't."

Jake laughed. "Well, I'm not inclined to be sharing tonight as I'm purty damned gant my own self. Guess I'll head that way."

It was about a hundred yards east from the barn and the pole corrals on the south side of it to the cook shack. The ground between the two places was hard packed and had been mostly denuded of all vegetation due to the years of foot and wagon traffic on it. As he walked along, Jake felt a sense of belonging, of being safe here. However, his mind would not let go of the worry that after tomorrow, when he saw the sheriff, he might not be coming back.

It was a warm evening. The door to the cook shack stood open. As he approached it, Jake could hear the clink of dishes as Greta washed and dried them before putting them back in the cupboard. She had her back to him when he stepped through the door. Jake said, trying his best to be cordial, "Rumor has –"

Greta suddenly spun around, almost dropping the plate she was drying. Her blue eyes locked onto Jake's in a mean but frightened sort of way. "Dammit, Mr. Lafarge, I don't like being snuck up on like that."

Jake came back as quick as she had come at him. "I'm sorry, Greta. I shudda knowed better." She looked at him, her anger and fear having subsided a little. "I don't like being this skittish." She sighed. "I wish I were different but I doubt that will ever be."

Jake had never known Greta to be anything but melancholy and distant. There had been a number of cowboys on the Rockin' C that had approached her with the notion that they could cure her of this malady, but they got nowhere. Because she was a pretty woman, about 35 Jake guessed, with long blonde hair and of medium height and shapely Greta had, in the beginning, drew men like flies to sugar. She rebuffed them all and in no time the word was out that she was a cold mystery woman to be avoided. She had shown up one day about two years ago when Cyrus brought her in from the mountains. The explanation that he had given everyone was that her husband's horse had fallen with him and he had been killed. Cyrus had then come along and found Greta grief stricken and in need of help. In turn, he brought her back to the home place. For a while she had stayed in the main house not doing much of anything except sitting on the front porch and mourning. And then one day Cyrus announced she was going to be the new cook, the old one having gone to town, gotten drunk and thrown into jail for breaking up a saloon. But from the outset, Greta's appearance at the Rockin' C had been suspicious. In Jake's opinion, and most everybody else at the home place, she had been traveling pretty light with only the clothes on her back. This, however, was not the most peculiar thing about her as both her horse and her dead husband's wore the Army's US brand. Jake had asked Cyrus point blank about this to which he adamantly claimed to have seen the bill of sale. But this did not ring true with Jake and others as both of the horses were young, strong animals. They were not old and used up and unable to stand the rigor of daily cavalry life. They were not animals the Army would surplus. Jake recalled that, after a time, Cyrus had gotten so short fused about the matter that no one brought it up anymore.

Jake said, "I hope Greta that one day you find happiness."

For a second she stared back at him, almost like, *how dare you judge me*? And then she turned away and went to the oven. Taking up a potholder she removed his plate of food and set it on the table along with a knife and fork. "I've got milk that was cold when Elmer brought it in from the ice house about an hour ago. I can't vouch for it now."

Jake reached for the back of his chair and began sliding it back. "That'd be grand."

Greta took up a pitcher from the counter along the wall behind her and poured a glass of milk.

She set it in front of Jake. "Can I get you anything else?"

There was roast beef, fried spuds and boiled corn on his plate. In spite of their rocky start a moment ago he was not too intimidated to ask, as he'd come to expect such drama from her, "Ah few biscuits and butter would go good." A slight frown came to Greta's face as she said nothing, but turned away. Jake added, "and maybe some ah that choke-cherry jam you made up last fall." Momentarily she returned with the additions to his supper and set them on the table.

"Thank you, Ma'am. I'm sorry to be the nuisance that I am tonight."

She appeared indifferent to his apology. "I suppose with the country being what it is, the dinner bell doesn't ring at the same time for everyone."

Jake had a mouth full of meat. He chewed a couple more times and swallowed so as to free his tongue up. "No Ma'am, I reckon it don't."

Greta stood on the other side of the big table. It had ten chairs, five on each side. Jake looked odd, even lonesome sitting there by his self. All of a sudden it had gotten quiet, the only sound being the occasional popping of the stove and a windup alarm clock sitting on a shelf near the door to Greta's room. The loud ticking drew Jake's attention that way and to the fact that she kept that door closed. Not one time since she had come to live in the cook shack had he ever seen that door open. No one on the place had either, not even Elmer. Jake supposed it was nobody's business what was in there or what went on in there but in a sense he'd already violated that standard. Elmer's room was right through the wall from Greta's. As far as Jake knew he was the only one that Elmer had told about what he heard late at night. *She starts out talkin' to herself and other folks that ain't there. And then purty soon she starts to cry and she gits mad and cusses the Indians up one side and down the other and the Army too. Those worthless blue belly sons ah bitches, she calls them. I'll tell ya, it makes the hair on the back ah yer neck stand up. That woman ain't right in the head.*

And then she broke the silence. "The talk is you hung a man."

A ripple of anger shot through Jake as all the bad images from that day cascaded like an avalanche through his mind. *Dammit, this woman generally don't say two words to most people and now here she is wantin' her share of the gossip.* Jake looked up from his plate. "I had a hand in it."

"I saw a hanging one time. I was a little girl in Abilene. My Pa took us. Like it was the circus. Wished I hadn't gone."

Jake paused from eating and looked into Greta's face. She appeared to be somewhere else, maybe Abilene. He came back, "It ain't a purty sight."

Greta scoffed, causing her head to bob ever so gently as she kept her gaze fixed to another place and another time. She said confidently, "I've seen worse, much worse."

Elmer's words came again to Jake. *She ain't right in the head.* He was reluctant to go where she was but it was like she

76

had purposely opened that door for him. He stepped inside. "What is it you've seen, Greta?"

Tears came to her eyes as her lower lip began to tremble. Her voice quivered like aspen leaves in the wind. "My – my family. My babies, my husband, they killed them, right in front of me. Made me watch. Butchered them is what they did, those dirty red devils. Hell is too good for them."

Jake was instantly taken aback. He'd heard stories of Indian brutality against settlers up on the Musselshell River. He'd even talked to other people who'd experienced it first hand, but none of them were as consumed by it as Greta appeared to be. And then as her words echoed in his mind one of them bobbed to the surface like a dry cork in water. *Husband.* At the same time he could hear Cyrus saying how her husband had been killed when his horse fell with him. Jake's gut told him that Greta wasn't lying now about her husband, so why had Cyrus? He said to her, "I'm sorry for yer loss, Greta. It –"

"Elmer's coming," she said quickly. "Don't say a word about what I've just told you. Please, it won't bode well for me." And with that she retreated to her room and closed the door.

Seconds later, Elmer stepped inside. It struck him right away that Greta wasn't in the room. "So where's the boss?" he said as he sometimes jokingly referred to her when she wasn't present.

"Said she had a headache and was gonna lay down for a little bit."

Elmer paused and looked towards Greta's door knowing that she'd probably heard him. "Oh, maybe it's this heat."

"Yeah, probably so."

"I was thinkin' if you was to take a pack mule with you tomorrow you could bring back a few sacks ah oats."

Jake laughed sarcastically. "Yer more confident than I am that I'll be comin' back."

"Well, if you don't come home I'll just go to town and fetch the mule and the oats, but at least that ornery mule will already be there."

CHAPTER SIX

There were still a few stars that had not yet gone dark when Jake slipped out of the bunkhouse and headed towards the barn. The morning air was cool but not cold. Across the way he could see blue smoke trailing off from the chimney of the cook shack. Through its two front windows he occasionally caught glimpses of Greta in the soft yellow light flowing from the kerosene lanterns on the big table. She no doubt was busy getting breakfast ready for the men who would soon be up. Jake was craving a cup of hot coffee but he kept on toward the barn. After last night's session in the bunkhouse, he'd made up his mind he didn't need additional speculation at breakfast concerning the prospect of him and Cyrus going to jail.

It was not a problem to catch Rusty, but even with a bucket of oats Gus the mule took some time before he allowed himself to be cornered at the far end of the pasture. It was starting to get light by the time Jake got him back to the barn. As he adjusted the pack saddle on Gus' back he could see the men trailing from the bunkhouse to the cook shack. He mumbled quietly. "Damned Elmer snookered me on this one."

The other hands and Elmer had just sat down to breakfast when Jake rode by leading Gus. There was not the guilty silence he'd hoped for as the cook shack door was open. He heard above the din of the men talking, maybe for his benefit, "Well hell, looks like Jake is anxious ta git ta town and try out some of that jail chuck." This was followed by loud laughter. Jake did not look their way but nudged Rusty into a trot. Under his breath, he said, "Sons ah bitches."

Owing to his early start, Jake arrived in Miles City shortly before noon. The ride in had given him plenty of time to consider all of the opinions rendered last night but it was to no good end as his stomach was tied in a knot. The town, excluding the stock yards and train depot, was not large. It ran about two blocks long and sprawled out in varying distances to either side of Main Street, which on this day was dusty. There were the usual assortment of businesses located here; saloons, restaurants, a barber shop, hotel, grocery stores, a newspaper, doctor's office, bakery, livery stable and banks. Most of the structures were wood frame with many having oversized facades. There were also a couple of parlor houses on side streets where a man, for a price, could enjoy the short term company of one of the ladies who resided there. Also, on a side street, but no less conspicuous, was Sheriff Melvin Nye's office. Just like the parlor houses, everybody knew where it was at. Jake tied Rusty and Gus to the hitching rail outside the red brick building. It had one four pane window in front. In the event it rained, a boardwalk ran from the hitching rail to a paint chipped door that was intended to be white. Jake opened the door and stepped inside. The walls were a waxy yellow which, even for a man's taste, didn't mesh with the dark wood floor. To his left was a small stove with a wooden box full of coal next to it. There was a desk on either side of the room. Beyond them was a solid door.

On the right side, a three high stack of oak filing cabinets sat behind the desk and wooden chair. Above them was a calendar with a picturesque setting of cattle grazing in belly high grass and in the background a train with smoke rolling back over its length. Below the picture was the caption; Serving The West – Northern Pacific Railroad. Below that was the white calendar page with dark black letters and numbers for June – 1886. Behind the desk on the other side of the room was a rack that held guns in an upright position. There were three lever action Winchesters and one pump action Winchester shotgun. In the wooden chair behind that desk sat Sheriff Melvin Nye. He was fortyish with short dark hair and clean shaven except for a black handlebar moustache which seemed to fit his more than ample belly. A silver star with the word sheriff clearly imprinted on it was pinned to the right side of his gray shirt. He said in a voice so deep that for a second Jake thought he was purposely manipulating it to sound that way, "I'd be willin' to bet you're Jake Lafarge."

Jake nodded. "I am."

Nye pointed to a chair against the wall behind Jake. "Have a seat."

Jake brought the chair over and sat down across from the Sheriff. And then before Nye could speak, Jake blurted out, "You got Cyrus locked up."

A wry look came to the lawman's face suggesting he was thinking of messing with Jake, but then he eased away from it. "No, not yet I don't."

Jake felt a sudden but partial easing of the tension within him. He came back, "So what's yer intention regarding him and me?"

There were a clutter of papers, an ash tray and a coffee cup on Nye's desk, but in the midst of all of it was a copy of today's paper. He picked it up and tossed it across the desk towards Jake. "It appears the local gossip sheet thinks yer boss has performed some kind ah public service, like he got rid of ah coupla wolves or some such."

Jake looked down at the bold headline; STOCKMAN RIDS RANGE OF RUSTLERS. Beneath these words were two long columns of smaller print with details supplied by Cyrus. Jake had not yet found his name when the Sheriff interrupted him.

"The judge allowed Cyrus to post bail yesterday. So what does he do but trot his self over to the newspaper. I'll tell ya, yer boss, that fella," said Nye sardonically, "he ain't stupid."

"No, I reckon he ain't," said Jake. "But, where does that leave me?"

Nye gave Jake a sour look as he reached into the shirt pocket opposite his badge and pulled out a can of Prince Albert tobacco and cigarette papers. He peeled a paper out of the tiny folder, formed a trough and began sprinkling tobacco into it. He said, barely looking at Jake, "Well, why don't you tell me what your part in hanging Nate English was?"

"Didn't Cyrus already tell you?"

"He did, but I figure if you had a hand in killin' ah man the least you can do is own up to it."

The fear in Jake that a moment ago had greatly subsided now flared up. His mind flashed back to when Cyrus had given them all the choice to ride out with the understanding if they did they were done on the Rockin' C. He wanted to think that he'd been tempted more than he had to do this but, truth be told, he was fearful of having to start over somewhere else. So here he was for thirty and found trying to talk his way out of jail. He looked back at the Sheriff. His voice had a tone of defiance. "I helped Cyrus with it all. I held my gun on Nate while Cyrus tied his hands behind his back. I helped Cyrus put him on the horse and after Cyrus put the noose around Nate's neck I tied the rope off to the tree."

"But it was Ellsworth that actually slapped the horse?"

"Jake hesitated for a few seconds and then sighed. "Yeah."

Nye looked at Jake intently as if to gauge the veracity of what he'd just said before striking a match with his thumbnail, a trick that Jake had never mastered, and lit his cigarette. He shook the match and tossed it into the ash tray while taking several deep puffs and spewing the blue smoke into the space between them. He came back. "Ellsworth says he sent you with these dead fellas' possessions to find one of 'ems widow, that right?"

"Yes sir, Ellie English is her name. Her and her boy live a ways up Deer Creek."

And then Nye asked like he already knew, "How'd that go?"

It came instantly while his mind was scrambling for a way to generate sympathy from the Sheriff and before he'd had a chance to consider how it would sound for Ellie. "Well Sir, she shot me."

"She shot you?"

"Yes Sir, another two – three inches to the right and she'd ah punctured ah lung."

Nye frowned and shook his head. "I can't say as I blame the woman, but I suppose I'm gonna have to visit her."

A sense of guilt that bordered on betrayal came over Jake. "I don't know that you need to do that, Sheriff. It all worked out."

Nye scoffed. "So whadda we got laws for if people can just go around shootin' and hangin' whoever they think needs it? Hell, if that's the way people want to have it I may as well go find myself a regular job. Quit wastin' my time."

Jake knew the Sheriff was right, which made it all the more perplexing to him why he'd helped Cyrus hang Nate. He said, "I reckon I don't need to tell you Sheriff, that woman has got a lot on her plate already."

Nye took an agitated, quick drag from his cigarette and then exhaled the smoke forcefully towards Jake. The smoke had barely finished leaving his mouth when he said tersely, "Yeah, thanks to you and Cyrus Ellsworth." He paused before adding angrily. "Don't you go trying to make me feel like some shit heel for doin' my job."

"I'm not Sheriff. I was just-"

"I know what yer sayin'. Let it rest."

"I'm sorry."

Nye suddenly became silent in a deliberate way. The expression on his face was smug, almost haughty. He leaned back slightly with his right elbow resting on the arm of the chair so that his cigarette was cocked up at an angle where the both of them could monitor the sinewy ribbon of smoke and the progression of the red glow on the end of it. A clock with big black Roman numerals encased in oak and glass hung on the wall behind Jake. The bronze pendulum hanging beneath the clock face clicked loudly back and forth. It was obvious to Jake that Nye seemed to be taking some satisfaction in the fact he held Jake's fate in his hands. He took another drag off his cigarette while looking straight at Jake. Finally, he said, "I'm of the opinion that I'm the only one here that's interested in applying the law as it was intended." He paused, his expression becoming irritated, even angry and then he said, "I believe, Mr. Lafarge that I will save myself some paperwork and not indulge either one of us by putting you in jail so that yer boss can bail you out. I have no illusions that a jury in these parts would convict you or him. In my opinion, it is sad to say that Cyrus Ellsworth has had his way in matters such as this for far too long. The country's civilized now."

Jake felt relieved, almost emboldened. He came back. "I'll grant ya, Sheriff, Cyrus is old school but it's what got him what he has."

The Sheriff appeared deflated. "Times are changin', Mr. Lafarge. Yer boss needs to make note of that."

Jake nodded. "He's a proud man."

Nye snorted, tossing his head slightly. "Pride can be a dangerous thing. Ellsworth needs to recognize that 'fore it's too late."

"I'll tell 'im."

Nye laughed. "I'm sure you will," he said sarcastically. His eyes shifted to his cigarette. It had burned down close to his fingers. He drew it into his mouth and milked a final uptake of smoke before leaning forward and exhaling as he crushed the cigarette in the ash tray. Without looking at Jake, he said, "Go on. Get the hell outta here."

Jake stood up. "Thanks, Sheriff."

Nye looked up at Jake. His eyes were dead serious. "Just know, Mr. Lafarge, next time I have cause to arrest you we will play that hand out."

Jake thought to say, *there won't be a next time*, but for some reason he couldn't bring himself to concede that to the Sheriff. He said simply, "All right."

Jake untied Gus and then Rusty before climbing into his saddle with Gus' lead rope in hand. Even though he'd not been locked up, the sunshine had a different feel to it now. He savored it and being able to do the simple things that he had just done of his own accord. Prodding Rusty, he headed back towards Main Street, conscious of his heart still beating faster than usual. He said to himself, *you got lucky ya damned fool.*

At the intersection with Main Street Jake turned right, his destination being the Tongue River Café. He was some distance from it when he recognized McClellan saddles on two of the horses tied out front. The sight of them prompted him to recall what Cyrus had said about Greta and her husband riding Army horses and the doubts he still had about how they come to be in possession of those animals. But, he'd missed breakfast and it was now past noon. He had no intention of purposely missing a second meal. His suspicions of Greta were soon lost amongst his considerations of what he would eat.

He'd just opened the door and stepped inside the busy diner when off to the right he heard his name. He looked that way and was temporarily distracted by two Army officers who were likely from Fort Keogh, which was just west of town near the mouth of the Tongue River. But then he saw Cyrus wave his hat from a table at the back of the room. Jake advanced past a small counter where money was taken and then right along a clear path between a counter for eating and five round topped stools in front of it and the scattered square top tables and chairs to the right of it. There was a steady hum of voices and scraping and clinking of silverware upon dishes and occasional outbursts of laughter such that Jake's arrival garnered virtually no attention at all, except for the Ellsworth clan. With the exception of Hope, they were all there; Cyrus, Agnes, Ben and Walter. Their eyes followed him all the way back until he stood before their table next to a big rock fireplace with the head of a huge bull elk overlooking them from the wall above. Cyrus had a prominent grin on his face as he gestured towards an empty chair next to him. "Sit yerself down."

It was easy for Jake to accept Cyrus' invitation. He felt comfortable around the Ellsworth family but today, he sensed, was going to be different. He'd barely got seated when Cyrus said, "Well, I see Nye didn't lock you up." And then he and Ben laughed.

It flashed in Jake's mind. *They're not seein' it. This is like a family outing.* But then, just for a second, his eyes caught those of Agnes and he could tell that she saw today for the omen that it was. Jake said in a somber voice that was absent any tone of celebration. "No, I guess he figured it wouldn't do any good."

"Well, the damned fool should have known better than to go against what people want," said Ben in a hostile tone.

Jake looked over at Ben but said nothing. He knew better than to stoke his temper. At twenty years of age, with short black hair and a full beard he resembled a younger version of his father. His temperament, Jake suspected, was probably like Cyrus' when he was that age. Jake purposely left Ben waiting for a response and shifted his focus back to Cyrus. He said, "I took the Sheriff to be dead serious about next time, if there ever is one he won't be so accommodating."

Cyrus leaned slightly toward Jake. "It ain't just up to Nye. His job is to execute the will of the people. They're the ones who elect him, who give him a job." He paused and then added. "Did you see the paper?"

"I did."

Cyrus grinned in an arrogant, almost condescending way, "Well, so did the judge and district attorney."

Ben laughed while looking straight at Jake. Walter, three years younger than Ben with a cherubic face, kept quiet. Agnes, on the other hand, with pretty auburn hair piled beneath a brown hat adorned with feathers and a paisley yellow dress appeared weary of the talk already.

Jake glanced at Ben in a cursory offer of respect meant only to keep him out of the discussion. Regret that he'd come here flooded his mind. But, there was little he could do about it now except to surrender to Cyrus and Ben's way of thinking. However, he'd already formed words in his mind that his ego wouldn't let go of, he said, "Times are changing, Cyrus. Lots ah new folks comin' into this country."

"Don't I know it. They're the ones causin' the trouble."

"The old ways won't do anymore."

A hint of anger flared in Cyrus' eyes. "It was the old ways that made this country what it is now. If we -"

"That'll do, Cyrus," said Agnes in a sharp, curt voice. "You've killed more men than I'd want on my conscience and you're still a free man. Count your blessings."

Cyrus' expression became one of hateful incredulity. He looked at his wife as if she was the only one at the table. He said with as much indifference as he could muster, "Just you know, that pretty dress you've got on and that nice house you live in and Hope going off to that fancy school back east has come at a price."

Agnes' blue eyes suddenly got an awkward, almost embarrassed look to them as she shifted beyond Cyrus.

"Here we go folks," said the waitress oblivious to what she had just interrupted. She began setting plates of food on the table.

It occurred to Jake, that since he hadn't ordered yet and the mood at the table had pretty much gone south, he would excuse himself. He slid his chair back and stood. He said, like it had been planned all along that he would leave now, "I believe I'll git underway. Elmer wanted me to pick up some oats."

For a moment Cyrus appeared uncertain what to say but then he played along, just wanting the situation to be over. He nodded, his eyes looking apologetic. "Glad you're doing that, Jake. I know we're just about out."

"Yeah, we are." Jake looked in the direction of Agnes and touched his right hand to the brim of his hat. "Ma'am."

Agnes smiled politely. "We'll be seeing you Jake."

Jake turned and started back through the crowded room. He'd just come next to the table where the Army officers were seated when he paused to allow a waitress to go past him to his left. In those few seconds, like the calm before a storm, the clamor in the room died away enabling the words of one of the officers to float up to Jake as clear as a robin at dawn. "Yellow Wolf says he knows where that Peterson woman is at."

Jake was abruptly gripped by surprise if not mild shock. He could not help but look over at the soldier who appeared to be a Captain and about thirty years old. His curiosity was such that the officer suddenly returned Jake's stare. "Can I help you?"

Embarrassment covered Jake's face. He stammered, "No, no I guess not. I thought for a second I knew you but I don't." And with that Jake walked on leaving the Captain to watch his departure. It wasn't until he was outside that he asked himself, *how many women named Peterson with ties to Indians and the Army can there be*? Greta was the only one he knew.

CHAPTER SEVEN

The trip back to the Rockin' C was slow going as the pace was dictated by Gus who was now carrying four bags of oats. Large panniers that hung off either side of his pack saddle each contained one bag. Two more bags were laid across the top of the saddle and tied down. At 50 pounds per bag, Jake figured it best to not push Gus beyond a slow walk. It was a rate of travel that was mostly agreeable to the big black mule. So far, he had made no attempt to prematurely unload his cargo, as he sometimes did when things were not to his liking. For Jake, however, it was a long time for him to be alone with his thoughts and the relentless deer flies. He was conflicted in his opinion of Cyrus and his almost cavalier attitude at having avoided jail. Some years back, when the country had been much more lawless than now, Cyrus had gone off with the vigilantes. Being a green kid, Jake had not been invited. For some months they went on a rampage giving notice for rustlers to vacate the country or suffer the consequences. Foolishly, many did not heed the warning and they were hanged. But then, as it was now, Cyrus had said, *it was a necessary thing. It had to be done.* Jake did not question it then as he took everything that Cyrus said as gospel, but he also wasn't involved in the hangings. Jake shook his head. He said aloud, "I don't see how he can live with all of it." He rode on with images of Nate constantly pestering him. For a good ways his conscience remained in *control* of his mind's eye berating him for that day at Jawbone Springs until, finally, his curiosity about Greta's past took charge. *Why would this Indian named Yellow Wolf care about where Greta was at? The Army wantin' their horses back makes more sense, but this Indian and Greta? That's peculiar as hell.*

It had been a hot day, cooling only slightly in the early evening shadows cast by the big cottonwood trees that grew next to Dead Horse Creek. Nonetheless, Jake appreciated the minor respite from the heat as he rode along the wagon road that paralleled the creek. But whatever gains in comfort he made from the shade of the trees was offset by the mosquitoes and gnats. It was the time of day when they were the worst. Just downstream from the house was a ford in the creek. It was across from the barn and the bunkhouse beyond it. As he started into the water Jake could see some of the men lounging in front of the bunkhouse pitching horseshoes. Probably all of them had been at breakfast this morning and shared in the laughter as he rode out. But they were quiet now, merely glancing in his direction, one of them waving. Near the barn, Jake could see the buggy that the Ellsworth's had taken to town. *They beat me back. Cyrus musta told'em I ain't goin' ta jail. He ruined their fun.* Jake rode on to the barn and began unloading the oats. He had just removed the last bag from Gus when he sensed someone behind him. Before he could turn around Greta said, "Cyrus told me you'd likely want to eat when you got in."

Jake looked at her and smiled. "I surely would, Ma'am."

Greta did not return the smile but the look in her eyes seemed to brighten just a bit as she rattled off what was for supper. "I've got pork chops, fried spuds, string beans and biscuits. There's peach cobbler for dessert with fresh cream."

Jake could hear the pride in her voice. He came back, like he had forgotten she was this pretty mystery woman who had turned away all suitors, "I'll tell ya Ma'am, if you continue to put out fare such as that some buckaroo is gonna put his brand on you." He then started to laugh as if to finish his compliment but stopped almost before he started. Greta's expression had turned to stone. She said, "It's ready whenever you are."

Jake washed his face of emotion so as to be on par with her look. He said, "I'll be along just as soon as I tend to the animals."

She nodded, "all right." And then she started back across the hard, bare dirt to the cook shack.

From deep in the shadows of the barn Jake allowed himself to watch Greta's departure. She was a handsome woman. If things were different, he'd be drawn to her but, as they were, he was reluctant to even go to supper as it would be just the two of them and the demons of her past. On the ride home, he'd vacillated between feeling he had an obligation to tell her what he'd heard at the café in town or mind his own business. It was a quandary that he hoped would either go away or resolve itself while he brushed and grained Rusty and Gus, but it did not.

The windows of the cook shack were more dark than not. Its door was open. As he neared it, Jake cleared his throat so as to alert Greta that he was coming. He stepped inside. In the poor light he could see, right in front of him, that she had set his food on the table. From the shadow to his right, she said, "I was watching for you."

Jake looked toward her. In the dim light it was difficult to gauge her emotion. His voice was weary, almost perfunctory, "Sorry I took so long but I believe a man needs to take good care of his animals if you want them to do the same for you."

"Unfortunately, not all men understand that."

Jake nodded. "I know." He began to eat. He thought to make idle conversation but his fatigue and frustration with the day's events made it easy to leave the burden of filling the void between them to her.

But she said nothing, allowing the water within the kettle on the stove to purr as it heated to just short of a boil. From outside the laughter and banter of the men at the horseshoe pit near the bunkhouse could be heard. And then came the harsh cry of a raven flying overhead, carrying with it images of Nate English's scavenged body. Jake said, mostly to purge his mind of Nate, "This is real tasty, Ma'am."

The silence, accentuated by the windup clock on the shelf across the room continued. An untoward feeling started to well up in Jake. *Did she not hear me?* He glanced in her direction. She was looking back at him. It was, he thought, almost like she could see what was in his head. It made him shiver. He fell away from her eyes and took up another fork full of spuds.

She said, "I'm glad they didn't lock you up. It wouldn't have been right."

Jake hesitated and then said, "No, I suppose it wouldn't."

Anger came to her face. "You suppose? What kind of a fool are you? Did you want to go to jail?"

Jake was taken aback by her response. Nonetheless, he came with what he truly felt. "No, it's just I believe we cudda stopped short of hangin' Nate."

"That was his name, Nate?"

"Yeah, he had a wife and son too."

"I can imagine their pain. I've felt it."

93

Jake laid his fork down, his mind's eye having gone to Jawbone Springs. He said, "They went with me to bury Nate and the wife's brother. I'll never forget that day."

Even in the poor light, Jake could see the shiny, watery look Greta's eyes had taken on. She said as she began to sniffle, "At least they got to see them buried."

He absorbed her words and then said cautiously, knowing the probable answer he would get, "Your kin didn't get a proper burial?"

She shook her head, her face contorted into a painful grimace. A profusion of tears overflowed her eyes and began to stream down both cheeks. She started with a gulping sob before an apparent surge of anger allowed her to collect herself. "They were left for the vermin. Like so much carrion to rot in the sun; my husband, my son and my daughter. What kind of people could be so wicked and cruel?" And then she began to openly cry, not caring that Jake was seeing this side of the cold mystery woman.

The torrent of her grief was daunting to Jake. It was as if he was standing alone in front of a raging forest fire. It was obvious there was nothing he could do to stop it. Human compassion, however, dictated that he at least try. This was a woman he'd known for two years and not until now had she chosen to reveal her sorrow. That had to mean something. He got up from the table and went to her, uncertain if he should touch her. He stood before her. "I'm sorry for your loss, Greta."

She looked back at him crying, trembling, her face contorted in extreme anguish. And then she reached out and wrapped her arms around his neck, holding on tight allowing herself to sink against him. Sensing she might collapse, Jake put his arms around her. And then she began to babble in a halting, sobbing voice. "I'm no better than they are, Jake. They made me into them."

Jake was torn if he should draw her out. He wondered if she would later see this as a moment of weakness that she would prefer forgotten. His gut told him that she wanted to be free of this, whatever it was she had chosen him to share it with. She pushed back from his chest so as to be able to see his eyes. For a brief moment, she measured his receptiveness and then said in an arbitrary, almost indifferent, tone, "I killed two Indians. They were under lock and key and I shot them like caged animals."

Jake struggled to not show the shock he felt, but he failed. Greta removed her arms from him and took a step back. Her emotions had begun to harden. "You think less of me, don't you?"

Jake was uncertain what he felt but, in this case, telling her that would be as good as saying, *that was a hideous thing you did, Greta.* Instead, he told her what she wanted to hear. "No, no I don't. It's like the good book says, an eye for an eye and a tooth for a tooth."

"Yes, that's how it was, Jake. Just like that."

"I'm sure you had good cause."

A distant forlorn look came to Greta's face before she grimaced and said slowly, as if she was watching the cruelty play out in her mind's eye, "I hear them every night. Sometimes even during the day when I'm here alone and it's quiet. I hate the silence, Jake. You don't know what it's like to hear your child cry out, Mama, Mama and there's nothing you can do to help them." And then the tears flooded from her eyes and she looked away.

Jake felt helpless to fix such immense sorrow. He didn't know what to do so he parroted what he'd heard others say to the grief stricken. "Time heals all, Greta." But he didn't believe that himself.

Greta locked eyes with him and scoffed. "How much time, Jake? How long does it take before you can erase the memory of some savage bashing your child's head in?" She paused, glaring at him, before adding sarcastically, "And then to be defiled and tortured by the same heathens, Jake. Tell me, how long does it take to put that out of mind?"

Jake felt overwhelmed. *A person might not ever be shed of that.* Aloud, he said, his voice sounding defeated. "I don't know."

"Those fools at Fort Laramie were going to let them go. Said it was the only way they could get the rest of 'em to go back to the reservation. Can you believe that? I'm certain those Indians had killed soldiers too."

Jake recalled the decision he'd made on his way to the cook shack to not tell her about the Army officers in town, but now he questioned if that was the right thing to do. He did not want to upset her any more than she already was, but he also reckoned that to not tell her might put her in danger. He briefly tried rehearsing the words in his mind but there didn't seem to be any good way to say it so he just put it out there. "Do you know an Indian named Yellow Wolf?"

Fear instantly consumed Greta's face. She became pale. "How do you know that name?"

"I heard it in town. Supposedly, he claims to know where yer at."

Greta gasped and then whimpered as she shook her head from side to side. "I knew it would never last here."

"And this Yellow Wolf? What does he want with you?"

"Revenge, I suppose. He's a Sioux chief. It was renegades from his village that murdered my family and abducted me. The Army killed some of his people when they rescued me."

She paused to collect herself and then added, "One of the men I shot in the Fort Laramie stockade was his nephew."

Jake sighed. "How is it you were able to get away?"

"A soldier, a good man who could see this travesty of justice for what it was helped me."

"He's the fella that Cyrus found you with a couple years ago?"

Greta nodded. "Yes, we'd made good our escape from Fort Laramie for over a month when we ran into an Army patrol that saw the brands on our horses. One thing led to another and my friend was shot, but not before he shot a couple of those troopers. We managed to escape and made it as far as the Rockin' C before my friend succumbed to his wound. And then Cyrus found me and took me in."

Jake now viewed Greta in a different light. He felt guilty for ever having thought she was strange or cold. He said, "Do you think this Yellow Wolf really knows where yer at?"

Greta scoffed and tossed her head back slightly. "He could, I don't know. I live my days in fear that some new hand will come to work here that was at Fort Laramie when all of this went on and he will recognize me. And my nights, well I've told you about those. I'm a prisoner here, Mr. Lafarge."

"Maybe there'll come a time when you can move on, California or someplace where there's little chance of anybody recognizing you."

"Some things you just can't rid yourself of. I'm afraid this is one of them."

"Do you suppose we should tell Cyrus about Yellow Wolf? Maybe you should hide out for a while. You could go to one of the line shacks."

Greta smiled ruefully. "It'll be the Army that comes. If they do, they won't go away quietly. Cyrus will have even more trouble on his hands."

"But to just wait for them to come? You've got to try and escape."

"It'd never work, Jake, me going to a line shack to hide out. There'd be too many hands here that would find out and question it." She paused and forced a weak smile onto her red, tear stained face. She added facetiously, "Besides, who would cook?"

Jake was at a loss as to how to comfort her. Her demeanor was beyond sad, it was pathetic. It caused the voice in his mind to become irrational. He suddenly heard himself say, "I'll help you get away."

For a brief moment she appeared to entertain this idea, but there was nothing between them to bond them in that way. The forlorn smile returned to her face. "No Jake, but I appreciate the offer."

"You can't just give up."

"If they come, so be it. I'm tired of being me."

Jake went quiet, his mind less burdened than when he had first got there. He was pondering if he should leave when his eyes took it upon themselves to follow a big black fly that landed on one of the pork chops on his plate. Instinctively, he swished it away with his hand as if it mattered that the fly crawled over his food. Regret struck him like a boxer's jab as Greta said, "I'm keeping you from your supper. Eat Jake."

"No, that's alright. We need to figure you a way out of yer predicament."

Greta shook her head. "I don't feel well, Jake. I believe I'll just go to my room and lay down. There's more on the stove if you want seconds so help yourself."

Jake felt guilty eating when Greta's world, such as it was, appeared to be on the verge of caving in. He said, "I hope you feel better tomorrow."

She smiled. "I'm sure I will." And then she went into her room off of the kitchen, gently closing the door behind her.

It became eerily quiet and seemingly darker as Jake began to eat. His food was barely warm and not really enjoyable, but he ate anyway as he was hungry and didn't know what else to do. He'd picked through most of his plate when he heard her, just as Elmer had described, crying and talking to herself. *Surely she knows that I can hear her.* He considered knocking on her door, but she'd already rejected his help. *In two years Elmer has never saw need to knock*, he told himself. *But this is different.* He pushed back from the table and got almost to her door when she went silent. He stood there, listening to his heart thump and an occasional sniffle from her. His conscience spoke to him, *she don't want yer help.* Finally, he walked away allowing his steps to be heavy on the wooden floor so she would know that he had made the effort, that he cared. As he passed by his place at the table he looked over at his un-eaten cobbler but kept on going out the door.

He'd pitched horseshoes with Elmer and some of the other hands until it got too dark to see. One of the men had a bottle of Old Crow and had offered it up to celebrate Jake and Cyrus not going to jail. Everybody, including Jake, got a few nips off of it. Between the liquor and the comradery of the horseshoe game, the gravity of Greta's situation began to fade from Jake's conscience. The Old Crow and the fatigue of everything that had happened to him over the past several days had caused him to sleep hard. It was still dark outside when he felt a hand on his shoulder. He opened his eyes. It was Elmer's voice. "Git up, Jake. Come over to the cook shack when yer dressed."

Jake propped himself up on one elbow. He whispered so as to not wake the others. "Whaddaya need, Elmer?"

Elmer leaned close and whispered back, "Greta's dead."

Jake's heart catapulted into his throat. He hissed, "What?"

"Just come to the cook shack. Cyrus is waiting there."

Elmer had barely closed the bunkhouse door behind him when Jake's mind began spinning the possibilities of what could have happened to Greta. None of them were good and all of them were siding with his conscience for not doing more last night. His conscience was giving him hell. *You cudda knocked on her door and just flat out insist she accept your help. Hell, you shudda went and got Cyrus. He knows her best. Anything but pitching horseshoes and drinking.*

Both of the lanterns on the eating table in the cook shack were lit. A shaft of light poured out the open doorway making it easy for Jake to see inside. His dirty plate, his white bowl of cobbler, everything was just as he'd left it except the door to Greta's room was now open. For two years that door had not been open to anyone except maybe Cyrus. It struck Jake as he stepped into the tiny room and his eyes began to pour over this forbidden space, that the dead have no privacy. Her sanctuary would become a morbid curiosity subject to speculation, stories and avoidance by the living as no one would want to sleep in a dead person's room. Greta was fully clothed, lying on her narrow brass bed. Cyrus and Elmer were standing beside it looking down at her. She was on her side, her left arm outstretched to the point her hand extended beyond the edge of the bed its fingers curling down, drooping like they were the leaves of a plant in need of water. Her right arm was bent back in a natural position as if she were clutching her chest in a deep sleep. Even though her eyes were closed, Jake was certain he could still see the anguish in her face.

Cyrus looked back. He appeared sad, more so than Jake had ever seen him. He said, "Greta has killed herself."

Jake recognized the two empty laudanum bottles on the little night table next to her bed. One stood upright, the other lay on its side next to the lantern and a small bible. *His conscience had already started working on him. You shudda knocked. You shudda went to her last night. Got Cyrus, something. But no you just walk out.* He sighed heavily and shook his head. "I'm sorry Cyrus."

Cyrus said, like he knew it for a fact. "You were the last one to see her alive, how was she?"

Jake hesitated not wanting to tell how it had been last night. He began, "She told me her secrets, all of it I reckon. It caused her to become purty upset."

Cyrus frowned as if he were puzzled. "But to kill herself, why now?"

It was tempting to not tell Cyrus about Yellow Wolf as Jake was certain it was that information that had pushed Greta over the edge and for people to know that would, he figured, start the second guessing as to why he hadn't done something more. In hind sight he wished that he had but there was no changing last night now, just like he knew that he couldn't live with himself if he wasn't honest about Yellow Wolf. He said, "Yesterday in town, I overheard a couple of Army guys talking about one of the Indians that had a hand in murdering Greta's family and mistreating her. This -"

"I guess she did have reason to carry on in the night," interjected Elmer in a surprised tone.

Cyrus glared at Elmer as if to silence him and then looked back at Jake who went on, "This Indian named Yellow Wolf claims to know where Greta is. I told Greta this. Told her I'd help her get away. I told her purty much anything I could think of that would give her hope, but she wouldn't hear any of it. Said she wanted to go lay down so I left not long after that."

Cyrus scowled. "Damn Jake, I wish you would have come got me."

"I offered to, but she didn't want it."

Cyrus looked at Jake in a stern, disapproving way. He said in a somber voice, "When people get the way Greta was last night you have to think for them, just do what you know is best."

"She was purty dug in on what she wanted and didn't. I guess you wudda had to have been there to know how she was. I reckon you can call me a fool but I did not see this coming. I figured come this morning she'd talk to you about what to do."

Cyrus snorted. "Well, that's not going to happen." His anger was haughty and readily apparent. It was hurtful to Jake. In the nine years that he had known Cyrus he could count on one hand the times that they'd been angry with each other. But even then, those times had been akin to a passing storm cloud that was followed by blue skies and sunshine. This time it was different.

CHAPTER EIGHT

Later that day after Elmer had constructed a coffin and Jake had dug a grave, they buried Greta next to a couple of cow hands that had died on the Rockin' C. One of them had gotten killed trying to break a mean horse and the other had been found with a half a dozen arrows in his body. Greta did not know them and they did not her, but they had all been buried on the closest thing they knew as home at the time of their deaths. Everybody at the headquarters place came to the burial. Cyrus said words over her. He got a little choked up near the end, probably more so than Agnes thought was necessary. Besides Cyrus, no one but Elmer and Jake knew what had likely motivated Greta to take her own life. There was some talk among others at the bunkhouse that, *the crazy cook finally killed herself.*

It was two days after they had put Greta in the ground that the Army showed up. Jake and Cyrus were loading a wagon that was backed part way into the barn with rolls of barbed wire from a storage room inside. Jake saw them first as their horses splashed through the creek at the ford below the house. He hollered at Cyrus. "Got some soldiers headed our way. And the Sheriff too."

Cyrus frowned but said nothing as he emerged from the supply room with a heavy roll of wire resting on his right thigh. His steps were exaggerated and labored due to the concentrated weight of the tightly wound roll. Upon reaching the wagon he gave the wire a heft into the back of it causing it to shudder slightly with a loud thump. He then went along side of the wagon to just outside the barn door where Jake was watching the soldiers advance. Cyrus laughed. "Hells bells, you figure there is enough of 'em?"

There was an officer, six troopers, and the Sheriff. Jake's mind went back to that night and Greta's certainty that the Army was determined to find her. *These boys have come fixed for a fight if need be,* he said to himself. He scoffed aloud and then said derisively, "Maybe they git lonely."

The soldiers had started toward the house when Sheriff Nye, apparently having recognized Cyrus, pointed in the direction of the barn causing them to change course.

Jake sighed. *Shit, I just git clear ah the Sheriff and all that business with Nate and here he comes again.* He said to Cyrus, "What do we tell them?"

"Beyond Greta's name, you didn't know a thing about her past. Not a thing."

Jake looked over at Cyrus who was staring intently at the soldiers coming their way. He said, "Maybe we should just be honest with them."

Cyrus snorted. "They want revenge and to save face. We'll get no quarter from the Army or the Sheriff on this so you can put away your principles of honesty, Jake."

They were just about within normal conversation distance when Jake recognized the officer as the one in the café who'd said what he had about Yellow Wolf. He was about to whisper this fact to Cyrus when Sheriff Nye called out like they were friends, "Afternoon boys. She's a hot one today ain't she."

"What can I do for ya, Sheriff," asked Cyrus indifferently.

The Sheriff nodded toward the officer. "This is Captain Bouchard. He's looking for a woman that we've heard is employed by you."

The Captain, who was tall and slender with dark mutton chop sideburns and a bushy moustache cut in. "Her name is Greta Peterson. Is she here?"

"She is."

"Well could you take us to her?"

"All of you?" replied Cyrus with a hint of insolence in his voice.

The Captain, who had likely been briefed by the Sheriff about Nate and Roy's hanging, was in no mood for Cyrus' attitude. He flashed an annoyed look before saying sternly, "Where's the woman?"

Cyrus took a couple of steps towards Bouchard and the Sheriff and then pointed up the canyon to a big cottonwood tree with three wooden crosses beneath it. "She's the one with the fresh dirt."

At first Bouchard appeared surprised but that soon turned to anger, maybe even disbelief. "When did she die?"

"Couple days ago.

"What was her cause of death?"

"She drank too much laudanum."

"Are there others here who can verify that?"

"You saying I'm lying."

The Sheriff cut in. "In a situation like this, people who are mindful of the law would fetch me so I can make the determination as to the cause of death."

"Well, next time I'll ride that 40 miles to town and back so I can bring you out here and have you tell me how a dead person with two empty laudanum bottles on her nightstand got that way."

Bouchard moved on. "Any idea what brought this on?"

"Couldn't live with herself, I reckon. Indians murdered her family. Took her hostage. Raped her. I found her wondering by herself out east of here in the hills."

"She was by herself?" asked Bouchard suspiciously.

"That's the way I found her. Half out of her mind. Didn't make any sense for a coupla weeks."

"She never said anything about a soldier being with her?"

"Not to me, she didn't"

Bouchard paused briefly and then looked straight at Jake. "What about you? Did she ever tell you anything different?"

Not wanting to incur their ire in any way, Jake came back respectful. "No sir. Till she died a coupla days ago, I hadn't known any of this business about the Indians killing her family. Greta could whip up some really fine chuck but she wasn't much for talking."

The air was still and unmercifully hot. Beads of sweat ran down the trooper's faces as they swatted in vain at the horse flies buzzing around them. Bouchard had gone silent as he stared up the canyon at the big cottonwood and the graves beneath it. He'd anticipated success in finding this woman who had eluded capture all this time, but now it was clear he would get no satisfaction in that regard.

At last the Sheriff said, "Do you suppose Yellow Wolf will believe you?"

Bouchard frowned. "He's got no choice. The Army, on the other hand, will still require justice for those two troopers that were killed trying to apprehend Mrs. Peterson and Corporal Saunders. So my search will go on, I suppose."

From the corner of his eye Jake snuck a peak at Cyrus to see if he was tempted to throw himself upon the mercy of Bouchard and the Sheriff and tell them that he had buried Saunders, and the Army's horses that he and Greta had been riding were at this very moment in a remuda not three miles from where they were standing. But, his face was blank. There wasn't a hint of anything like that happening. And then Jake shifted his full attention to Bouchard and the Sheriff, thinking that they would soon be leaving as their business was finished when the Sheriff threw a rock in that still pond. He said, "Whaddaya aim to do with that barbed wire, Cyrus?"

Cyrus came back like cold water dropped on hot rocks, his words sizzled. "What the hell do you think I'm gonna do with it?"

"Most likely piss off some legitimate homesteaders by fencing them out of open government ground. You know you can't do that."

"You're mistaken Sheriff. This wire is for building a drift fence to keep my cattle outta those places where the Grangers has got so thick that a cow can't stay outta trouble."

The Sheriff snorted in disbelief. "Well, I hope at some point down the road we don't lock horns over this."

"If it weren't for the big ranchers settling this country these Grangers wouldn't be here. It's the cattlemen that's made it so folks can live on this land. They opened it up."

Bouchard appeared insulted. He jumped in. "I think Mr. Ellsworth you need to review your history. If it weren't for the Army and the railroad this country would be totally uncivilized. It wouldn't be safe at all."

Cyrus laughed. "I wish you could have told that to Greta. I suspect she would have had a different view on the matter. She was under the impression you soldier boys wasn't around when she needed you. "

The Captain's expression was now clearly one of anger. His eyes were like bubbling caldrons ready to erupt. And then the Sheriff, not so affected as Bouchard, said, "We should go, Sir. I don't think we're going to see common ground here today."

Bouchard glared at Cyrus who was un-phased, if anything he was amused, which further angered the Captain. He said, constrained by the decorum of his position, "I suspect, Mr. Ellsworth, I'll be seeing you again."

"I hope so," replied Cyrus in a cocky tone. "These reservation Indians been butchering my cattle whenever the mood strikes them. Seems the government hasn't been giving them the beef they was promised."

Bouchard stared at Cyrus for a few seconds before snorting in a contemptuous way and tossing his head back. "Let's go, Sheriff."

Jake and Cyrus watched as the soldiers and Sheriff Nye swung around in a column of twos and splashed back across Dead Horse Creek. Jake said, "I believe you've put a permanent burr under that Captain's saddle blanket."

Cyrus said nothing as he continued to watch the riders. When they had disappeared beyond the trees along the creek, he said, "I want you to catch them Army horses of Greta's and take 'em south. Maybe down around Jawbone Springs. I suspect somebody will steal them. If they don't, we'll know where to find 'em if we ever feel the nerve to use them."

Jake nodded and then his conscience, and maybe a little of him being a young red-blooded guy, prodded him. "You suppose I should pay Nate English's widow a visit? See how she's gittin' along."

Cyrus said, so as to sound more serious than flippant, "She might shoot you if she finds out the law let us go. And if that damned Nye goes down there and starts preaching the law to her about how she shouldn't ah shot you in the first place, she could be a little ornery."

Jake smiled. "Guess I'll take my chances."

CHAPTER NINE

They were now into July. So far, it gave no indication that it would be any more merciful in terms of rain or even some relief from the heat than the preceding months of May and June. There were some springs that had gone dry that Jake had never known, in the time he'd been in the country, to ever do so. Fortunately, Jawbone Springs was still putting out the same trickle of water that it always did. It was more than enough for the two Army horses that Jake turned loose there. He suspected it didn't really matter though as he was fairly certain they would end up on Pumpkin Creek where the feed was better and there was lots of water and Grangers. It seemed to him there was a decent chance that someone, if they were law abiding, would see them and alert the Army as to their whereabouts. He smiled as he watched the horses begin to graze. He said to himself, *if that Captain gits wind of these horses he'll likely be beatin' the bushes around here for his Corporal Saunders.* In a way Jake wished that he could be truthful with Bouchard and the Sheriff and put an end to all of this deception, but he knew that wouldn't bode well for Cyrus.

He'd purposely not allowed himself more than a fleeting glance up the hill at Nate and Roy's graves but he knew

Ellie would ask about them and as much as he didn't want to go up there, he didn't want to lie to her either. Jake urged Rusty on towards the graves going past where he'd originally piled rocks on the dead men and where they'd later found their scavenged bodies. The memory of that day and its horrific images and the smell came back to him as plain as if it was happening right now. But he went on trying his best to crowd out the bad things in his mind and focus on the blue sky and the white puffy clouds and the good birds, what few there were, singing in the juniper trees and the grass already starting to turn yellow. At last when he was about 15 feet from the graves he stopped. From atop Rusty he could see they were as they had left them. Nothing, absolutely nothing had changed. It came to Jake, *being dead is damned lonely*. It made him shiver and then he began to be fearful of how it would be for him when he was dead. The feeling was building within him until he felt as if he might get sick. Abruptly, he looked away and started Rusty back down the slope and away from all that had happened at the springs.

Jake was hopeful that George McDonald's anger at Rockin' C cattle having gotten into his grain field had subsided and should he encounter McDonald along the way to Ellie's it would not result in him making good on his boy's threat to give Jake a thrashing. Nonetheless, he dropped down to Pumpkin Creek and the trail that ran along the east side of it. Right away he ran into Rockin' C cattle, not in large numbers which he took to be a favorable sign as the grass was getting short along the creek, but enough to push over some of the rickety fences he was seeing around the grain and pasture fields. He was nearing McDonald's place when he stopped and studied a barbed wire fence surrounding a wheat field on the other side of the stream. He laughed out loud. The fence had three strands that were often loose and spaced such that a cow could easily stick her head between the top two strands and eat away at what grain she could reach. Jake snorted and said aloud, "Shit, they're just baitin' 'em in. Least they could do is build a decent fence." A ditch had been cut from the creek upstream and carried water to the field. The wheat was green and stood about two feet tall. Jake said to himself, *if this damned drought goes on this field is gonna be the only green thing for a cow to eat. It'll be like setting a steak and all the fixin's in front of a bunch of hungry men and telling them to not touch it.*

As he neared the spot on the trail when he would be straight across from McDonald's place on the other side of the creek, Jake became a little uneasy. He wondered if Mc-Donald or his boys saw him if the fight would be on. There was smoke coming from the chimney of their log cabin. *Those boys are probably inside eatin' supper*, said Jake to himself. However, no sooner had he drawn this conclusion than one of McDonald's sons appeared in the doorway. For a time, he stood dead still with his hands cupped over his eyes trying to make out who the stranger was on the horse across the creek. Jake reckoned it was a good 400 yards beyond the distance for someone to immediately recognize a horse and rider unless the horse was different like a paint or palomino, which Rusty was not. But then in the stillness of the evening air, the words, "Hey Pa, come here," carried across the creek as clear as if that person was standing right in front of Jake. Soon, there were more voices talking over one another. Jake could not see their owners as he had not slowed Rusty and would now have to turn in the saddle to look back at the cabin. But he did not look as he had no desire for a confrontation. He smiled when he saw what appeared to be McDonald's saddle horses grazing along the creek about a quarter mile below the cabin. He sighed, feeling somewhat relieved. He whispered aloud, "Now, if our cows don't push over their sorry fences we'll be alright."

Jake continued on at a walk so as to not give the impression that he was running from a fight but when he had rounded a bend in the trail and was out of sight of the cabin he nudged Rusty into a trot, just in case the McDonalds decided to go catch their horses and come after him. He maintained this pace for a little over a mile at which point he was at the mouth of Deer Creek. Slowing Rusty to a walk again, he turned onto the trail that went up the canyon. It wouldn't be long and he'd be at Ellie's place. Since he'd been gone from her he'd thought about her often. It was, he knew, when he was honest with himself, more than just her offer of work or guilt that he should look out for her. Decent white women who would be interested in a cow hand with nothing to his name but a bedroll and horse were hard to find in this country, or for that matter, probably anywhere. He'd known a number of saloon girls, even becoming serious about one of them a couple of years ago, but too many other hands at the Rockin' C had done business with her for it to work out.

Deer Creek was a well-defined drainage with fairly steep slopes coming up on either side of it. The bottom of the canyon, however, was wide, a quarter mile or more in places. It was these wider places, Jake figured, that had probably attracted Nate English as the soil was dark and rich and the creek water was right there. To his credit, Nate had mostly fenced off about ten acres of natural meadow just down from his cabin. He'd strung wire from the trees around the meadow's perimeter, just as they had at Jawbone Springs. Jake scoffed and said to himself as he looked at the portion of the fence not completed, *Nate probably took the wire he needed for this to build his rustler trap. What a fool he was.*

There was about half a sun still visible on the western horizon. It was well past supper time. Ellie's cabin, from the down canyon side appeared dark to Jake, even unoccupied but Nate and Roy's horses were in the corral along with Daisy the milk cow. And then suddenly, Bella came running from around the corner of the cabin barking wildly. Rusty stopped of his own accord.

Jake called out. "Hey Bella dog, you remember me don't you?"

Bella stood her ground, squarely in Rusty' path and continued to bark.

Jake continued to indulge the dog. "Where's Ellie and Henry? Why don't you take me to 'em?"

"Mr. Lafarge, what are you doing here?"

Jake looked up and beyond Bella to see Ellie and Henry coming at a fast walk. He was instantly reminded of Ellie's beauty. She was wearing a blue ankle length gingham dress with her hair tied back in a ponytail. She had Nate's rifle cradled across her chest and appeared slightly out of breath. Henry was trailing behind her. Jake said, "Evenin' Ma'am."

Ellie smiled as she lowered the rifle to her side, holding it with her right hand while shading her eyes from the setting sun with her left. "We were down by the creek working in the garden. Seems almost impossible to stay ahead of the weeds."

Jake laughed. "If there is one thing that will grow in a drought, it's a weed."

"Oh yes, how well do Henry and I know that."

Jake could see the hope, the excitement in her eyes. It suddenly occurred to him that maybe he shouldn't have come as he wasn't here to take Ellie up on her offer to work for half the crop. In the short time since he'd started up Deer Creek or essentially what was Nate English's homestead, it appeared to him that nothing had changed since he was last here. The sage flats further down the canyon needed to be cleared and plowed and planted. The meadow fence needed to be completed and the grass hay cut and hauled in. A barn needed to be constructed for the milk cow and horses and storing the hay. There was lots of work to be done and he was here just to see how she was getting along. It was akin, he thought, to giving a man dying of thirst a sip of water from a full canteen and then taking the canteen away.

Ellie went on, "Come inside, Mr. Lafarge. I've got apple cider. A neighbor further down Pumpkin Creek brought me a whole gallon. It's sweet, very tasty. You've got to try it."

He came back, "If it's all right Ma'am, I'll tend to Rusty 'fore I come in."

"Why certainly. Are you hungry?"

Jake smiled. "I never turn down a free meal."

Ellie smiled back, happy seemingly, at least on the surface she was. She said, "Fine, it'll be ready when you come in."

Jake nudged Rusty and rode on past Bella who was now content to sit on her haunches and observe. As he went by Ellie and Henry he sensed their desperation. It did not give him a good feeling knowing that he was partially to blame for it. He smiled and waved at the boy, but he did not wave back. At the corral he unsaddled Rusty, fed him a few handfuls of oats from his saddlebags and then picketed him a short ways up the canyon from Ellie's cabin. In a way, he was in no hurry to get back there and enter into discussion as to why he was here. Before starting out he took a moment and rolled a cigarette. Sometimes a smoke helped him to think. After lighting it, he spit on the match and dropped it on bare ground where he then shoved it deeper into the soil with the heel of his boot. It was a good 300 yards to the cabin on account of the horses and Daisy had pretty much grazed off all the grass out to that distance. He set off at a slow pace meandering through the aspen and ponderosa puffing on his cigarette. It was peaceful and quiet except for the Steller's jays who screeched their disapproval of his presence. The tranquility caused him to feel better about being there almost to the point of seriously considering Ellie's offer. He said to his self, *I can see why Nate wanted to settle here. A fella could fence off the mouth of the canyon and have water and graze and some farm land too. Doesn't make any sense that he'd go to rustling.* But then in the next instant it all felt peculiar, almost dirty or wrong for him to be there thinking and feeling as he was. Even now, in his mind, he could see Nate begging for his life and then struggling, kicking, gasping at the end of the rope. They'd walked away so as to not have to watch Nate die, but he knew now that a man can never walk away from a hanging soon enough to avoid being haunted by it. He sighed. *I'll never be free of that day if I stay on here.*

Smoke was coming from the cabin's stovepipe. It was a vigorous column going straight up into the stillness of the evening air. *She musta stoked the fire up on my account*, said Jake to his self. *She's wantin' in the worst way for me to stay on.* Henry and Bella were playing outside. They caught sight of Jake as he came out of the trees about 50 yards away. Henry briefly stared at him, like he was something to be feared, and then ran inside the cabin. Bella, on the other hand, ran towards Jake and began barking.

Shortly, Ellie appeared in the doorway. "Bella, that's enough. You come over here." Instantly, the dog went quiet and started back towards Ellie.

Jake laughed and called out, "I hope yer dog's memory improves."

Ellie smiled and reached down to pet the top of Bella's head. "I think in time she'll take to you."

Jake latched on to the '*in time*' part of what Ellie had said. His inner voice came back, *She's countin' on you staying*. He thought to say, *Well, I probably won't be around long enough for Bella to git to where she won't bark at me*, but before he could Ellie said, "I've got hot beef stew inside and biscuits and fresh butter. Honey too. Henry found a bee's nest up the canyon."

Jake laughed and looked down at Henry who had come to his mother's side. "I'll betcha that was a trick gittin' that honey and not gittin' stung."

Henry broke his silence. "Willy showed me how."

"Willy?" asked Jake.

"George McDonald's son," said Ellie. "He and George stopped by a couple of days ago. They brought us some fresh beef."

Jake felt as if he'd just been hit with a left right combination. He instantly felt a pang of jealousy that George McDonald had come to see Ellie. It was a feeling that he immediately tried to discount, but in his mind it got jumbled with an equally unforeseen impulse and that being anger. The fresh beef that McDonald had brought was likely from a Rockin C cow that he had shot for having gotten into his grain field. But before Jake could sort through these emotions and respond to Ellie in a way befitting the fact he was about to eat this beef, Henry threw a little more kerosene on the fire.

"Willy says if you was to come around anymore they were going to whip you good."

Ellie blurted out. "Henry, mind your tongue. I told you that was just idle man talk. Foolishness, nothing will come of it." She then looked at Jake. "I hope you don't take the McDonalds seriously, Mr. Lafarge."

116

Jake scoffed. "No more serious than the other day when they told me to my face they were going to whip me."

Ellie became embarrassed. "I'm sorry but I really think they just talk a lot."

Jake heard the words in his mind before he said them. He knew in that instant it would be best to let them die, but he didn't. He put them out there, without arrogance or spite. "Well Ma'am, I believe yer eatin' Mr. Ellsworth's beef. That's the end result of McDonald's threat. So you see the man might just follow through on what he says."

At first Ellie looked indignant but that quickly gave way to hurt. Her eyes began to tear up. She said, "I suspected it but we had no meat." She paused and then said in a tone that came close to blame. "I'm now at the mercy of other's generosity, Mr. Lafarge."

Shame flooded Jake's face. "I'm sorry. If it wasn't for me and my boss you wouldn't be in this fix."

Ellie laughed. "We were in a fix long before this. Why do you think Nate and Roy were doing what they were?"

Jake looked at her, trying to decide if she really wanted to go on talking as they were in front of Henry. Ellie pierced his stare. "Let's go inside, Mr. Lafarge. Your stew is on the stove." Looking down at Henry, she added, "Why don't you and Bella play outside?"

Henry frowned at being excluded from what would be said, but he always minded his mother. However, he did not look up before starting to walk away. He said, dejectedly, "C'mon Bella."

Jake followed Ellie into the cabin and sat down at the table in front of a bowl, a pint Mason jar that appeared to contain cider and silverware. Biscuits, butter and honey were within arm's reach. Moments later, Ellie set a steaming pot of stew on a pot holder in the center of the table. It smelled good to Jake.

"Help yourself, Mr. Lafarge."

"Thank you, Ma'am. This looks mighty fine."

Ellie smiled, trying to ease the awkwardness of it. "Well, it's your beef and my potatoes, carrots and onions."

Jake forced a laugh as he spooned some stew into his bowl. "I reckon we're even then, Ma'am. They complement one another, for sure they do." A sudden lull descended upon them as Jake began to eat. Neither of them wanted to go back to where the conversation had been heading outside.

Just out of the blue, Ellie said, in a coy halting voice, "You know Mr. Lafarge, I have no objection if you address me by my first name."

Ellie's words caught Jake by surprise. His face gave away the fact that he had immediately begun to ponder her intent, such was his expression and hesitation in answering that she became embarrassed. "I'm sorry, Mr. Lafarge. I didn't mean to be forward."

"You weren't, Ma'am. Not at all, it's just I don't associate too much with ladies. Most women I call by their first names are, well – saloon girls and yer definitely not in their class."

At first, Ellie looked hurt, then angry. Neither reaction was what Jake had expected. Finally, she said, "I guess they can't be all bad. Nate seemed to have an eye for them."

Jake was taken aback. He said, "Some men are that way. In Nate's case, I would say he was a fool."

Ellie blushed slightly, but then the anger returned to her eyes. She said, her voice beginning to crack, "This place is the way it is on account of him and my no account brother gallivanting all over the country drinking and gambling and then trying to make up for it by stealing. Why is it do you think that we're farmers without a plow or mower, or for that matter, a team to pull them. Nate would've told you that Indians stole the team, but I know better. Him and Roy, they'd be gone four or five days at a time. " And then she began to quietly cry.

"They left you and Henry here alone?" Ellie nodded but did not look up.

It was callous and cold but Jake heard the voice in the back of his mind call out, *Maybe Nate and Roy was deserving of what they got.* He'd known men like them. They were never content with what they had, always looking for easy money and a good time. Monte dealers loved their kind. Jake shook his head and sighed. He said the obvious. "It'll be tough to make a go of it here alone."

Ellie wiped at her eyes and sniffled. "I'm not alone. George McDonald has offered to take care of me. Him and his boys would do everything, put up my hay, build me a barn, break out new ground, plant it, harvest the crop, everything. But, it comes at a price."

"And that is?"

"He's a widower. I'd have to agree to marry him."

Jake snorted. "He doesn't waste any time."

Ellie laughed in a sarcastic tone. "He made me this offer months ago when Nate and Roy were off doing whatever mischief they could find."

"I take it yer not tempted by his offer."

"No, not in the least, but the way he sees it now that Nate's gone I've got no good reason to refuse him."

As Ellie's words sunk in, it became clear to Jake that McDonald would have even more reason to give him a whipping if he were to step in as Ellie's partner.

And then Ellie said, "I need your help, Jake. I come from poor people. This place would be the first thing of any value that I ever had."

When he first got there, he'd known deep down that he wanted to help her but logic and his commitment to Cyrus had over rode him telling her. The words were like a bunch of yearling calves that trailed along a fence until they found a place they could slip through. He heard himself say, "Well, maybe I can help you out for a couple of weeks."

Ellie's face immediately brightened, like the sun breaking through dark clouds. "That would be so kind of you, Jake. But you should know, I have almost no money for materials."

It was not lost on Jake that she had started addressing him by his first name. He welcomed the familiarity, knowing full well that he may have just stepped off into quicksand by agreeing to stay on, to no doubt incur the wrath of George McDonald. He said, "You've got those weapons I brought you. If you can find a buyer, they might bring enough to get some lumber for a barn."

Ellie, who had been standing, pulled a chair out and sat down at the table across from Jake.

She said, "The man who gave me the cider, Mr. Halverson, is a genuinely kind person. He has a small sawmill. I suspect he might be willing to take the guns in trade for lumber. He never cared much for Nate but I think he would do it for me."

Jake had just taken a spoonful of stew. He chewed a couple of times like he was thinking as much as he was eating. He said, "Probably won't be much of a barn for that kind ah money but it'll be better than nuthin' come winter. Henry will appreciate milkin' in out of the snow and cold."

Ellie smiled. "I suspect he will."

Jake reached for a biscuit, cut it in half and began to butter it. He said, with his attention more on the biscuit than her eyes, "I'll need some help building the barn."

Ellie came back quick. "I can help you. I'm strong, Jake. You may not think it, but I am."

Jake grinned as he teased her, "That may be but can you drive a nail?"

It took a second for her to gauge the tenor of his words before replying in the same vein as him, "I'm good at holding boards."

Jake laughed. He could see in her face that all the bad emotions that had been there since he'd first met her were gone, certainly not forever but they had sunk beneath the surface of the quicksand. It played in his mind that what might be his dilemma was her salvation.

CHAPTER TEN

They had talked about what needed to be done and how they would go about it until the sun was out of sight. To see the hopefulness, maybe even happiness in Ellie helped to ease the nagging pain and regret in Jake's mind of that day at Jawbone Springs. And, in that sense, he was able to reconcile his decision to stay for a couple of weeks knowing that Cyrus was going to be upset with him.

After retrieving Rusty from where he'd been picketed and putting him in the corral, Jake took his bedroll and rifle and went down by the creek. In the off chance that it should ever rain, he constructed a shelter from a piece of canvas that Ellie had given him. It was simple, consisting of a rope between two aspen trees with the canvas hung over it. The corners of the tarp he tied to wooden stakes driven into the ground. His makeshift tent was open on either end but it was better than nothing and it defined his place, kind of like his bed in the bunkhouse back at the ranch. As he lay there in his blankets listening to the gurgling of the creek and the chirping of the crickets, his mind was awash with what he had committed to. He wondered if, at the end of the two weeks, he would be able to leave.

Jake opened his eyes. It seemed that he'd just heard the Great Horned Owl up the creek a ways and now there were a host of daytime birds singing. He threw back his blanket and crawled out of his shelter. He stood next to it in his union jack underwear. Through the trees he could see the corral and that Daisy had been tied to one of its poles. For a moment, he was puzzled by this as it was barely light enough to see, but then he caught a glimpse of Henry squatting on his milking stool beside Daisy. It came to him, *that boy is likely not cut from the same bolt of cloth as his old man.* He wondered too, if Henry would ever warm up to him.

Jake had just finished dressing and was heading across the open ground between the trees along the creek and the corral when the gate opened and Daisy came trotting out, behind her came the boy lugging the heavy milk bucket. He set the bucket on the ground momentarily while he closed the gate. As he turned around, Jake hollered out, "Yer gonna end up with cow milker hands. Why you'll be able to squeeze ah broom stick in two." And then Jake laughed but Henry acted like he hadn't heard him. He picked up the bucket with his right hand and proceeded to walk as fast as his heavily tilted posture would allow towards the cabin. As he watched the boy it came to Jake what Ellie had said last night. *Henry had his father up on a pedestal and you knocked him off. It's going to take time for him to get over that.*

With the way the Indians had been lately, Jake was reluctant to leave Rusty unattended all day. But, it didn't make sense to have him trail behind the wagon and he didn't want to put him under harness to pull it, that he was leaving to Nate and Roy's horses, Trixie and Jiggs. And so, he turned Rusty out along the creek to graze.

It was close to nine o'clock by the time they'd had breakfast and Jake had dealt with the minor rodeo in getting the saddle horses harnessed and hooked to the wagon. He and Ellie sat on the driver's seat while Henry stood in the back and Bella ran along side. Jake had a peculiar, but good, feeling sitting there next to Ellie. He could see them in his mind, kind of like a family, traveling as they were. They'd not gone very far when she said, "They're pulling well, don't you think?"

Jake glanced over at her and grinned. "The wagon's empty. Be a different story comin' back."

"Yes, of course. We'll have to make it a light load."

"We will, assuming we can trade guns for wood."

They went on being quiet mostly save for Ellie commenting occasionally on the wildflowers. There were places where the purple of the lupine and the yellow of the mule's ear dominated the open spaces on the sides of the canyons. The color came down to the toe of the slope being held out of the creek bottom by the wild plum and boxelder that grew in profusion there.

Ellie said, "The plums are coming on in spite of this cursed drought. Do you like plum cobbler, Jake?"

Jake's mind went back to a time last year when he had picked some plums and taken them to Greta so that she could make cobbler for the men. She baked up enough so that they had it with thick cream and sugar for dessert two days in a row. And then just as he had formed the words to tell Ellie how much he liked plum cobbler the image of Greta laying there, on her side dead, invaded his mind. He came back, his voice having been robbed of its enthusiasm, "Yes Ma'am, I do."

Ellie went on, not knowing where Jake's mind had gone off to. "Fine, Henry and I will pick some for that purpose. They should be ready by the first of August I would think."

The naysayer in his mind suddenly burst into the solemnity of Greta's room and her being there dead and Jake wishing he'd gone for Cyrus the night before; it shouted out to him, *August is almost four weeks away. You ain't gonna be here then. You need to tell her 'fore she gits herself all built up for a big letdown.* But he weighed the moment against how it would likely go if he told her now and kept quiet. *Maybe tonight, after supper*, he told himself.

It was a little before noon when they arrived at Otis Halverson's sawmill. It was situated about a half mile up a side canyon off of the Pumpkin Creek road. Ponderosa pine, big and old and tall grew on the north facing slope hence the reason for the sawmill being where it was. The air smelled strongly of fresh cut pine and smoke with just a hint of grease as one neared the actual machinery. The sawmill had been in existence for about two years and already any tree bigger than about four inches in diameter was gone from that area within a quarter mile of it. There were more stumps than trees. But surrounding this devastation, at least to the ridgetop, there was a sea of trees that appeared like a heavy green rug had been laid on the ground.

A huge iron wheeled tractor with a large boiler about ten feet long by about four feet in diameter was parked beneath an open-ended wooden shed. Dark blue, almost black smoke poured from its stack. The boiler fed a steam powered engine attached to it. A long thick belt composed of rubber and canvas ran from the flywheel of the engine to another wheel that drove a large round saw blade so fast that Jake could not make out its individual teeth. The blade was just entering a huge ponderosa pine log. Its high-pitched whine faltered just slightly before recovering as the wickedly sharp orbit spewed sawdust behind it slabbing off a board about an inch thick by ten inches wide and twelve feet long. A young man wearing a flat cap picked up the board and carried it over to a large stack that was about up to his chest. He set it on top of the stack making sure it lined up perfectly.

Jake caught Ellie's attention before pointing to the boards. "We could use that whole pile about four times over."

Ellie's eyes widened. "How big of a barn are you figuring on building?"

"Big enough."

From the seat at the rear of the tractor a man shouted over the rhythmic chunking and hissing of the steam engine and the whirr of the saw, "Dinner time." The board stacker as well as Otis Halverson's other two boys who had been feeding logs to the saw did not hesitate. They started towards the cabin where a plump middle-aged woman stood in the doorway knowing their father would be doing business. Otis cut the power to the saw blade and got down from the tractor. He was a big man, a little over six feet tall and heavy set. His Levis and gray cotton shirt were coated with sawdust, dirt, grease and pitch from the trees. His shirt, in particular, was heavily stained with sweat. On those days when he shaved his face was devoid of whiskers save for a black droopy moustache. But that day had been some time ago as he looked scruffy and unkempt. His short-billed miner's cap was as dirty as the rest of his clothes.

Ellie called out. "Good morning, Mr. Halvorson."

Otis came back, his dark eyes mostly on Jake, "Mornin' to you, Mrs. English. You come for some more cider?"

Ellie laughed. "No thank you, but it was very good." She paused as if to acknowledge his curiosity which had become close to a stare. She glanced at Jake and then back to Otis. "This is

Jake Lafarge. He has agreed to help me out for a while."

Otis stepped towards Jake and extended his big meaty hand. Jake noted the ground in dirt and grease in the folds of skin on his knuckles and under his finger nails, but he did not shy away in the least from giving him a firm handshake. "Pleased to make yer acquaintance, Mr. Halvorson."

"Likewise," said Otis. "Where do you hail from?"

"Originally Louisiana, but for some time now, I been punchin' cows for the Rockin' C."

Otis looked as if he'd just heard a rattlesnake buzz. "That's Cyrus Ellsworth's outfit, ain't it?" Jake sensed trouble. "It is."

Otis hesitated like he was thinking. The friendly at ease look that had been on his face just a moment ago was now gone. He said, "I was talkin' to a feller just yesterday that had come from town. Said the talk there is all about how Ellsworth and one of his hands hung Ellie's husband and shot her brother." He paused and then demanded, "You have any part in that?"

"He did," said Ellie quickly. "But, it couldn't be helped. He just did what his boss told him to." "You really believe that?" asked Otis in a doubtful tone. "Ain't no amount of money would allow my conscience to hang a man."

"Trust me, Mr. Halvorson," said Jake in a curt tone, "if I could take that day back I would."

From the corner of her eye Ellie could see the anger in Henry's face and the tears that were building in his eyes, but she felt helpless to address them as equally apparent was the disgust on Halvorson's face. She said, "Nate and Roy were up to no good. You know how they were."

"That may be true," said Otis coldly, "but it ain't up to this fella and Cyrus Ellsworth to decide their fate."

Jake cut in. "I agree, but there ain't no takin' it back. I'm here now to try and make amends. Ellie has been kind enough to accept my help in gittin' her place ready for winter. We need lumber."

Otis snorted and shook his head, his opinion of Ellie clearly having changed from when he had taken her a gallon of cider. He said, "Well, I'll tell ya, with Nate and Roy barely cold in their graves the two of ya make ah fine pair."

"People may judge me," said Ellie sternly, "but I have forgiven Mr. Lafarge. I think he is sincere in his offer of help. So please, Mr. Halvorson, we need to negotiate a deal for some lumber so I might build a barn."

Halvorson sighed and shook his head as if it was difficult for him to look at Ellie and Jake. His eyes suggested that he was uncertain if he wanted to even do business with them. Finally, he said, "How much do you need?"

"As much as we can get for a rifle and two pistols," said Ellie in a pleading tone.

Halvorson laughed. "I got guns. I don't need anymore."

"Oh, please Mr. Halvorson. I've got to get a barn put up before winter," said Ellie in a shaky voice. And then she paused, her eyes becoming slightly watery before adding, "There's a saddle scabbard for the rifle and holsters and belts for the pistols too."

Halvorson scowled. "If I take those guns in trade I'm gonna haf ta do what you shudda before comin' here and that's find somebody that wants ta buy 'em. Most folks that need a gun has already got one."

Ellie began to cry causing Jake to jump in. "Sir, the general store in Miles City I believe would take them in trade for goods."

Halvorson scoffed. "They won't give you anything near what they're worth."

"I suspect not," said Jake, "but, maybe you could come over to the wagon and take a look at them. You tell us what they might be worth to you, knowing what you would be up against in disposing of them."

Halvorson purposely reinforced the scowl on his face and sighed impatiently. "Alright, let's go. My dinner is waitin' on me."

"Thank you, Mr. Halvorson," said Ellie in a now steady voice. "I appreciate your taking the time."

As they all started towards the wagon it was obvious that Mrs. Halvorson had emerged from the cabin and was coming towards them. She was just about to normal speaking distance when Otis shouted, "Edna, you can go back inside. I'll be along shortly."

But she did not retreat as her husband had ordered. She said, "I came to invite Mrs. English and her companions to dinner."

Otis came back quickly, his face already turning red from shame, "They don't have time. It's a long drive back to Deer Creek."

Edna went quiet but stood her ground, watching the group proceed to the wagon.

Under normal circumstances Jake knew they would've been invited to eat. He felt bad for Ellie and wondered how many of the other neighbors would judge her because of him. He wanted to call out to Edna and thank her for the offer so that she might be relieved from the insubordinate vigil that she was maintaining, but he knew better.

As they reached the wagon, Otis turned towards Edna and shouted, "Dammit woman, this matter does not concern you, now go inside."

Jake could see that Ellie and even Henry were greatly embarrassed at the blatant rudeness of Halvorson. Reaching into the box beneath the wagon's seat he brought out Roy's .44 Caliber Henry in its leather scabbard. Otis unsheathed the rifle and tried the action, dry firing it once before returning it to the scabbard. He said nothing. Jake then handed him Roy's .45 Caliber Army Colt and Nate's .44-40 Caliber Remington.

Otis hefted the pistols but did not cock them, his examination being mostly cursory. He said, "I ain't never had much use for six-shooters." He paused and then added like it was intended for Jake, "I ain't like these buckaroos that parade around with these things strapped on. I doubt if most of 'em could hit a barn wall if they was standin' inside the barn.' He laughed. "A rifle will do me just fine."

Jake ignored the slight and said, "You got a number that comes to mind, Mr. Halvorson?"

Halvorson sighed. "Thirty dollars."

"Thirty dollars," blurted Jake. "With the scabbard and gun belts they're worth way more than that."

"Maybe to somebody that needs them, but not me," replied Otis with a cold indifference.

"Thirty dollars will be fine," said Ellie. "How much lumber will that get us?"

Halvorson thought for a moment and then nodded towards the pile of boards that he'd been adding to when Ellie and Jake had arrived. He shrugged, "About 80 or 85 of those boards over there."

Ellie looked at the lumber stack and then at Jake remembering what he'd said about needing four of those. "That won't do will it?"

Jake shook his head. "We'll just have to git by with it."

Eighty-five boards, twelve feet long didn't take much time to load. Jake and Henry were through with it before Otis or any of his boys came back out from dinner. But that didn't really matter as there was nothing more to be said. Jake snapped the reins over the backs of Trixie and Jiggs.

"Giddup." The horses strained under their new burden. They did not rebel as Jake had feared, but instead moved the wagon along at a slow and steady pace. When they were down the road a ways, Jake said without looking at Ellie, "I'm sorry for causing this ill will between you and Halvorson."

"It's my doing, Jake. I knew your being here would set tongues to wagging, but they were wagging before all of this. It got back to me what people were saying, *Oh, that poor Mrs. English and that scalawag husband of hers and her no-account brother. That poor, poor woman. Leavin' her and that boy alone like he does.* So now I reach out and play, I suspect on your conscience and for that I'm sorry, but it was either that or share a man's bed whom I have absolutely no interest in."

"There'll likely be more Halvorson's."

Ellie slowly nodded her head while staring down at the rise and fall of the horses' hooves and the tiny puffs of dust with each step that they took. She said simply, "I know."

CHAPTER ELEVEN

The exchange at Halvorson's sawmill had been unpleasant. Before he came, Jake had considered the possibility that people would think poorly of Ellie for accepting his help let alone seeking it out. He could see how folks might read something else into it but, as was so often the case, he didn't listen to his inner self. Whatever happened, he would be riding away from it in two weeks. Ellie, on the other hand, would have to live with it and that included Henry, who hadn't said a word to him since leaving the sawmill.

They had just turned up Deer Creek. It was miserably hot and as usual the horse flies were relentless in their pestering. They swarmed around the horses and the wagon refusing to leave a good thing, no matter how many of their number died under Jake's hand or the horses' tails.

"I feel so sorry for the horses," said Ellie. "Being confined to their harnesses like they are, they just have to endure not only the flies but the heat."

"I guess that's the good thing about winter," said Jake.

"Winter is not without its challenges, otherwise we wouldn't need this lumber," replied Ellie.

Jake sensed the sudden bitterness in Ellie's voice. He considered briefly just keeping quiet the rest of the way home, but he had been worried about Rusty to the point the angst it had created within him would not allow it. He said, "I just hope my horse is still at your place when we get there."

"You think he might have strayed too far?"

Jake laughed derisively. "Yeah, with a little help from the Indians –" He stopped short, for her benefit, of adding, *and thieving white men*. He went on, "the Crow and Cheyenne can come off their reservations any time they want with written permission from the Indian agents. All they gotta do is say they're goin' huntin' for game. The truth of the matter is that game quite often ends up being horses and cattle. Like that day down on Pumpkin Creek when they was butchering that steer."

Ellie said, with some hesitation, "We did take their land and it was just one cow."

"So it'd be ok with you if they was to take Daisy and Trixie and Jiggs. That ain't too many."

Ellie frowned. "You know what I meant. Mr. Ellsworth has lots of cattle, and horses too I imagine."

"And there's lots a people tryin' to take 'em." The edge in Jake's voice was not lost on Ellie. She suddenly went mute and looked away. Jake noted it and came back, "I'm sorry, Ellie. I didn't mean to git preachy about this."

Ellie looked back him. "I know, I didn't mean to be so naïve about it."

"It worries me, you and Henry being here by yerselves. Why the Indians or whoever could just come and take yer animals and whatever else they wanted and there wouldn't be a thing you could do about it."

Ellie smiled. "Well, I shot you didn't I?"

Jake blushed and then laughed. "You sure enough did," he said in a mock tone of anger.

They went on, the conversation perhaps on a different plateau flowing more freely now. But, in the back of his mind, Jake couldn't help conjuring up a worst case scenario involving Indians and Ellie and Henry. The paranoia it generated in him was only slightly lessoned when he saw Rusty not far from the cabin down by the creek. His harder side shouted out to him, *Ya damned fool, you wouldn't be worryin' 'bout none ah this if you'd just stayed put.* He reckoned time would tell if this was good advice or not.

Breakfast talk had been dominated by Jake and Ellie discussing his plan to cut poles to frame out a small shed. It was about a half mile on up Deer Creek to a stand of lodge pole pine that he had discovered several years back while gathering cattle. It was before Nate had settled in the canyon or, for that matter, a good number of the Grangers that were in the area now. Jake was hoping, with the demand for posts and poles being what it was, that the trees had not been found. The sun was just coming above the horizon when he went out to the chicken coop to get the rusty whip saw hanging on its back wall. As he took it down, for some strange reason, he felt as if Nate was watching him doing the things Nate should have done. For a second, the hair on the back of his neck stood up and then from behind him, he heard steps.

"I could send Henry with you. He could be of some help, I'm sure," said Ellie.

Jake turned to face her and lowered his voice. "I don't think he really cottons to me. I'll be alright by myself."

Ellie sighed. "He just doesn't understand how things are."

"I suspect yer neighbors don't either."

For a moment she looked uneasy, almost agitated. "I've got to move on, Jake. I guess people expect me to sit here and pine over a man who left me for days on end. I'm sorry Nate and Roy are dead but the manner in which they died does not come as any surprise to me. No, I intend to make a life here for Henry and me."

Jake said purposely to gauge its impact, "Maybe after I'm gone people won't be so quick to judge."

Sadness came instantly to Ellie's face as she absorbed Jake's words. "I was hoping you'd stay on."

"I've already got a job."

Ellie paused as if she was thinking how best to convince him to stay, but then she said simply, like it didn't have the importance to her that it did, "My offer stands if you change your mind."

"I'll put some thought to it but I've been at the Rockin' C a long time."

Ellie immediately turned and began walking towards the cabin, she said over her shoulder, "Come by the house before you go. I made sandwiches for you."

Jake stood where he was for a moment and followed her with his eyes. She was a pretty woman who he sensed was offering him something more than thirty and found. He could see, if he allowed himself to fantasize, it might even turn out to be the family he'd never had. But no sooner had he gone there than the naysayer in his mind spoiled it with images of Halvorson and the look of contempt that Henry had given him. And then the dam broke with sights from Jawbone Springs and Nate and Roy's ghosts everywhere he looked and to top it off, his abandonment of Cyrus. Jake took a deep breath and exhaled noisily. He said to himself, *this is a bog hole I don't need to step off into.*

The stand of lodge pole pine was as Jake remembered it three years ago. The trees were tall and uniformly straight, which made them desirable for cutting if a person didn't need big logs. It was cool in their shade and quiet save for the chatter of the pine squirrels, Steller's jays and a lone raven circling overhead sending out the alarm that something was amiss down below. By noon Jake had felled what trees would be required for the shed and a few more that, when bucked up into eight foot lengths, would provide enough posts to finish the hay field fence. But before the trees could be skidded down to the canyon bottom where they could be cut to length, they needed to be limbed. He had just picked up a double bitted axe to start this task when he heard a horse nicker downslope from him. Thinking it might be Indians he lowered the head of the axe to the ground and let the handle slowly and silently fall over onto the boughs of the tree he was about to limb. He then took his pistol from its holster and moved behind a good-sized Douglas fir tree. For a short time he could hear nothing but the birds and the hammering of his heart. And then it came. "Hello up there."

In his mind Jake listened to the voice a second time before shouting back, "Afternoon to ya."

The voice came back. It had the ring of a cowpuncher. "Mind if I come on up."

Jake shouted into the trees below. "Help yerself, but I might put ya ta work."

The voice laughed. "Well hell, maybe I better head on down the canyon." But it was clear he was working his way up the hill to where Jake was at and then, all of a sudden, he came out of the trees. The man saw that Jake had his pistol out and stopped abruptly. He said in a light hearted manner, "I'm generally pretty neighborly when I ain't looking down a gun barrel."

Jake felt sheepish and quickly holstered his pistol. He hollered back. "Sorry, ah fella just never knows these days."

The stranger, who was on foot started up the hill again. He was wearing a sharply peaked Stetson with a long sleeved blue cotton shirt and Levis with, Jake figured, a good two inch cuff rolled up on them. There were streaks of gray around his temples and in his otherwise brown moustache as well. His face looked weathered like he worked for a living. He had black leather cuffs about six inches long that laced up on the underside on each forearm. Around his waist he had a gun belt that held an Army Colt .45. Most of the cartridge loops on it were full. When he was within about ten feet of Jake, he said in a cordial tone, "Cuttin' ya some fence posts, are ya?"

"A few," said Jake. "I'm mostly after some timbers for a little shed."

The stranger came closer and extended his hand. "Name's Harry Bovill."

"Jake Lafarge, pleased to make yer acquaintance."

"I take it your place is nearby?"

"No, I don't have a ranch. I'm just helpin' a widow woman down the canyon here."

"Oh, well I'm new to this country. I brought 5,000 head, give or take, up from Kansas this spring. We're just gittin' settled in to the east of here over on Antelope Creek."

Despite his initial take on Bovill, that he was a decent fellow, Jake felt a sudden pang of anger upon hearing that the man had brought a big bunch of cattle to a range that was already over stocked and now being carved up for farm land. Besides that, Antelope Creek was country that the Rockin' C had always claimed. But, it also occurred to him that he did not need to aggravate his present situation by telling this man he was not welcome. Jake did his best to hide his resentment and said, "Antelope Creek has got some good graze to it. Too bad you come in a drought year."

"Wasn't my call. I'm just runnin' this place for these ole boys back east. They heard about all this easy money to be made up here and I reckon it had 'em bustin' their cinches ta git here 'fore the other fella."

Jake laughed. "Yeah, that kinda tells it how it is purty good."

And then off in the distance towards Pumpkin Creek came the dull thuds of gunfire, five all together. Four of them sounded alike, louder, and one was different. They came quick taking no more than a few seconds.

Bovill said, "That don't sound friendly."

"No, it don't," replied Jake. "It's a long ways off. Hard tellin' what it might be."

"Could be somebody got confused about what belonged to 'em and they got caught," said Bovill with a grin. "A while back we had problems with that sort of thing down in Wyoming. Got to be quite a row before it was all said and done with."

Jake sensed he might have a sympathetic ear in Bovill concerning the Jawbone Springs affair, but he did not go there. He moved on. "Ya had yer dinner yet. I got ah coupla sandwiches and some apples and cookies. Yer welcome to some of it."

"Well, I am a bit gant so hell yeah, if yer offerin' up yer feed bag I'll try it on. I ain't never been one to turn down free chuck."

Jake retrieved the flour sack with the food that Ellie had prepared along with his canteen from beneath some snowberry bushes a short distance away. He held the sack out to Bovill, "Help yerself."

The stranger dug into the sack and pulled out a sandwich that was wrapped in wax paper and then handed the bag back to Jake. "Much obliged."

Jake sat down on the ground with his back against a big fir tree that had died and turned gray before being blown over by the wind. His head barely cleared the top of the tree whose bark had mostly sloughed off long ago leaving its surface smooth. After getting his sandwich, Jake tossed the bag midway between him and Bovill who was sitting cross legged on a bed of pine needles about ten feet away. "Help yerself to dessert when yer ready for it."

Bovill, whose mouth was full, nodded, swallowed and then he said, "I can't recall the last time I had a bacon sandwich."

"Does it suit ya?" asked Jake as he un-wrapped his own sandwich.

"Oh, hell yeah. I ain't got nuthin' against hogs."

Jake took a bite of his sandwich. It tasted good to him. The slices of bread were about three quarters of an inch thick. Between them were six pieces of bacon mired in heavy fresh churned butter.

Bovill looked up so as to catch Jake's attention. He said, with a grin, "I'll tell ya if this is the kind of chuck this widow woman puts out, you might be well advised to drop yer bedroll right here."

Jake laughed politely. "Naw, I already got a job."

Bovill persisted. "Is she ah looker?"

"She's purty easy on the eyes."

"Well hell, point me in the direction of her place. I'll ease her loneliness."

And then as his mind was wont to do it flashed an unpleasant image, as if he didn't have enough of those already, of Bovill having his way with Ellie. It was for Jake, like pulling the trigger on a gun, there was a quick reaction. He said, with some edge in his voice, "She ain't like that."

Bovill suddenly went silent as a weak, half grin came over his face. He appeared to be measuring the true intent of Jake's words and was about to apologize when Jake sensed it and cut him off, lest he draw any more attention to his conflicted feelings. He said, like the sun had long since set on their discussion of Ellie, "So, are ya gittin' purty well settled in over there on Antelope Creek?"

The uneasiness drained away from Bovill's face as he moved on. "We are, be better though if we could git some rain and the Indians would quit stealin' our cattle. They try to git our horses too but we generally got them close to the home place so they're a little more leery if they think there might be some hot lead comin' their way."

"Yer wise to keep yer horses close. Folks been losin' quite ah few."

Bovill, having finished his sandwich, reached into the sack for a cookie before tossing the bag closer to Jake. He took a bite of the cookie and said as he chewed, "I got to go up to Miles City in a coupla days to pick up some haying equipment. I thought I might go to Fort Keogh and see if the Army can help me out."

Jake laughed. "I wish you luck with that. A while back some Crows stole some horses and the Army caught 'em. Course the Crows said the horses was theirs. Some ranchers got wind of the deal and went into Keogh. They asked to see the horses so they could claim the ones that was theirs but the Army wouldn't let 'em even look at 'em. Said they had to go all the way down to the Crow Agency and the Indian Agent there would settle the matter. The Army then escorts the Indians and the horses back to the reservation. Far as I know, the ranchers lost most of their horses. So yeah, you just go right on over there to that fort and talk to those boys."

Bovill shook his head. "I'm beginning to wish I had stayed in Wyoming."

"You mentioned yer going after some haying equipment?"

"Yes sir, it's comin' in on the train. Gittin' a brand new mower and a buck rake." Bovill paused to laugh sarcastically. "Now if it would rain we might have something to cut."

Jake knew there were some meadow areas along Antelope Creek that could produce good grass hay but the fact there wasn't enough to cut this year was due more to being overgrazed, and not just by Rockin' C cattle. "You really think a good rain storm will fix you up?"

Bovill snorted. "Maybe every day for a month it might."

The wheels had begun to turn from the very moment that Jake had heard Bovill mention the haying equipment. He said, "I got a proposition for ya."

Bovill became a little more serious. "What is it?"

"Well, I believe yer gonna haf ta come right by the mouth of Deer Creek on yer way to Miles City. So, if you was agreeable to it I could take yer team and wagon on into town, pick up the equipment and come back to my place with it. The widow English down here has got a little patch of grass hay – maybe ten acres that needs to be put up. Again, if yer in agreement I'd take care of that for her and then I'll bring the equipment on over to yer place."

Bovill sighed in a mild way as if he needed to think on it. He reached into his pocket for his Bull Durham and papers and began rolling a smoke. When he was done he popped the head of a stick match with his thumbnail and touched the flame to his cigarette. He drew heavily on it a few times as he gently waved the life from the match. Seeing nothing but tinder dry pine duff all around him he spit on the match and put it in his shirt pocket. He shook his head. "I'll tell ya, it's drier than dust on a frog's ass."

Jake nodded, wondering if Bovill was going to get to the haying equipment. "It is. Thank God we ain't had no lighting or this country would be nuthin' but ashes."

"Yeah, we'd all be up shit creek if that was ta happen."

Jake looked at Bovill. He seemed content to just smoke his cigarette. He said, like Bovill needed reminding, "So whaddaya think about that?"

Bovill removed the cigarette from his mouth. It had about a half inch of ash. He tapped it into the cuff of his Levis and pressed the sides of it together to smother the ash. At last he said, "It ain't no small chore to load and unload that mower and buck rake. A fella 'bout needs ah loadin' dock of some sort. So, I guess it'd be alright but I can't let ya have it for more than a week. These boys that's bankrolling this outfit is comin' on the 18th and I gotta have some hay cut by then. The only problem is I don't know where I'm gonna find it."

"I'm much obliged for the loan," said Jake. "You ain't alone in not having any hay to cut. The truth of the matter is, there are so many cows in this country a fella would be hard pressed to find much ground that hasn't been grazed."

"There'll be hell ta pay if a hard winter comes."

Jake scoffed. "It ain't like anybody is plannin' for that. What hay that gits cut is mostly for saddle horses and milk cows and such."

Bovill took the last drag off of his cigarette, savoring it like it was the last bite of chocolate cake on his plate. He then ground the butt into the heel of his boot before spitting on it and flicking it away. "Just between me and you and the fence post, I can see it was a mistake to have brung more cattle to this country but these ole boys I work for has got more money than sense."

Jake laughed. "Don't ya wonder sometimes how rich people got that way when they do such things."

Bovill sighed as he leaned toward the dinner sack and came away with an apple and took a big bite. He chewed it a couple of times to the point he could talk. He laughed. "Kinda makes a fella hope he never gits rich so he doesn't git struck down with stupidity."

Jake grinned and bobbed his head in agreement. "I reckon I won't have to worry about it."

Bovill took another big crunchy bite of his apple. He said in between chewing and swallowing, "You said your name is Lafarge?"

"Yeah, I'm a Cajun."

Bovill gestured with the apple as he looked straight at Jake. "You got any kin in these parts?"

Jake tensed up as the prospect that Bovill might know his father came into his mind. For years, he'd wondered whatever had happened to him. It had gotten to where neither he nor his mother really cared, at least he told himself that. He said, "I might have. It'd be my Pa, Pete Lafarge."

A sudden peculiar, un-wanted look came over Bovill's face. It was such that he appeared confused as to what to say.

Jake leaned slightly forward from the tree and looked Bovill in the eyes so as to ensure he would tell him the truth. "You know my Pa?"

Bovill nodded his head several times like he was working the handle of a water pump to prime it. Finally, he said, "I knew a Pete Lafarge down in Wyoming."

Jake's stomach had begun to churn. "Where'd ya come across him?"

"South of Buffalo a ways."

143

Jake cut to it, lest Bovill surprise him with what he already suspected. "Was he up to no good?"

"He was. For a time he worked on a ranch down there and then I reckon he decided that didn't pay enough. He fell in with a bad crew. We caught some of 'em and strung 'em up. Your Pa though, his horse was better than ours that day. I won't lie to ya, Jake. I was one of 'em that threw lead at him. He's a scalawag."

Jake snorted as he tried to hide his shame. "It don't surprise me. He ran out on me and my ma when I was just a kid. Never heard a thing from him after that."

Emboldened by Jake's admission, Bovill came back, "One ah the boys workin' for me that knows yer pa said he saw him about a month ago down at Ashland. Rumor he heard there was yer pa was sellin' whiskey to the Cheyenne."

Jake looked away. Selling whiskey to the Indians was despicable. It wasn't good for the Indians or the white people who lived around them. In spite of their years of disassociation Jake felt humiliated. It was bad enough that his father had deserted him, but to leave this kind of legacy in his wake was only adding to Jake's contempt for him. He felt stymied. There was no defending his father but, at the same time, he couldn't bring himself to go on a rant and criticize him any further, at least not to Bovill he couldn't. His mind, however, knew no such limits. It was privy to images of his mother crying and the depravations they endured until he struck out on his own. And then he heard his inner voice say, *that bastard, that no account bastard, is there no end to his deviltry?*

Bovill said in a humble tone, "Sorry to be the one to tell you these things."

"It's alright," said Jake trying to feign indifference. "I always suspected them."

CHAPTER TWELVE

Jake's chance meeting of Harry Bovill had been a good thing for Ellie. He had not intended to go on about how destitute she was, but some facts do not lend themselves to secrecy or humility, especially when exposing them is being driven by a guilty conscience. The fact that Ellie had a total of $5.14 to her name with winter coming on was one of them. And so it came to pass that, *these ole boys back east who had more money than sense* would not only loan Jake haying equipment but they would give him barbed wire and staples for the hayfield fence and nails to build the shed. It was, as Bovill said, *the neighborly thing to do.*

About mid-morning on the third day since they'd talked up in the woods, Bovill showed up at Ellie's place driving a big flatbed wagon, the kind a person would haul or feed hay from. It was pulled by six Percheron draft horses, two of them white and the others black. The harnesses and tack that constrained them was all brand new. *Just the horses got to be worth a coupla thousand dollars*, said Jake to himself. Bovill brought the wagon to a stop next to where Jake was working on the frame of the shed. He hollered out, "You got your bedroll together?"

"You musta got up with the chickens. I didn't expect you till after noon."

"Well, she's two long days from my place to Miles City. I don't wanna make it three."

Jake was a little taken aback as he thought he was going by himself. "I take it yer coming along."

"I am. It's been a while since I been to town."

Jake sunk the axe he'd been notching the posts with into one that lay on the ground. "I'll fetch my bedroll. It's down by the crik. I won't be but a minute."

Jake started at a fast walk towards the creek and his canvas shelter. He was about half-way there when he heard Bovill call out, "Mornin' Ma'am." He glanced over his shoulder. Ellie, who had been helping him but had gone to the cabin to check on some bread in the oven, had now come outside. She was dressed as a man in Levis and a brown loose-fitting shirt that had the sleeves rolled up to the elbows on account of the heat. Her long dark hair was gathered into a single braid that hung down to the middle of her shoulders. The fact that she was distracting to Jake caused him to quicken his pace as he was certain that she would be to Bovill as well.

Ellie's voice sounded next, cheerful and inviting. "Good morning, you must be Mr. Bovill."

Just inside the cover of the trees, Jake stopped and turned to look at Bovill and Ellie. Bovill had jumped down from the wagon seat. They were within a few feet of one another. Bovill was removing his hat, they were talking but Jake could no longer hear what they were saying. And then Ellie tossed her head back and laughed. She never did that with him, at least not like that she didn't. And Henry, he appeared to be in awe of the big horses. In that instant Jake regretted not having given Ellie some reason to hope that he'd be there longer than two weeks, but he owed Cyrus and then there

146

were the images of Nate. If only he could be shed of those, but would it matter, Henry would always be there to remind him of what he'd done. Jake pressed the palm of his hand against the smooth slick bark of a large aspen tree in front of him. He gripped it hard as if doing so would bleed off the frustration he was feeling. *Yer thinkin' with yer tallywhacker and not yer head.* But then the naysayer in his mind came back at him with a glimpse of the future. He was still on the Rockin' C, too broke down to sit a horse all day, he would likely follow in Elmer's footsteps as the chore boy. He'd never have a family except what crumbs of emotion the Ellsworth's might toss his way. Finally, he pulled away from the tree and sighed heavily. *Hell, she's got to be fair game. Too much bad water has gone under our bridge.*

By the time he got back up to the big wagon, Bovill had unloaded two rolls of barbed wire, a coffee can containing staples for the fence and another with nails for the shed and a sack of oats for the horses and Daisy and another of wheat for the chickens. He had set it all within the framework of the shed as if it had walls that afforded some protection. Ellie was beside herself with happiness. She said, "Jake, look at this bounty Mr. Bovill has been so kind to bring. It's like Christmas in July." And then she laughed again.

Jake looked over at all that Bovill had brought. *I wonder if those old fools back east knew how their money was being spent if they would agree.* And then he looked back at Ellie and the revealing nature of her attire. *Hell, maybe they would.* He said aloud, "It was right nice of him."

Bovill stood next to the wagon soaking up the accolades. "It's no problem, Ma'am. Just tryin' ta be neighborly."

It seemed to Jake that Bovill was in less of a hurry now. Regardless, he put his bedroll and rifle in its scabbard on the back of the wagon. He then climbed into the driver's seat and slid over so as to make room for Bovill.

"You fellas don't want to stay for dinner?" asked Ellie. "It won't be long till it's ready."

Jake cut in. "Harry's wantin' to push on, Ellie. So, I reckon we'll git on down the road."

Ellie looked disappointed. She stepped toward Bovill with her right hand outstretched. She said as he shook her hand, "Thanks again, Mr. Bovill. This is most kind of you."

Jake wondered if Bovill would give any credit to the *ole boys back east with no sense* but he did not. Bovill came back. "If there is anything else I can do just let me or Jake know, or me since I guess Jake will be leavin' soon."

From the corner of her eye Ellie could see the impatient, almost irritated look on Jake's face. She did not fuel it but said simply, "Thank you Mr. Bovill, that's most generous of you."

Bovill touched his hand to his hat, nodded and smiled before beginning to climb up on the wagon. Jake had to look away lest he reveal his jealousy. He said to himself, *holy shit, is there no end to the pleasantries between these two.* Bovill took up the reins and released the brake.

Ellie called out. "Be safe."

Jake caught her eye and gave her a casual wave that didn't involve any more than his wrist and hand. Conversely, Bovill called out like he and Ellie knew one another far better than the last fifteen minutes would suggest, "Be seein' ya Ma'm."

Ellie waved back, even Henry who had known of Bovil no longer than his mother waved.

For a long time they rode in silence. Neither of them approaching the topic of Ellie since they would be sitting side by side for the next four to five days. In a way Jake resented Bovill using his employer's money to bring her things that he couldn't, even though he'd made the pitch for those very things that day up in the woods. Ellie had told him that she appreciated his asking Bovill for the supplies but it paled in comparison to when she thanked Bovill, or so Jake thought.

It was early evening. They were about ten miles down Pumpkin Creek at a place where the road crowded right up next to the creek. The wagon had a predictable rhythm of squeaking and rattling in response to the roughness of the ground. Occasionally, one of the big horses would give a weary snort as if to remind Bovill that it was hot and it had been a long day. And had it not been for the no see-ums it would have been almost soothing. The no-seeums, as Jake called them, were out in force. They were tiny gnats that a man generally felt before he saw them.

Bovill turned his head to the side and launched a stream of tobacco juice off into the willows. No sooner had he done this than he slapped at the back of his neck. He said, "I'll tell you what, I've 'bout had a gut full of these iddy-bitty bastards. It wouldn't be so bad if they'd just take yer blood and that was the end of it, but it's the itchin' that I can't take. I know sure as I'm sittin' here downwind ah these horses I ain't gonna sleep fer shit tonight. I'll be scratchin' everywhere."

Jake was about to chime in with his disdain for the gnats when he caught sight of a group of riders coming around a bend in the road up ahead. It caused him to draw back the words he had formed in his mind. He said instead, "Yonder comes my boss and some hands from the Rockin' C."

"You reckon he's upset?"

"He might be."

Cyrus stopped his horse off of the road on Jake's side of the wagon. His face was serious, troubled in some way. Bovill, seeing the intent, halted the wagon so that Jake and Cyrus were looking straight at one another. Cyrus said, almost before the wheels of the wagon had stopped. "You seen Ben?"

At first Jake felt relieved as he was certain that he was in trouble as this was day six since he'd left to check on the widow English. But then the worry in Cyrus' eyes spoke to him. Jake said, "I ain't. He come down this way to see that girl he's been ah courtin'?."

Cyrus nodded. "He left the day after you did. It was Sally Harper's birthday. There was gonna be a party that night at her folks' ranch and he was gonna come back the next day. When he didn't come home we just thought he decided to stay a while, spend some time with Sally since they seem to be gittin' all gooey eyed for one another, but then her brother, Ned, came by the house last night on his way to Miles City. He said they ain't seen Ben."

Jake thought to reassure Cyrus, but he could not think of any logical reason that didn't involve something bad happening to Ben as to why he had not shown up at the party. He said, "I'm sorry Cyrus but this sounds peculiar as hell. If I had my horse I'd go help ya look for him."

Cyrus glanced at the wagon and Bovill. "You headed to town?"

Jake came back. "This is Harry Bovill. He's new to that Antelope Creek country. He's offered the loan of his haying equipment to the widow English. We're on our way to pick it up at the train station."

Cyrus did not acknowledge Bovill. It was as if his worry had taken him elsewhere and that Jake and Bovill and their mission was of no consequence to him. He said, like he couldn't be bothered with having to, "Fine Jake, I'll see you next week." He did not wait for Jake's response but touched his spurs to his horse and moved on past the wagon followed by his men.

When the last of the five cowboys with Cyrus had passed by the wagon Bovill gently snapped the reins over the backs of the horses. "Giddup." They'd gone only a short distance when he said, "Whaddaya make ah that?"

From the moment Ellsworth had told them that Ben was missing Jake's mind had begun to spin with the probabilities of what could have happened to him. None of them were good. He sighed and shook his head. "It's worrisome. If he's alive, I can't figure where he'd be."

Bovill came back. "I don't know the man, but that's how I read it. If his horse throwed him and he was able he coulda walked somewhere for help by now."

And then Jake's conscience spoke to him. *You shudda warned him 'bout McDonald. He might ah stumbled into that clan butcherin' ah Rockin' C steer for having gotten into their grain field and things went sideways from there.* He said aloud, "You recall those gunshots we heard that day up in the woods? That wudda been the same day that Ben was comin' down here."

Bovill turned to the side and spit tobacco juice in a carefree way before answering Jake. He said, "Well, I guess this fella coulda ran across some Indians up to no good. Like I told ya the other day, them damned soldier boys need to patrol somewhere besides the inside of their fort."

There was a part of Jake that told him not to say it but he had the words right there on his tongue. He said, "If I was to wager who might know somethin' about what happened to Ben I'd put my money on George McDonald. He's got it out for the Rockin' C."

"I've heard the name but I don't know the man."

"He's put up some half-assed fences around his crops and he expects them to turn hungry cattle. I've had words with him in the past over Rockin C stock."

The progress of the wagon jostled them in a steady sort of way. Bovill appeared almost mesmerized by it as he pondered what Jake had said. Finally, he said with some reluctance, "That McDonald fella coulda been like a wounded grizzly all primed for a fight when this friend ah yours came along."

Jake had been afraid that Bovill would see it that way and now he regretted telling him about McDonald. He'd started this picture and now Bovill was being quick to finish it.

CHAPTER THIRTEEN

It was early afternoon of the next day when they reached Miles City. The Northern Pacific railroad depot was on the north side of town. Although he could have avoided it, Bovill chose to drive the hay wagon pulled by its six expensive draft horses up Main Street. The boardwalks in front of the businesses to either side of the dusty thoroughfare were crowded with people carrying their belongings. Some had actual suitcases, others a sack, but all of them had a bewildered look about them as they gawked at their new surroundings.

Jake nodded towards the slow moving mass. "Train must be in. Here's another crop ah Grangers come west to make their fortune."

Bovill laughed in a sneering sort of way. "Yeah, I reckon we'll be slicin' the pie a little thinner out here."

It came to Jake's mind as quick as a wolf trap snapping shut, *Well, you'd be one ah those slicers.* But he held his tongue and did not point out that hypocrisy to Bovill, he said instead, "When the railroad first come to town folks hereabouts was pretty happy about it. A man could ship his cattle from here instead of having to trail 'em down to Ogalalla. And it made it easy to git lots ah goods here and if ah fella wanted to go back east why all he had to do was buy a ticket and off he went. But the hell of it was, that track runnin' both ways like that brought lots more people here. It allowed the white man to purty much strike that final coup on the Indians but, truth be told, it might do the same for the big rancher. This country can only hold so many people, especially the ones that want to plow it up or graze it off."

Bovill appeared to be having another one of his silent, pondering moments. His face suggested that Jake's words might have rubbed him the wrong way. He said, while looking at Jake kind of cold like, "Well, we could probably git rid a one Granger by not helpin' the widow woman. I'd bet she'd fold her tent right after the first snow flies."

Jake allowed his face to go blank as if Bovill's sarcasm was a viable option. He said, "I suppose we could. You can just tell her that you changed yer mind."

Bovill snorted. "Sure I will right after I tell her kid there ain't no Santa Claus."

Jake manufactured a brief laugh so as to break the tension and then moved on, pointing up ahead to the street off to the left. "That'll take us right down to the train depot."

Bovill remained silent as he glanced towards the side street and then shook the reins over the backs of the Percherons as if they needed encouragement, which they did not. Momentarily he made the turn to the depot still collecting the desired head turns and finger pointing from the newly arrived homesteaders. However, one of those taking note of their arrival was Sheriff Nye. He was standing out in front of his office when he caught sight of Jake perched on the seat of the wagon.

Bovill was first to see the Sheriff staring at them. He said, "That lawman over there sure seems interested in us."

Jake picked up on Nye's presence just as Bovill had started to speak. The Sheriff was making no effort to disguise his interest in Jake which made it difficult to not make eye contact with him. For a moment, Jake returned the hard stare he was getting from Nye but then he turned away lest he antagonize him. He kept his focus over the backs of the horses as the wagon moved beyond where it was natural to look in the Sheriff's direction. From the corner of his eye he could see that Bovill was still waiting for him to explain the Sheriff's behavior. He hoped it wasn't due to the Jawbone Springs affair as he'd just as soon Bovill not know that he'd had a hand in making Ellie a widow. Finally, he said simply, "We had some dealings with the Sheriff and the Army a while back. Might be that."

Bovill seemed less than satisfied with Jake's response but did not probe it any further. He parked the wagon next to the loading dock, which was immediately adjacent to the train tracks so that wagons or heavy machinery could be offloaded onto it and from there down a ramp to the ground or straight across on the dock and onto another wagon. After setting the brake he handed the reins to Jake. He nodded towards an iron wheeled mower with a six foot cutting bar that was locked in an upright position and a buck rake that had the wheel assembly detached from the rake. He said, "I reckon that's our machinery. I'll go inside and settle up."

"Fine," said Jake. "I'll wait here."

Jake watched as Bovill jumped down to the ground and began meandering his way through the milling homesteaders towards the depot. He'd just about reached the door of the little white building when a voice sounded off to Jake's side. "Mr. Lafarge, can I have a minute of your time?"

Jake instantly recognized the voice. And even though he'd been half expecting it, he spun around in his seat like he'd been startled by some life ending thing. He said, trying to not act like he just had, "What can I do for ya, Sheriff?"

Nye looked up at Jake and for a few seconds he said nothing, but allowed a smile that bordered on sinister to spread over his face. For a time he purposely let the effects of it work on Jake's fears and then he said as if being sheriff entitled him to make such judgements, "I hear you're parkin' yer boots these days under Mrs. English's bed. That's a helluva note you hang a man and then take up with his wife. Course I guess it don't say much for her either." He then laughed knowing that he was likely immune from fisticuffs on account of the tin star on his shirt.

Jake came back quick and angry. "You got some bad information, Sheriff. I'm helpin' Ellie out and that's all."

Nye scoffed. "Ellie? "

"What do you want, Sheriff?"

"Ned Harper was in to see me. Said Ben Ellsworth never made it to his sister's birthday party. You know anything about that?"

"I know Cyrus is plenty worried. He's out lookin' for Ben now."

Nye snorted and tossed his head. "Hell, he probably ought to be lookin' in some sportin' house somewhere."

"Ben ain't like that anymore."

"So you say. That boy's got a wild streak in him."

"I'm tellin' ya, Sheriff, he cudda came to no good end. I heard gunshots in the vicinity of where he mighta been about a week ago."

"That don't mean nuthin'. Coulda been somebody shootin' at a wolf."

"I don't think so," said Jake in a stern voice. "It was an exchange of two different guns except one of 'em only got off one shot."

It appeared that Nye was about to come back with something flippant but caught himself at the last second. He sighed. "So where was it you heard these shots?"

"My best guess is it was near the McDonald place."

Nye's expression suddenly changed. It was like Jake now had some credibility. He asked, "Ben ever have any trouble with McDonald?"

"Not that I know of but I had harsh words with him and his boys over Rockin' C cattle gittin' in his grain. They've threatened to whip my ass if the opportunity ever presents itself."

Nye eased back on his hostile attitude. It was like Jake had made friends with a mean dog by tossing him a bone. Nye said, "Sounds like I need to take a ride up Pumpkin Creek."

It occurred to Jake to ask the Sheriff to not mention his name to the McDonalds but then the defiant side of him shouted out, *to hell with them.* He said aloud, "Be careful of those boys Sheriff. They're well-heeled and bent on shootin' somebody I think." Nye nodded. "Much obliged." And then he walked away.

Jake sat where he was for a bit pretending to be studying the haying equipment on the loading dock while inwardly the naysayer in his mind was criticizing him for having told the Sheriff about the McDonalds. His mind began to paint pictures of the future as only a mind can. *I shouldn't ah sicked Nye on those boys. It'll be ah guaranteed ass whipping or worse if the lot of 'em catches me out alone.* He sighed loudly trying to bleed off some of his frustration as he reached for his tobacco and papers. The cigarette came together quickly. Anxiously he put a match to it and filled his lungs with its soothing powers. He held the smoke for a second before expelling it in a concentrated stream, as he did Ellie and Henry invaded his mind negating somewhat the narcotic effect he'd hoped for.

Bovill shouted up to him. "The stationmaster's roundin' up ah coupla bohunks to help us load this. A lot of 'em don't know much English so he might be a minute."

Jake made eye contact with Bovill and then jumped down onto the loading dock. It was only then that he became aware of the mixed languages being spoken by the people around him who were waiting to retrieve their things from the train. He said to himself, somewhat sarcastically, *between the railroad and the government they've done a fine job in luring all these folks out here to bust up the land.* As he looked around at the people he saw plenty of flat caps and derbies on the men and flowery and feathered hats on the women, but there wasn't a single cowboy hat.

The stationmaster was of little help in loading the equipment. He was short and rotund with gray hair and walked as if it hurt him to do so. But the men he found were good sized and strong and spoke more German than English, it was enough, however, to get the job done. Bovill gave them each a quarter and they were greatly appreciative.

They left the wagon at the depot and walked to a diner on Main Street where they had a good steak dinner at Bovill's expense. Not a word came up about the Sheriff eyeballing them until that night when they were camped, drinking coffee and mostly listening to the crickets. It was like Bovill surprised himself in thinking about it. He blurted out, looking right at Jake, "Say, what did that law dog want? I saw from the depot he was ah twistin' yer arm."

Jake's mind quickly went to what he thought best to say and not. He said, "Oh, he was just wonderin' if Ben ever showed up."

Bovill snorted. "Is he gonna lend ah hand in lookin' for him?"

"Yeah, said he's gonna make a swing through that Pumpkin Creek country."

"Did ya tell 'im 'bout those gunshots?"

"I did, but he figures they was probably just somebody shootin' at wolves. He didn't put much stock in it."

Bovill shrugged. "Well hell, maybe he's right."

"Yeah, maybe so," said Jake.

CHAPTER FOURTEEN

It was early the next morning. The sun was not up but it was plenty light enough to see. Jake and Bovill had camped off the road right next to Pumpkin Creek. They were in the process of harnessing the horses and hooking them up to the wagon when they heard a rider coming at a quick pace from the direction of town. Jake was first to make out who it was. "Looks like the Sheriff is makin' good on what he said he'd do."

Bovill glanced over at the Sheriff's approach but continued with getting the team ready. He shrugged. "Well, it's what he gits paid to do."

Jake had worked his way through the rye grass which was mostly eaten down to the ground, chest high sagebrush and a few scattered wild plum bushes over to the edge of the road. He hollered out. "Mornin' Sheriff."

Nye reined his horse in near where Jake was standing. He had a serious look on his face, before he could speak, Jake added, "Yer a long ways from yer bed for so early in the day."

The Sheriff came back, his voice cold and somber, "Cyrus brought his boy into town late last night."

"Well, how is he?'

"Dead. He had two bullet holes in his chest."

Jake was taken aback. He'd known Ben since he was a little boy. He was mired in a flood of recollections of him when he was alive causing his voice to be unsteady. "Where 'bouts did they find him?"

"Up the Tongue about five miles. A coupla homesteader kids that was fishin' found 'im floatin' in the river."

"Well, I'll be go ta hell," said Jake as he shook his head.

"I'll betcha it was Indians that did it," proclaimed Bovill who had come up behind Jake. "It's just like I said, if the damned Army would quit playin' soldier inside their fort and git out in the hills the Indians would be more fearful, but hell they do as they please."

Nye shot Bovill a hard, somewhat angry, look. "Hold on there, Mister. Don't git yerself all worked up."

Bovill snorted. "You don't have to defend what's yours day in and day out. You can sit there in town and stroll up and down the street and have yer dinner in the café and collect yer check.It ain't quite that easy for us folks livin' out here on the land."

Nye scowled at Bovill. He said sarcastically, "I hope yer there the next time some hard case pulls a gun on me so you can remind me how easy I got it."

Bovill drew back in a haughty sort of way in response to the Sheriff's anger. He said, his voice feigning contrition, "Sorry Sheriff, didn't mean to offend you."

Nye scoffed. "This ain't yer problem so don't you be addin' fuel to the fire. You git the Indians riled up and there'll be more than one white man dead."

"So it was the Indians that did it?"

Nye appeared uneasy, he replied, "I never said that."

Bovill laughed. "You don't play poker do ya, Sheriff? If you do let me know when yer next game is cause I wanna play." And then in spite of the dirty look Jake gave him, Bovill laughed some more. Suddenly, his eyes lit up like he'd just had a revelation. He blurted out, "So tell me Sheriff, was this boy scalped?"

The question took Nye by surprise. It was obvious by his face that he was not going to give Bovill a straight answer. Bovill started to grin even before Nye opened his mouth. Nye said, "I can't divulge those particulars out of respect for the family."

Bovill burst into a full blown laugh. He said loudly and emphatically, "Shit Sheriff, you already done told us he had two bullet holes in his chest. What kinda school boy fools do you take us for? You think Jake here ain't gonna find that out just as soon as he goes back home?" Bovill put his hands on his hips and snorted defiantly before looking away.

Nye looked at Jake and the expectant but respectful expression on his face. He said in a tired voice, "Indians ain't the only ones that scalp people." And with that he spurred his horse and headed on up the road towards George McDonald's place.

"Can you believe that?" shouted Bovill. "Him tryin' ta cover up for the Indians."

Jake shifted his eyes from the Sheriff's distant image to Bovill. He said, "Don't git me wrong cuz I've had my problems with the Indians, but there's something about this that just don't seem right."

Bovill looked puzzled. "What's that?"

Jake grimaced and shook his head slightly. "I can't figure the Indians going to the trouble of dumpin' Ben's body in the river. It's like whoever killed him wanted to hide his body. I reckon they thought it would just sink and nobody would find it for a long time. That don't seem to me like something

Indians would do. They'll scalp ya alright, but they're gonna leave ya where ya lay."

"Well, I reckon it don't really matter," replied Bovill. "This boy isn't the first fella to turn up dead out here with no hair and no one with any idy who took it."

Jake nodded. He said quickly, in a dismissive tone, "I suppose so." And then he started back towards the horses to finish hitching them to the wagon. His mind, however, had drifted to the McDonald's and their reaction when the Sheriff showed up at their place. *They're gonna be mad as hell if they figure out it was me that put the Sheriff on to 'em. I'll haf ta watch my back or I'll be the next one floatin' down the Tongue.*

Bovill, who had followed Jake back to the horses called out from the other side of one of the big animals. "Ya ever seen a scalped man?"

It was a memory that Jake had tried to bury. But now, thanks to Bovill, it was center stage in his mind. It was as clear as mountain creek water. Jake shot Bovill a dirty look even though he could not see it because of the horses between them. He said abruptly, "Yeah."

There was a sudden, obvious silence from Bovill's direction. Save for a meadowlark off in the distance it grew, expectant of something more from Jake, but he was not forthcoming. Bovill, however, lacked the sense to let it alone. He came back, "So where was it you saw this?"

Jake sighed. He said, making no attempt to disguise the irritation in his voice, "It was some years back down on the Platte."

Bovill persisted as if Jake was about to show him a risqué photo of some girl in a sporting house. "Settlers was it? Wouldn't surprise me, a lot ah those folks don't know their left foot from their right when it comes to ways ah the frontier."

Jake was there now. His mind's eye was locked onto those cowboys' arrow riddled bodies and the grotesque, painful expressions on their faces. He was just a kid then. It'd been right after he'd hired on with Cyrus and they were trailing cattle north to Montana. The herd had stampeded during the night going off in a number of directions. The men chased after the cattle, sometimes for miles. All of the cowboys came back but two. Jake helped to bury them and until now he'd managed to keep that memory mostly at bay. He said, "You ever scalp ah man, Bovill?"

The awkward silence between them came back. Jake let his words stand until finally Bovill responded, "Why do you ask?"

Jake spoke into the side of the horse as if it were a curtain between them that would allow Bovill to confess. "I can't abide the practice but you seem to have a peculiar interest in it."

"So you think less of a man if he's taken a scalp?"

"I don't see a need for it, that's all."

"Sometimes, Mr. Lafarge, a man's gotta send his enemies a message."

Jake said, "I suppose so." He then walked away to get another harness, leaving Bovill's past a secret. He wondered, though, if George McDonald or one of his hot headed sons was capable of scalping a man.

CHAPTER FIFTEEN

It was early evening when they arrived at Ellie's. She came out of the cabin still drying her hands on the plain white apron that was tied around her waist. Even at a distance, it was apparent to Jake that something had changed with her, at least as far as the way she looked at him it had. As she neared the wagon her eyes became more intense like she was trying to pry him open and then she said, "I've been keeping your supper warm in the oven. I wasn't sure you would make it tonight."

"It'll be a while before we're ready to eat, if that's ok?" said Jake. "We need to tend to the horses and unload the machinery."

"Not too long, I hope," replied Ellie. "Your food will get dry."

Since their conversation about scalping, Bovill had been anything but upbeat. Now, however, he shouted to Ellie in a jovial tone, "We'll be quick, Ma' am. I'm so hungry I'd wrastle ah bear for supper."

Ellie smiled. "No need, Mr. Bovill. I'll gladly surrender it to you." With that she turned away, her eyes going past Jake like he wasn't there.

Ellie's behavior, her body language towards him anyway, was perplexing to Jake. It was like she'd had time to really think about the fact he'd made her a widow and the subject of some scorn by her neighbors and maybe too that Nate wasn't such a bad man; after all, he was Henry's father. Regardless of her motive it was an emotion he didn't need. He was torn as to whether he should be there now or if he should go back to the Rockin' C headquarters, that was home, it was where he belonged. The Ellsworth's would be grieving. He supposed they'd bury Ben in the next day or so. Jake's conscience shouted out to him, *you should be there. Look at all they've done for you.* No sooner had he begun to consider this, when Ellie, and what only a woman could offer him, came to mind. It was a strong draw, but not without its complications.

Bovill invaded his thoughts. "Ya wanna unload it right here?"

"Yeah, that'd be good," replied Jake. But then he added, anxious to re-engage Ellie to see if she would warm to him. "Maybe we could just tend to the horses and leave unloading the equipment till morning."

Bovill did not question Jake's motivation. He said, "I suppose we could but just know I intend to git an early start. I been away too long already."

"As do I," said Jake. "I aim to git a fair amount of that meadow, if not all of it, laid down tomorrow."

Bovill grinned. "You might be able to. It'll be the fetching it in and stacking it that'll take time."

"Like I was telling ya on the way here, since I'll have a shed for the horses and milk cow I can use the corral to store the hay."

Bovill laughed. "Gonna be ah lotta pitchforkin'."

"Ellie's a stout woman and Henry's a good worker."

"They'll need ta be ta fork that much hay."

"Maybe I'll need to teach Ellie to run the buck rake and I fork the hay."

A smug look came to Bovill's face. "In my experience, that could be ah tall order."

"I reckon we'll see," said Jake as he jumped down from the wagon seat to the ground.

The sun was no longer visible by the time they had un-hitched the horses, taken them to the creek for water, grained them, and hobbled them a short ways up the canyon. It had gotten shadowy to the point Ellie had lit a lantern inside the cabin. On a small bench just outside the door she had placed a tin wash basin, a bar of soap and a towel. Henry had brought up a bucket of creek water that rested on the ground in front of the bench.

The day had been hot. Its heat had relented little with the onset of evening making the necessity of maintaining a fire in the stove to keep the food in the oven warm a sacrifice of some magnitude, as the inside of the cabin was sweltering. Ellie had brought a chair outside and was sitting to the right of the cabin door as Jake and Bovill approached. She glanced at the wash basin. "You can wash up if you like."

"Much obliged, Ma'am," said Bovill struggling to keep his eyes from the fact that Ellie, owing to the heat, had left the top two buttons of her blouse unbuttoned allowing a hint of where her cleavage began. He drank it in for a few seconds before picking up the bucket and pouring water into the tin pan. He added, in that same good old boy tone that he could bring to bear in a heartbeat, "Always makes chuck taste bet-ter if ah fella gits the trail dust off ah his lips." Bovill stooped over the basin and lathered his hands and then his face. It was while his eyes were closed and he was working the dirt from the pores of his skin that Jake sensed Ellie was staring at him. No sooner had he picked up on this than the mystery of her demeanor began to unravel. She said, "The Sheriff was by today. He told me Ben Ellsworth was murdered."

"Yeah, we ran into him early this morning," said Jake. "It's ah real sad deal. I knew Ben since he was about Henry's age."

Ellie looked straight at Jake, her voice somewhat cold and indifferent. "Yes, it is sad when you lose a person you've known for a long time."

Had Bovill not been there Jake would've just asked Ellie what seemed to be troubling her. But there was no need as she said, just as Bovill stood up and began drying his face and hands, "The Sheriff told me I was lucky he didn't arrest me for shooting you."

Bovill's eyes suddenly grew big. The words exploded from his mouth, "You shot him? How come?"

Ellie ignored Bovill. She said, "For some reason, I thought that you hadn't told the Sheriff about me shooting you. All this time I thought that was so noble of you, but I know now you were trying to keep yourself out of jail."

Jake struggled to keep his thoughts afloat in the shame that had flooded his mind. He said, "I'm sorry, Ellie. I guess I was just –"

"I know what you were doing. I suppose it wouldn't have bothered me as I thought you had kept this to yourself but then here comes the Sheriff all high and mighty and tells me, *you people can't go around doing as you please.* Like I didn't have some justification."

Bovill had a look of expectation on his face, like he was about to receive a treat. He said to Jake, "Did you kill her husband?"

Jake hesitated, looking for the right words to water down the effect of what he had to say, but there were none. "Yeah, I had a hand in it."

Bovill looked first at Jake and then Ellie. He appeared insulted by them for having deceived him, on purpose or not. He was still searching for a response when Ellie said.

"It's in the oven. You fellas help yourselves. I'm going up the canyon and help Henry bring in the horses and Daisy." And with that she turned and began walking quickly away.

It had not been lost on Jake that Bovill never missed an opportunity to leer at Ellie's backside, and now was no exception. He made no effort to disguise his action, knowing that his generosity with the *ole boys back east's* money would keep Jake at bay. After he'd satisfied his voyeuristic lust to the extent he could, he turned to Jake. He smiled in a derisive way and said, "When we was up in the woods and you told me you was helpin' this widow woman out I thought you were a right decent guy. And then when I saw what a looker Ellie is I thought you was still an alright guy that was lookin' to git some fringe benefits for his trouble. But now, I ain't sure what to make of either one of ya."

Jake's eyes danced with an anger he could not suppress. He said to himself, *yer ah sorry bastard, Bovill. Your moral compass ain't never pointed any direction but south.* But Bovill had him and the both of them knew it. A smirk spread over Bovill's face as he watched Jake muster sufficient humility to sieve the anger from his voice. At last he said, "Yer wrong Bovill, as soon as I git these chores done for her I'm headed north."

Bovill called his bluff. "Ya ain't comin' back?"

"As of today, it ain't in my plans."

Bovill came back quick, like he'd been successful in baiting a wild horse into a corral trap and he needed to close the gate before it realized its mistake. He said, "Well then, you won't mind if I come calling on her?"

Jake doubled down on his earlier words. "Help yerself." He paused and then added, "But, I can tell ya she ain't no hussie."

Bovill smiled. "Winters can git purty long and cold."

CHAPTER SIXTEEN

It was more dark than light when Henry came out of the house with an empty milk bucket on his way to the corral. Bovill had done as he said he would the day before. He'd not slept anywhere near Jake, preferring instead to lay out his bedroll near the corral. His back was towards Henry as he tied his gear to one of the saddles on the corral fence.

"That's my Pa's saddle," said Henry.

Bovill spun around, searching the early morning darkness for the voice. Henry challenged him again. "Did you ask my Ma if it was ok to take that?"

Henry's black crushed felt hat shrouded his face such that Bovill could not read his eyes. Bovill said, "No, but your friend Mr. Lafarge said it would be alright."

"He's not my friend."

"Why's that?"

"He hung my pa."

Bovill feigned ignorance as if he didn't already know this. Finally, he said, "Oh, no wonder you don't like him but yer Ma likes him, don't she?"

Henry could not bring himself to say the words but nodded instead.

Although Bovill's voice carried enough for Jake to hear, he could not, in the poor light from the distance he was, make out Henry's reaction. But then Bovill said, "You don't like that, do ya?"

Jake's approach had been silent. Sarcasm coated his words. "You coachin' the boy to suit yer purpose?"

"He's just statin' how he feels."

Jake snorted and for a time glared at Bovill, his response being tempered by the fact that Henry was watching. Finally, he said, "Maybe we should just git the machinery unloaded." Turning to Henry he said, "Daisy's waitin' on ya."

Henry frowned in Jake's direction. It was the first time that he had been openly defiant of him, but since his mother had taught him better than to be disrespectful, he said, "Yes sir," and walked away.

It was in that instant, while he stood there between Bovill and Henry, that regret so intense it bordered on panic, gripped Jake. *I shudda never come down here*, he said to himself. He looked beyond Bovill to the corral where Rusty was confined. *I wish ta hell I could just saddle up and ride out.*

"We gonna unload this or not," said Bovill brusquely. "It ain't gonna be easy with no loadin' dock."

Jake tried his best to ignore Bovill's temperament. He said, his words absent any emotion such that if they'd been in a glass it would have been empty, "I believe we can make a ramp out ah some of the poles I cut."

Bovill glanced in the direction of the poles lying on the ground. He studied them for a moment. It was between them now as if each was making a concession to be civil. "I reckon we could if we was to lash a couple of 'em together for each wheel to roll down on."

"Yeah, maybe tie a rope onto each piece ah machinery so we can let 'er come down slow."

171

Bovill nodded. "Oh, hell yeah. We wouldn't want them things ah rollin' off there full throttle."

And so without saying it was what they needed to do, they set aside their differences. The machinery was unloaded by the time the sun was about half way above the eastern horizon. The two of them having to work together had diluted some of the tension between them. After breakfast, and when Bovill had Jiggs saddled and ready to go, it was almost like nothing had happened between them. It may have been this feeling or possibly the fact that Ellie and Henry's existence on Deer Creek was ensured for a little while longer, but she was profuse in her gratitude. She said, "I can't tell you, Mr. Bovill, what this means to Henry and me. I'll always be indebted to you."

Visions, illogical or not, of how Ellie would repay Bovill roared to life in Jake's mind. They were disturbing and erased the fragile comradery they'd just achieved.

Bovill stepped towards Ellie. He said, "Ma'am, you don't owe me ah thing, but if you was to invite me to Sunday dinner at some point I'd be here lickity split."

Ellie smiled. "Yes, Mr. Bovill. That's the least I could do. Why don't we just plan on two weeks from this Sunday?"

"That would be real fine, Ma'am. I'll be here."

In spite of telling himself and Bovill that he didn't care a pulse of anger, maybe even hurt, surged through Jake. The naysayer in his mind laughed and shouted out at him, *well, ya damned fool you told 'im it'd be alright ta come callin'*. And then it was as if Bovill had listened in on Jake's thoughts. He stepped toward Ellie with his right hand outstretched, intent on shaking hers. She started to take his hand but at the last second she said, "You're more deserving than a handshake, Mr. Bovill." She then grasped him loosely by the shoulders and gave him a brief hug. Bovill grinned at Jake over her shoulder.

It was difficult but Jake did his best to act as if he were looking at strangers. To have shown any emotion at all would have allowed Bovill to gloat more than he already was. Jake's association with Bovill was not yet over as he had to return the equipment when he was done with it. He said, as Bovill withdrew from Ellie's embrace, "I reckon I'll see you in five or six days."

"No need," he said trying to disguise his true intent with graciousness, "I'll come git it."

Jake instantly thought, *I'll bet you will you sorry sonovabuck.* Aloud he said, "Well, suit yerself but I've no problem with bringing it back."

Bovill got on Jiggs. He said to Jake, "I'll see you in a week." He then looked at Ellie, smiled, and doffed his hat like he was a gentleman. Nor did he neglect Henry. He waved. "Be seein' ya, son."

Jake turned away, unable to watch as Ellie and Henry waved back. He went to the corral and began harnessing the two Percherons that he'd kept behind to pull the mower. The other horses and Daisy they'd turned out to graze on up the canyon. He'd been at it a short time fully expecting Ellie to come to him and talk, but she did not. From the corner of his eye he could see that she and Henry had gone to the chicken coop to gather eggs, as if it took both of them to do it. Jake scoffed and whispered sarcastically into the side of the big horse he was working on. "I reckon some things is just more important than others." And then he went on hooking the team up to the mower. It was a McCormick-Deering with a six foot sickle bar and a doubletree hitch that would accommodate a singletree on either side of the tongue. Jake was bent over the second singletree when Ellie came up behind him. She said, "Can I be of any help to you?"

Jake stood upright and looked at her. "No Ma'am, I'm just finishing up."

She appeared uncomfortable, knowing that her offer of help had been disingenuous. "I would've come earlier but Henry wanted to talk."

Jake thought to ask what about, but he did not. He said, "I guess there's just times when a boy has got to talk to his Ma."

"Henry's a smart boy. Older than his years I think." Ellie paused and then she said, "Up until now he'd never known anyone but his father to be in my life. It scares him."

Jake wondered if she was talking about him or Bovill, or the both of them. He said, "I reckon so."

And then, like she'd needed to work up to it, anger pooled in her eyes. "The other thing that scares him, that makes him cry, is the possibility the Sheriff will arrest me."

"I don't think that'll ever happen. Nye knows folks 'round here wouldn't cotton to him arrestin' ah widow woman."

Ellie's face showed mock indignation. "I would hope not, seeing how you and your boss got off with nothing but a tongue lashing."

In light of how things had gotten to be he was inclined to debate her, even though they'd plowed that field in the past, but he checked himself. He said, "I'm sorry to have turned yer life upside down and for causing Henry to worry. I'll talk to 'im if ya like."

Ellie shook her head. "I doubt he would be receptive to it. He's got it in for you."

"I'm sorry to hear that."

"I am too."

Jake's mind went to wondering about the intent of Ellie's words. Was her concern only for Henry or was it how his animosity would affect her and Jake's relationship. But then it came to him. *What does it matter? Within a week, I'll be gone from here.* He said, "I reckon that hay ain't gonna cut itself."

"You'll be in at noon for dinner?"

"Yes Ma'am."

Ellie nodded; her demeanor business like still, not as it had been before the Sheriff had come, and now Bovill. She said, "Fine, it'll either be trout or sage chickens. It just depends on what Henry captures."

Jake had already started climbing onto the mower. He said over his shoulder. "Matters not to me." By the time he was settled into its iron seat and looked over to where Ellie had been standing, she was well on her way to the cabin.

The big Percherons easily pulled the mower with its six inch wide cleated iron wheels. Within a few minutes Jake was at the upper end of the meadow where Nate had not completed the fence choosing instead, Jake surmised, to use the materials to build a rustler's trap. The sight before him hit Jake like a sucker punch. He said angrily, "Well, I'll be ah sonovabitch." There were a dozen or so cows with calves scattered throughout the meadow. Jake's rage was quickly growing as was his suspicion. One of the cows with a broken horn he recognized from the day before about a half mile down the canyon. It and the other cattle were wearing the Rockin' C brand. Jake set the brake on the mower and climbed down. He was no sooner on the ground when he noticed, standing there in the unfinished part of the fence, that there were shod horse tracks amongst the cow tracks. He said aloud, "Somebody drove these critters in here. Must ah been last night." Jake sighed a frustrated breath and started walking briskly towards the cattle. *This is ah helluva note*, he said to himself, *a cowpuncher on foot.* The pasture was longer than it was wide. It was Jake's intent to go to the far end of it and gather the cows and their calves as best he could and push them back up the canyon to the opening in the fence. The day was already hot. The deer flies and no-seeums were out in force, constantly hovering and landing when they dared on Jake's exposed skin. As he walked through the thigh high grass he could see where the cattle had bedded down during the night and even where they had meandered to any degree. The grass was crushed and matted down and in places cow pies plastered it to the ground. By the time he got to the end of the field his contempt for the cows and whoever had pushed them there had grown considerably. It was like he was seeing things as a Granger would. His mind was beginning to conjure up sympathy for them. He was allowing himself to become immersed in these thoughts until images of McDonald and that day suddenly appeared, causing the cowboy Jake to come back. He started towards a white-faced cow that was staring at him while lying down contentedly chewing her cud. When he was within 30 or 40 feet of her Jake clapped his hands loudly and shouted, "He-yah, git up you sorry cuss."

Reluctantly, the cow got to its feet and trotted off for a short ways in the direction of the gap in the fence whereupon it slowed to a walk. Jake scoffed and said aloud, "Why you old blister you ought ta be damned glad I ain't ah horseback, if I was you'd be dancing to a different tune."

And then from behind Jake came a dog's bark. He turned quickly to see Henry and Bella standing at the edge of the trees over by the creek. He wondered how long they'd been there. At first, he thought to just wave and not press the boy to talk to someone that he didn't like but impulse took over and he shouted out, "Is Bella ah cow dog?"

For a time Henry acted like he was afraid or simply didn't want to talk to Jake, but then he said in a timid voice, "She's been known to put the run on cows."

"How 'bout we try 'er on these 'fore they eat up anymore of yer Ma's winter feed?"

Henry looked down at his dog as he started towards Jake. "C'mon Bella."

Jake met them at the fence. Henry, who was carrying an old single barrel shotgun, handed it over the fence to Jake without being reminded that was the thing to do. "Will you hold my gun while I crawl through?"

Jake took the gun in his left hand and with his right he pulled up on the second wire down so that Henry could slip through without snagging his shirt. Henry glanced at the gesture but said nothing and stepped over the bottom wire to the other side. Jake came back, "Ya ain't run across no sage chickens this mornin'?"

"No," said Henry as he took his gun back, "but I got a coupla nice trout on a willow stringer in a beaver pond back in the trees over yonder. Got my pole set too. I'll have a nice mess a fish by dinner time."

Jake grinned. He suspected that when times were better, when he had been happy, that Henry was a talker. Jake said, "Well yer Ma was right. She said you'd have fish or sage chickens."

Henry glowed under the modest praise. He said, "Most days I do ok."

Jake laughed briefly. "I'll bet you do." And then he went on, "Should we see if Bella can help us push these cows outta here? We just need ta send 'em to the other end of the pasture and that gap in the fence. It might be we won't need to use Bella too much with the both of us herdin' 'em."

Henry looked at Jake as if he was bored or Jake had misspoken. He said, "Me and Bella have herded cows before."

For a few seconds Jake was undecided if he should laugh or apologize but then he said, "Well, let's git 'em movin'."

And so they started with shouts and whistles and hand claps and Bella roving from side to side behind those cows in the rear. Things were going well. The cows and their calves were bunching up as if there would be strength in numbers and they were moving along toward the other end of the pasture. It was about this time that two un-fortuitous events occurred. A rider came out of the trees on the outside of the fence. It struck Jake right off that the guy was following the tracks of the cows and the horses mixed in with them. It also occurred to him that the rider might think that somebody had stolen the cows and he had just found them. The other unfortunate event was that an ornery old cow had charged Henry when he walked up on its calf lying in the grass. Bella, of course, was not going to let Henry get hurt. She was after the cow in what appeared to be a vicious way which caused the cowboy at the edge of the trees to draw his Winchester from its saddle scabbard. At about the same time, Jake and Henry saw the rider lever a round into the chamber of his rifle and take aim at Bella who was a hundred yards or more away. Jake hollered out, "Don't shoot." The sound of his plea, however, was mostly obliterated by the report of the rifle. This was followed by Henry running towards the cowboy crying and screaming, "Stop, stop. Don't kill my dog." The rider, however, seemed oblivious or uncaring as he jacked another round into his rifle and started to take aim on Bella who had not been touched by the first shot. And then there was another gunshot, but not from the rider. Black smoke roiled up from the end of Henry's 12 gauge shotgun. He was too far away for the shot to have been effective but the rider's reflex caused him to bring his rifle to bear on Henry. It was fortunate that Henry had lowered the shotgun after firing the only round it held as the rider hesitated, holding his fire apparently to see what the kid was going to do.

Jake screamed, "Put yer rifle down, Mister."

The rider looked to his left. Jake had a two handed grip on his pistol which was aimed at the cowboy with the hammer back. Instinctively, he started to bring his rifle around to Jake's direction. Jake shouted again. "Don't do it, Mister. You put that rifle back where it came from right now or I'm gonna touch this thing off. And don't think I can't hit you from here cuz I can."

Indecision precipitated by pride or ego generated a few tense seconds before the rider lowered his rifle and put it back in its scabbard. Seeing that the man had complied with his order, Jake holstered his pistol and started walking towards him. The cowboy had done likewise riding his horse in Jake's direction, neither of them speaking but keeping a close eye on the other one. They met at the fence. It was only then that Jake recognized the rider as a new hand at the Rockin' C. The rider however, seemed unaware of who Jake was. He was much younger than Jake being maybe 18 or 19, of slender build with a wispy moustache and short brown hair beneath a full crown gray Stetson that had been dimpled twice. It was clear to Jake that the kid was full of himself, like he had been at that age. The kid said in a haughty tone, "You need to control yer damned dog, Mister. The way it was going after that cow, why if it had got hold ah her milk bag and tore it I might ah had to put that cow down and then where would her calf be. You damned Grangers are ah blight on the land.

And that kid, that little bastard is lucky I didn't crease his hair for 'im."

Jake's heart was hammering away at a good pace, maintaining a steady flow of adrenaline in his system. Nonetheless, he said in a steady voice, "Mister, the boy ain't no bastard. I'd suggest you ease back on yer throttle 'fore yer train runs off its track."

It was apparent the cowboy was vacillating as to whether he should come back at Jake in the same manner or succumb to common sense. After an awkward moment of them looking at one another, he chose the latter. "There was horse tracks comin' outta Pumpkin Crik right across from yer neighbor's place. They fell in behind this little bunch ah cows and pushed 'em up here. That's how I came upon you folks."

Jake nodded. "I suspected as much."

"That McDonald fella has got it in for my boss."

"I know."

"How's that?"

"I work for yer boss. I'm Jake Lafarge."

A sudden look of surprise bordering on embarrassment came to the cowboy's face, but then it went away almost as quickly as it had come. He said, having apparently strayed from the decorum that went along with common sense, "Word back at the home place is yer shacked up with the widow of the Granger you and Mr. Ellsworth strung up."

From the corner of his eye Jake could see Henry and Bella approaching. There was little doubt in his mind that Henry had heard the cowboy. Jake frowned, "Ain't no truth to it. She's ah respectable woman."

The young cow hand recoiled slightly from Jake's hateful stare. He appeared uneasy like he was being forced to accept a lie. He said, absent any contrition in his voice, "Oh."

"When you go back you tell Cyrus I'll be home no later than one week from today."

"Alright, I'll tell 'im."

It was obvious that a pall of mutual indulgence had descended upon them. Neither respected what the other had to say. Jake said, "Seein' how me and the boy are afoot do you suppose you could come through the gap in the fence up the canyon and push these critters outta here?"

The cowboy looked up the creek for a few seconds and then came back to Jake. He said, "I reckon you want me to take 'em outta the canyon."

"Be nice if ya would. Grass is already short here and the widow's got two horses and a milk cow that needs ta graze till the snow comes."

The cowboy scoffed. "The grass is short everywhere. If it ain't the homesteaders plowin' it under its these big money people dumpin' more cattle in here where we already got more 'an enough lips and teeth workin' the country." And then his tone became like a rant. "Sure, I'll take these critters outta here, but I don't know where. There's new Grangers moved into the next two canyons to the south of here. Maybe beyond that there's un-used graze."

Jake thought to tell him that Bovill, or rather the *old boys back east with more money than sense* had moved onto that range, but he did not. He said, "We'll lend ya hand pushin' these animals out."

The young rider looked hatefully at Bella and then locked eyes with Henry who held his own. He then reined his horse around and jabbed it with his spurs. Jake and Henry watched as he trotted his horse alongside the fence until he disappeared into some box elder trees. Suddenly, they were left standing in the quiet of the hayfield. Things were different now between them. A raven began to circle overhead and call out its mournful cry. And then Henry said, "It was good that you was here, Jake. That fella had a bead on me. When I saw it I nearly peed my pants."

A sudden feel good sensation consumed Jake. He smiled down at Henry. It was, he thought, the first good natured thing that the boy had said to him. He took care to preserve it. "I was proud of you. It took spunk to take a shot at that fella, even if it was with yer scattergun."

"I couldn't let him shoot Bella."

"I don't blame ya. If I had a dog I wouldn't let nobody shoot it either."

"Ma's likely gonna be mad when she finds out."

"I'll tell her how it was. I'll tell her that buckaroo didn't give you no choice." Jake paused and laughed as a segue to what he would say next. "It damned sure got his attention."

Henry's eyes got watery as he reached over and began petting Bella on the head. Jake was uncertain if the tears were because of Henry's feeling for the dog, or a sense that hung heavy in the air between them that Jake had done and said something that Nate might have if he'd been there.

More often than not it seemed to Jake that cows at first acted like they didn't know what it was you wanted them to do and then, suddenly, when the odds were no longer in their favor to continue doing as they pleased they would comply with a man's whooping and hollering and arm waving and go where it was you wanted them to. It had been that way this morning. In a way Jake felt sorry for the bawling cows and their calves as he and Henry watched the young cowboy drive them along the outside of the fence and back down the canyon. They just wanted to be left alone so they could eat.

"Here comes Ma," said Henry.

Jake looked up the wagon road that ran along the creek. Ellie was walking down it towards them. Even at a distance she struck him as a handsome woman. She was wearing an ankle length blue gingham dress and a red and yellow paisley sun bonnet that was tied beneath her chin. Each step that she took in the flour like dirt caused a small cloud of dust to boil up around her feet. *That git-up has got to be hot as hell*, he said to himself.

Henry sighed. "She heard that cowboy's rifle shot, otherwise she wouldn't be coming. She knows the sound of my shotgun."

"I believe in this situation, Henry, the truth will serve you best. I was kinda like you growing up. My pa ran off when I was four years old. So it was just me and my Ma from then on. We was always truthful with one another. We had to be."

"Do you miss your pa?"

Jake shrugged. "Sometimes I do. It's mostly when other fellas go ta tellin' what they did with their pa growing up and such." He paused and then added with a dismissive laugh, "I hear my pa's a scalawag so maybe it's for the best."

"Kind of like my pa?"

Jake instantly regretted the last of what he'd said. He was searching for words to fix it when Ellie reached them. She said, mostly to Henry, "I heard shooting. I thought maybe I should come check on you boys, see if I needed to take some sage chickens back to the house and get them ready for dinner."

Henry appeared afraid to incur his mother's wrath. His eyes shifted to Jake for help. Ellie noted it and looked straight at Jake causing him to come to Henry's rescue. "We had ah little disagreement with a fella this mornin'."

Ellie nodded towards the young cowboy who was now visible only intermittently as he pushed the cows through the box elder trees at the edge of the field. 'That man over there?" Henry blurted out, "He tried to kill Bella."

"What?" shrieked Ellie, "Why?"

"She was chasing one of his cows."

Ellie looked down at Bella who was lying on the ground beside Henry. "Well, I'm glad he missed. I could've sworn though that one of the shots sounded like your shotgun."

From the corner of his eye, Henry could see Jake's expectant gaze. It caused his resistance to melt. "It was Ma. I took a shot at the guy."

Ellie's face exploded in shock. "You what? Why Henry? You know better than that."

"He was trying to kill Bella."

"Bella's a dog."

Henry teared up. "She's my best friend. Wouldn't you try and save your best friend?"

"This is different, Henry. You're lucky that man didn't shoot you."

"He was going to but Jake stopped him."

Ellie directed her anger onto Jake. "How could you let Henry be involved in such goings on? He's only *nine years old*, Mr. Lafarge. Too young to be a part of your silly man games."

"It happened purty quick, Ellie. This fella didn't give Henry much choice."

"Bella is a dog, Mr. Lafarge. I love her but I love my son more." And with that she went to Henry and grabbed the shotgun from his hands. Rage danced in her eyes. It was fueled by the possibility that she had just narrowly escaped losing the rest of her family. She shouted at Henry, "You can have this back when you show better judgement." And then she turned, her eyes settling on Jake, her breathing such that the rise and fall of her chest was noticeable. She opened her mouth to speak but nothing came out. For a moment, she held this look of exasperation before shaking her head and stomping off towards the cabin.

They stood and watched Ellie's departure and when she was beyond hearing, Henry said, "Ma gets this way sometimes."

Inwardly, Jake was angry that Ellie had not acknowledged the fact he may have saved Henry's life. He resented the blame she was placing on him. Nonetheless, he said, "Yer ma must care about you an awful lot to git this upset. I guess it's kinda like how you got when that fella tried to kill Bella."

CHAPTER SEVENTEEN

For whatever reason, nature had created an opening amongst the trees that covered the creek bottom. It was oblong with an irregular boundary due to, in places, the trees and wild plum bushes jutting out into the tall grass. Starting on the outer perimeter, Jake went round and round listening to the monotonous chatter of the sickle bar as it felled wave after wave of the grass and wildflowers before it. Perched as he was on the iron seat in between and above the wheels of the mower he had little choice but to watch the grass fall and the big horses' tails switching in their quest to rid themselves of the relentless horseflies. After a time these sights and sounds became mesmerizing, almost soothing, and would have succeeded in achieving these effects had it not been for all that Jake had on his mind. Talking about his father to Henry had taken him back to a difficult period in his life. It was one of those places he tried to stay away from as every time he went there it angered him. And then there was Ellie. He'd decided that he would pull out at the end of the week, but that was before he and Henry had talked this morning. Now he saw himself in the boy, just him and his mother down in Louisiana struggling to make a living. When it became clear that his father was never coming back he wished, even prayed, for a man to come into his mother's life that would take them on, but none did. He supposed, after enough time had passed, that Henry would think the same thing. Suddenly, Jake saw movement in the trees along the creek. He locked onto it with his eyes. Momentarily, Henry stepped into the open. He held up his willow stringer. There were six fish on it and a big grin on his face. He shouted, "I'm going to the house."

Jake hollered back, "They ought ta fry up real nice." It made him feel good to see Henry smile in his presence. In a way it chipped away at the burden his conscience had borne since that day at Jawbone Springs.

It took a couple of days following the hayfield incident for the tension in Ellie's demeanor towards Jake to go away. Aside from rehashing the events at dinner on the day it happened the two of them avoided talking about it. She just couldn't seem to acknowledge the fact that he might have saved Henry's life, as opposed to it was his feud with the McDonalds that likely caused the cows and the gun wielding cowboy to be there in the first place. Ellie was determined to make a go of it there, to have something in life, and to do that she needed Jake's help. In spite of the first day's tumultuous start he had managed to get the hay cut and, with help from Henry, finish the fence around the field and nail the boards onto the framework of the shed, all of this by the end of the fourth day since he returned from Miles City.

On the morning of the fifth day, the stars were just retreating from the sky when Jake finished his breakfast and went outside to begin hitching up the Percherons, four to the hay wagon and two on the buck rake. It wasn't long before Ellie and Henry joined him. Ellie was dressed as a man. She was wearing brown striped pants and a loose fitting red shirt that was open at the neck. Her hair was in a single long ponytail with a yellow bow tied at the end of it. A gray Stetson, somewhat soiled and tattered that was sharply peaked, sat atop her head. It was a look that would do nothing to dispel the notion among some folks that she was a hussy since she had her husband's killer living with her.

"It's gonna be hard work," said Jake. "By the end of the day yer back will be cryin' fer mercy."

"I've no doubt what you say is true," replied Ellie, "but we've got no choice. This is the task that fate has assigned us if our animals are going to have something to eat this winter."

Jake nodded. "Fine enough. If you wanna drive the wagon Ellie, I'll bring the buck rake. You can just park at this end of the field and wait while I scoop up a load of grass."

Ellie and Henry climbed onto the seat of the wagon. Driving a team was not foreign to her. When they had made the trip up from Kansas last year she had been at the reins almost every day. *It'll be a good thing to know,* Nate had told her. At first, his riding a horse when he could've tied it to the wagon infuriated her. Maneuvering a team was a significant departure from her life as a school teacher in Topeka. But now, Nate's insistence that she drive the wagon seemed prophetic.

The downed grass came right up to the edge of the fence that Jake and Henry had just completed. After several days of lying there in the hot sun, its color had gone from a bright green to a duller version with streaks of brown but that was the intent, to dry it so that it wouldn't spoil once it was stacked.

Ellie pulled back on the reins, "Whoa team, whoa." The wagon came to a halt just outside the wire gate. Right across the fence Jake was busily scooping the grass onto the wooden teeth of the buck rake. Ellie said, as if she needed to explain to Henry her reason for not going through the gate, "I don't want to get in Jake's way. Maybe the next load we'll go into the field."

Henry did not look at his mother but instead kept his eyes on Jake. "Boy, he sure can work that thing, can't he?"

Ellie watched as Jake kept the horses moving at an even pace. The rake skimmed over the top of the stubble collecting the loose grass. In its wake there was little that had escaped. She said, "Yes Henry, he's very adept."

"He's almost got a load, Ma," said Henry as he started to climb down from the wagon. "We better get ready to pitch it off."

Ellie smiled at Henry's eagerness and followed him to the bed of the wagon where they each picked up a pitchfork. In less than a minute, Jake arrived with a huge heap of grass. The rake was L shaped. It was ten feet wide with teeth that extended five feet and a back that was five feet high. It had railings too on either side that kept the grass from falling off.

"Jab yer fork into the ground behind the load," yelled Jake. "We'll try and slide it off."

It took a little while before they were able to thread their pitchforks into the seam between the load and the back of the rake and then straddle the teeth of the rake with the tines of their forks, but at last they were ready. "Brace yerselves," shouted Jake, and with that he started backing the horses. Within seconds, Henry gave way and his pitchfork slammed against the back of the rake. However, Ellie's side of the load was starting to slide off. It had moved about a foot when abruptly she also had to let go of her pitchfork. It was an effort for Jake to not show his disappointment. He had hoped they would be able to slide the load off and begin pitching it onto the wagon while he went back to the field and gathered another rake full. In that way they would never be waiting on one another, as he would gradually have to go farther for grass once he collected all that was on this end of the field. The process would be slowed enough when they would take the wagon to the corral and he would have to stop to do his own unloading.

Ellie hollered out, "We'll pitch off some of the grass and then let's try it again."

Ellie and Henry had already started to furiously stab and shove the grass off when Jake shrugged and said, "Ok."

In a short while they had reduced the load by about a third and were positioned to attempt another slide off. Ellie appeared, to Jake, almost desperate to prove to him that she could do this, that she could pull her weight. She said, "Alright, we're ready."

Jake began to gently coax the horses back, as he did the pile of grass started to move. It was a jerky motion at first, that quickly became smooth. Ellie and Henry broke into big smiles as the clump of hay now rested on the ground. Ellie laughed, clearly proud of what she and Henry had just accomplished. She looked at Jake. "I think we've got our technique down."

Jake too had a celebratory smile pasted on his face. He had just opened his mouth to tell her and Henry '*good job*' when his expression suddenly became fearful. Ellie spun around in the direction that Jake was looking. Just coming out of the trees were three Indians. She shrieked. "Henry, come here."

Henry saw the Indians and ran to his mother, as he did, one of the Indians laughed and pointed at him, saying loudly, "He runs like a scared rabbit." This caused the others to laugh as well. It was openly arrogant and hostile as if they were purposely goading Jake into doing something.

Jake got off of the buck rake and went to where Ellie and Henry were standing near the wagon. The Indians pulled up on the other side of it. No sooner had they done so than it became apparent to Jake that they had been drinking. The naysayer, that voice in his mind that always went to the bad side of things shouted out to him, *it was probably yer old man that sold 'em the whiskey.* Jake took a shallow breath lest his heart would run away with itself and held it for a few seconds before slowly exhaling. He quickly surveyed the situation. The Indians were all armed with repeating rifles and pistols. For the most part they were dressed like white men with dark colored pants, long sleeved shirts and boots, except for one who was wearing moccasins. Two of them were wearing black felt crush hats and the third a dark brown derby. All of them had long shoulder length hair worn loose. Their horses were of good quality and equipped with leather saddles and bridles, an observation that caused Jake's inner voice to offer up, *the owners ah that tack is probably missin' their hair too.* Jake made eye contact with the Indian wearing the derby hat. He was a skinny man with sunken cheeks and no whiskers of any kind. Three of his front teeth were missing, two on the bottom and one on top. He was the one who had started the laughter. Jake said trying his best to sound unafraid, "What can I do for you boys?"

The derby hatted Indian's drunken laughter dried up to a devious smile, "We hunting buffalo, you see any?"

Derby Hat's words caused his friends to giggle and look at one another.

Jake could see that he was being played. He came back, smiling his own hidden message, "There ain't been nuthin' but buffalo ghosts around here for about the past three years. You fellas must not git out too often."

"You sure? We heard there was some up here."

Jake indulged them in another exchange of nonsense. "There ain't no buffalo in these parts. The hide hunters got 'em all. You boys better 'n anybody ought to know that."

Derby Hat went silent. He shot Jake a dirty look. "We are not free to go as we once were. You, white man, should know that."

"This canyon," said Jake, "belongs to this lady. It's her homestead. The white man's council beyond where the sun comes up gave it to her."

The devious smile returned to Derby Hat's face. "Maybe she's got some cows she can give us since the white man made the buffalo ghosts. We are hungry. Our wives and little ones are hungry."

The critic in Jake's mind shouted out, *maybe you should have spent yer money on food instead of whiskey.* But aloud, he said, "I know the great white father in Washington has bought cattle and many other things for you to eat. I know this to be true because I have brought cattle myself to the agency at Lame Deer."

"Like the buffalo, they have disappeared."

"I'm sorry if that is true, but you need to take it up with the Indian Agent or the Army. It is not up to this lady, with what little she has, to feed you and your people."

Until now, Derby Hat had been resting his rifle across his lap with the barrel pointing slightly to the left of where Jake was standing. With no explanation he stood the butt of the stock on his right thigh with his finger inside the trigger guard. The gun was not cocked but Jake suspected it had a chambered round. To fire it, Derby Hat would need only to slide his thumb over the hammer at the same time he leveled the rifle at Jake and pull the trigger. It would be quick, maybe thought Jake, quicker than he could draw his pistol and shoot if it came to that. But then he saw that Derby Hat's friends were getting edgy, making slight adjustments in how they were holding their rifles, like they were a cat preparing to pounce upon a mouse. Jake said to himself, *hell, even if I git lucky and git Derby Hat 'fore he gits me his friends will shoot me dead.*

And then Derby Hat said, "Maybe your woman can fix us something to eat. Fill our bellies and then we will go."

From the corner of his eye Jake could see the terror in Ellie's face. In that same instant his mind's eye went to Greta's lifeless body and the empty laudanum bottles on her night stand. He knew from all the accounts he'd heard that this was a ploy to get the upper hand so that they could kill Jake and Henry and have their way with Ellie before they killed her too. Jake said, "We have no food to spare. You and yer friends need to be on yer way. Go back down the canyon."

Derby Hat's eyes radiated anger. He began to slowly rotate his rifle around to where he would have a better angle to pull its hammer back. The movement was not lost on Jake. Suddenly, his eyes locked onto the stock and the splinter of wood missing from it. He shouted, "Where did you git that rifle?"

The anger in Jake's voice appeared to momentarily unnerve Derby Hat. He said, "I trade with white man. I give him wolf pelts he give Pale Bear gun."

"Who is this man?"

Derby Hat suddenly became defiant. "You and your woman you do nothing for us. Why should Pale Bear tell you?"

"Because that rifle belonged to a friend of mine. He was murdered and I want to know who did it."

"You think Pale Bear killed your friend?"

"I don't know. You have his rifle."

"White man always think Indians do wrong."

"Just tell me who it was that you traded with for the rifle and we can go our separate ways."

Pale Bear giggled in an evil way. "Whiskey Pete. He friend to Indians. He bring us whiskey and guns and bullets."

Jake's mind instantly went back to that day in the woods and what Bovill had said about his father. It caused a sick, panicky feeling to come over him. "Is Whiskey Pete a Frenchmen?" From the corner of his eye, he could see Henry's eyes light up in a knowing way.

Pale Bear nodded. "Others have told me that is so."

"Do you know where I can find him?"

Pale Bear suddenly became angry. "No more questions. You do something for Pale Bear now. Give us a cow or a horse. You give to us or we take."

Henry cried out. "No, you can't take our animals."

Ellie grabbed Henry by the shoulders and pulled him to her. "Be quiet, Henry. Leave this to Jake."

Henry began to cry causing Pale Bear to look at him and laugh. "The scared rabbit now cries like a girl." The other two Indians joined in the laughter and humiliation of Henry.

Jake cut them off. "It is time for you to go," he said in an angry tone. "We are poor people and have nothing we can spare to give you."

Pale Bear glared at Jake for a moment as the anger in his eyes intensified and then, abruptly, he allowed it to drain away. Twisting part way around in his saddle, he said something in Cheyenne to his friends before coming back to face Jake. "Alright, white man, we go for now." And with that he reined his horse to the left, as he did Jake could see that Pale Bear was lowering his rifle so that it would be pointing at him. In the same instant he caught movement from one of the Indians beyond Pale Bear. He was taking aim at Jake. As he drew his pistol, Jake yelled at Ellie and Henry, "git behind the buck rake." They had barely taken a step when Jake's .45 roared and in that blur of time over the next second, two more shots sounded. One from the Indian to the side of Pale Bear that narrowly missed Jake and a second from Pale Bear that dug a deep furrow in the muscle of Jake's left side. And then Jake's pistol thundered again. The heavy slug emerged from the smoke at the end of the Colt's barrel and in less than a heartbeat it had plowed into Pale Bear's chest toppling his lifeless body from his horse. Terrified, the horse chased after the other two riders, one of whom was clutching his shoulder as they escaped towards the cover of the trees. Even then, in that adrenaline driven moment, the voice of caution in Jake's mind was screaming at him to keep shooting, to kill Pale Bear's friends lest he have to do it when they come back another day, but he did not. Instead, he watched them flee, gun in hand, ears ringing, his heart beating hard and fast so as to make the individual beats indistinguishable. Behind him in this sudden milieu of chaos, of unnecessary violence, he could faintly hear the whimpering of Henry and Ellie. He glanced at them but he did not go to them. He went first to Pale Bear, not to render aid, but to make sure he was dead. And then he turned to face Ellie. "You're shot," she cried.

As he looked back at her and Henry, Jake became aware that he was breathing heavily and that his hands were shaking. He filled his lungs with what he hoped would be fresh air to settle himself, but it was tainted with the acrid smell of gunpowder. He said, without looking at the growing bloodstain beneath his arm, "I'm alright."

"But you're not," said Ellie as she came toward him. And then the hysteria that she had just put to bay came back. "I should never have agreed to come to this God forsaken country," she sobbed. "It is wicked and unforgiving."

Jake stepped close to Ellie whereupon she settled her head on his chest. Over her shoulder he could see Henry looking at them. The disapproval that might have been there a week ago was no longer in his eyes. Jake extended an arm to him and placed the other around his mother's shoulder. For a time they stood there, huddled together in the aura of Pale Bear's death, quietly consoling one another by virtue of their presence, not making rash statements like, *it'll be alright*, because at the moment none of them believed that. At last, when they'd drawn what solace they could from one another, or at least Jake had, he said, "I'm going to drag Pale Bear's body over into the shade of the trees. They'll come back for it, probably tonight."

Alarm registered in Ellie's face. "But you're bleeding."

Jake looked at her and wondered if her concern was for him or more because he was all that stood between her and Henry and the Indians, should they return. He said, "Maybe if you've got something that will serve as a bandage up at the house you could fetch it while I tend to this fella."

Fear gripped Ellie. It caused her voice to be weak and uncertain. "Alright Jake, if you think it's safe to go there?"

"My guess is those other two have skedaddled on down the canyon. I hit one of 'em purty solid in his shoulder so they'll likely be wantin' ta tend ta that." Jake forced himself to smile. "If you ain't back here in two shakes of a lamb's tail I'll come huntin' for ya."

Ellie scoffed. "Trust me, we shall not tarry."

"Wished I had my scattergun," said Henry in a naïve bravado. "I'd fix 'em."

Jake was about to tell them that they just needed to be on their way and that they would be ok as he was confident the Indians were headed away from them when Greta and all that had happened to her came back into his mind. It pained him to think that either Ellie or Henry would ever withdraw into themselves the way that Greta had. His legs had started to move before he'd totally decided it was the right thing to do but he said, "Wait here." Even before he reached Pale Bear's body he knew the rifle next to it was Ben's. For one thing, it was a Model 76 Winchester in .45-75 caliber, there weren't many of those around as most cowboys preferred the .44-40. The telling proof, however, was a divot of wood about two inches long by a quarter inch deep missing from the butt stock. Ben had taken a nasty fall while crossing a rock slide last year and both he and the rifle had not fared well. It had been a present from Cyrus on his seventeenth birthday. Jake had attended the party and seen how happy and excited Ben had been to receive such a fine hunting rifle. And now here it lay in the dirt, stained with the blood of someone who couldn't possibly feel about it as Ben had. Jake bent down and picked up the rifle being careful to keep his back to Ellie and Henry as he wiped the blood from the stock onto his pants. He then walked back to the other side of the wagon and held the rifle out to Ellie. "Take this with you. It was my friend's. Have you ever fired one like it?"

Ellie was a bit taken aback. She looked at the rifle as if it were possessed, like it was some sort of demonic instrument. For a time these emotions held her tongue captive until finally she escaped, "Yes, Nate showed me how to shoot his."

"It works the same way. Just draw the lever down and then up to chamber a round. And then yer good ta go. But you should know this gun is much more powerful than Nate's. It'll really rock a wisp of ah woman like you, so have it tight to yer shoulder 'fore you pull the trigger."

Ellie appeared more fearful of the rifle. "I don't know, Jake. Maybe I-"

"Take it, Ellie. Ya need ta git used ta guns if yer gonna live out here." And then maybe it was his conscience prodding him, but he said, "Whaddaya gonna do when I'm gone?" He'd no sooner gotten the words out than he regretted saying them, at least right now he did with Pale Bear lying dead a short distance away. At some point she'd have to answer that question but now was not the time.

Ellie had begun to cry. Jake was at a loss as to how to repair the damage he'd just done. He said, trying to not sound indifferent to her pain, "I'm sorry. You can wait for me or go on your own." He allowed her a brief moment in which to answer, getting none he went to Pale Bear. After removing his gun belt and pistol he began dragging him, by his feet, towards the trees. It was an effort for Jake as his left side was burning and seeping blood at a steady rate. Finally, he reached the shade of some tall box elders where he released Pale Bear's legs, letting them drop to the ground. For a moment he stood there looking down at Pale Bear's eyes, wide open in that vacant dead man stare. Jake sighed heavily as if he could expel his anger. *He'll be there tonight with Nate and Roy and Greta. Damn him.*

Ellie and Henry were not yet back to the hay wagon. Jake glanced over at the buck rake and the big draft horses patiently waiting. He was considering raking hay until he saw, off in the distance, Ellie and Henry coming. It was hot causing their images to dance in the shimmering air. *Hell with it, I'm gonna have a smoke*, he said to himself as he plopped down in the dirt beneath the wagon. His fingers worked quickly and deftly in rolling a cigarette, a task that fifteen minutes ago his shaking hands wouldn't have been able to do. He drew in the smoke not quite filling his lungs to capacity before he pursed his lips slightly and sent it out into the space before him. Through the blue haze he could see them approaching. Mixed in with the crackling flight of the big brown grasshoppers that pervaded the field he caught snatches of their conversation.

I like him, Ma. I didn't used to but I do now.

That's good, Henry, but he'll soon be gone.

Well, you need to tell him not to go.

Ellie laughed. *I couldn't make your father stay home so I don't suppose I can convince Mr. Lafarge to stay either.*

Well, you need to try.

And then they went silent as they got close to being within normal speaking distance. Jake's conscience shouted to him, *you can't leave 'em now.*

"Maybe we should go over to the creek so we can wash your wound," said Ellie.

Jake tilted his head back slightly so as to be able to look up at her. In the sky overhead were two turkey vultures circling, waiting for when they would drop down and do to Pale Bear what others of their kind had done to Nate and Roy. Jake tried to focus only on Ellie, he said, "Alright, I'll follow you over there."

At the point they intercepted the creek it was below the beaver dam and shallow, maybe eight inches or so. The water ran over slick rocks that were orange-ish, blue-ish, red-ish, and if there were any true colors amongst them, it was white and purple. Jake took his shirt off causing Ellie to blush at the sight of his hairy chest and the bloody rawness of his wound. "I'll clean it up first," said Jake as he dipped the shirt into the water.

In spite of her embarrassment, Ellie said, "I can do that for you."

A surprised look came to Jake's face. The only woman who had ever touched him in that way had been a prostitute. To hesitate any more than he already had would only increase the uneasiness between them, so he held the shirt out to her. "The bleeding has eased off some so go easy."

It was fortunate that the heavy bullet had only grazed the outer edge of Jake's side. Ellie took the wet shirt and began gently dabbing at the dried blood surrounding the wound. There was a slight nervous tremble to her hands. Jake noted it and thought it was akin to the goose bumps on his chest. He said, "It don't look too bad."

"You were lucky."

"I reckon that's one way ah lookin' at it," said Jake with a laugh.

"You know what I mean."

Jake nodded. "We should be able to git a lot of the hay in the corral today. Hopefully, we'll finish up tomorrow."

Ellie ignored his talk of being done. She handed Henry a piece of towel that had been doubled over. "Hold this on the wound while I bandage it." And then she said, like the schoolmarm that she had once been, "Hold your arms up, Jake, so I can wrap this around you." She then began unrolling a long strip of white sheet and leaned in close to his chest. Her hair brushed against his chin. It was soft and smelled good to him, like wildflowers, he thought. She made two complete loops around his torso and over the towel covering the wound before tying it off.

Jake lowered his arms. "You make a right good nurse." And then he added, looking at Henry, "The both of ya do."

Ellie said, less serious now, "I guess we'll see if you survive." She then went to the creek and submerged his shirt in the cool water, kneading it to work the blood from its fabric. It was clear to Jake that she was trying her best to show her appreciation. After a time, she stood and wrung the water from his shirt and handed it to him, purposely allowing her eyes to linger on his bare chest. It caused Jake to say, "I reckon we better git back ta work."

Fear came to Ellie's face. "But what about the Indians?"

At first it came to him to dismiss her concern but then he saw himself down at the far end of the field, perched on the buck rake's seat scooping up hay when a bullet would come from the trees. He'd fall to the ground, maybe dead or not, but in his mind it was a minor point as the next thing he saw was an Indian rushing up to him, jerking his head back by the hair and starting at his forehead cutting away his scalp. An involuntary shiver surged through his body extracting him from the death he'd just experienced. He said, now regretting how he'd been with her earlier, "you and Henry wait here. Keep that rifle handy. I'm gonna make a swing down the canyon just to be sure those boys left the country."

"Alright Jake, but please be careful."

Jake nodded. He could see the concern in her eyes. He sensed that it went beyond just being her and Henry's protector. It was an emotional quagmire that he'd gotten himself into by coming here. Every day that he stayed he sunk a little deeper.

As he walked across the field and the grasshoppers flitted away under his feet, Jake muttered under his breath, "It ain't bad enough that things has stopped growin' cuz of this drought, but what little there is these damned things gotta eat it." He walked on past the wagon and the buck rake and had just entered the trees when the words escaped his mouth, "Those sons-ah-bitches." Immediately he bent down and picked up a stick and threw it at one of the turkey vultures that was pecking at Pale Bear. "Go on, git outta here." The birds ignored the stick as it went wide of them. Jake broke into a trot. "Go on, you devil birds. Git outta here." He was within about ten feet of them before they finally took flight.

It was inevitable that he would look at Pale Bear. The birds had ripped a couple of quarter sized chunks of flesh from his face. Right away his mind took him back to how Nate and Roy had looked, compounding what was before him. Jake turned away as if that would stop the images of Jawbone Springs from flooding his mind but it did not help. His conscience was trying to wade through this torrent of guilt when he heard himself say, "This ain't my problem. Pale Bear did it to his self." And then he willed his legs to move on down the canyon in search of the other Indians or sign of where they had gone. The horse tracks were not evenly spaced and sharply defined, but rather some appeared to have slipped throwing small clods of soil. They were running all the way to where a shallow pine filled draw entered the canyon. It was about a half mile from where Pale Bear lay. His companions had slowed their horses to a walk here and went into the thick trees. Jake stopped and studied their tracks. *They're in there sure as Christmas is comin' and if I go there I'll be dessert for those buzzards.* He sighed heavily as he clutched his rifle while staring off into the ponderosa pines and taking stock of his options. It made sense to him, like he'd originally thought before Ellie's fear had caused him to second guess himself, that with one of them hit pretty hard they'd lie up during the day and tend to his wound. Come nightfall, the healthy one would come for Pale Bear. But then it came to him, *if they're wantin' to even the score we'll be easy pickin's out there in that wide open field.* Jake turned away from the draw, certain only in that to enter it would be to die. He started back up the canyon trying to put his self in the Indian's place and how vengeful he would or would not be. His indecision stemmed mostly from not wanting to delay picking up the hay as Bovill would be back in two days to get his equipment. But then he snorted aloud and said to himself, it won't make much difference if I'm dead, or Ellie, or Henry. That settled it, he would get Ellie and Henry and they would go back to the house. He would give the Indians this day and night to retrieve Pale Bear and hopefully go away. It made him feel good to have arrived at this decision, Ellie, he knew, would welcome it. And then he came within sight of Pale Bear. The vultures were back. He did not hesitate but thumbed the hammer back on his Henry and took aim on one of them. As the front bead settled into the notch of the rear sight he squeezed the trigger. His rifle bucked upward, belching black smoke and a puff of black feathers as the heavy bullet knocked the vulture off of its feet. Its friend flew off having been warned as to the consequences of scavenging the dead. Jake stayed wide of the dead vulture and Pale Bear. His mind's eye had already confirmed what he would find if he went there.

CHAPTER EIGHTEEN

They loaded what hay had been on the buck rake when the Indians had come and returned to the cabin. Jake hoped that when Pale Bear's friends came for him they would see the dead vulture and know that Jake had tried to do the right thing. Nonetheless, the images of all that had happened at the hayfield fueled their worries. Ellie was sure the Indians would seek vengeance. *They'll come and they'll bring their friends. We can't stay here. They will kill us all. Oh, this God forsaken land, I hate it, Jake, I do.* By the time the sun had set she had begun to cry, quietly as she stood at the table washing the supper dishes in a big tin pan. Jake was at a loss as to how to reassure her. He could not tell her that everything would be all right because he'd known Indians to be unpredictable. But just before dark, he instructed her and Henry to stay in the cabin, bar the door and only open it for him. He then put the saddle horses and Daisy in the new shed and picketed the Percherons next to the corral. The moon was half full and the night was warm. Conditions for maintaining a vigil from the shadows of two wild plum bushes just beyond the shed would be good, assuming he could stay awake. And so he sat clutching his rifle, straining his eyes and ears, hoping to detect the Indians before they did him. A hundred times over they were there, at the corner of the cabin, coming for the horses and behind him in the trees. His legs had become numb from sitting in one place for so long and his back ached and the night air had cooled even more, chilling his insides. But finally, the birds began to sing as God peeled back a corner of the blanket he had thrown over the land last night. *Now is when they'll come*, said Jake to his self. *Git ya when yer groggy or going to the privy.* But more birds began to sing as it got lighter until finally Jake realized that his hiding place worked better in the dark than it did now. He was sitting cross legged on the ground. After taking a good look around, he rocked forward to his hands and knees. The stiffness in his legs was such that he had to use his rifle as a crutch to pull himself up, but even that was difficult due to the bullet wound under his left arm. The cabin appeared cold and dark. His heart was pounding as he hobbled across the bare yard towards it, all the while expecting a bullet from that unseen gun to find him. At last he knocked on the door. "Ellie, it's me." From the corner of his eye he saw the curtains in the window to his right move just slightly. Inside, he heard Henry's muffled voice, "It's Jake, Ma."

Momentarily, the door opened. Ellie's eyes were red and sunken. She appeared emotionally spent. Jake sensed, had things been different between them she would have hugged him, but she did not. She said, "Do you think they're gone?"

Jake shook his head. "I don't know. I'm gonna go see."

Her eyes widened, but not in a good way. "Maybe you should wait a while."

"If they intend to leave, they'll be gone."

Ellie sighed as if it hurt her to do so. "Be careful."

Jake forced a smile. "I always am." And then he added, "Bar the door."

He stayed in the trees and off the road all the way down to the new gate where the wagon had been parked and he had killed Pale Bear. The air was still except for the pleasantries of the songbirds' endless singing as they darted from one branch to another. But today, these were not the birds that interested Jake. Being careful to stay hidden in the willows near the creek he searched the sky for vultures or ravens over the woods where he'd left Pale Bear's body. For several minutes he maintained this vigil. He scoffed and whispered aloud, "hell, they might all be on the ground havin' their breakfast." He was reluctant to go there as he'd seen all that he ever wanted to of a vulture's handiwork. Nonetheless, he knew it wouldn't be right to leave a dead man like that. And so he started across the opening with the enthusiasm of a man climbing the steps to the gallows. He was about halfway there when down the canyon he saw smoke. It was white and diffuse, just lolling above the tops of the trees until it was absorbed by the sky. Jake quickened his pace. Pale Bear, the vultures, it all became secondary if this smoke wasn't coming from somebody's breakfast fire. Jake began to jog now. He felt foolish going towards a fire armed with a rifle, but he couldn't rule out the possibility that this was Pale Bear's friends drawing him into an ambush. On he went, pushed hard by massive amounts of adrenaline until, suddenly, he came to where Pale Bear had been. But he was gone, only the vulture that he had shot yesterday remained. The smoke was darker now and growing in size. Jake moved on, fighting through his fatigue from the night before, not knowing if once he got there, he would get a bullet in the chest. Running down the wagon road as he was it would be natural that the Indians would just wait for him, hidden in the trees. And then he rounded a slight bend in the road. Up ahead to his left was the wooded draw where the Indians had taken refuge, directly across the road from it was the fire. Jake studied the fire just briefly before going off the road and taking a knee in the brush. It was readily apparent to him what the Indians had done. Rather than risk another gun fight they had lit several fires between the road and the creek. They were mostly burning tall sage, grass and an occasional juniper tree. The flames were lively, at times being four or five feet until they reached the greener vegetation along the creek, whereupon they dropped to the ground. All together the fires totaled about an acre. However, as it was now, the flames were moving slowly down the canyon and away from the hay field due to a gentle breeze from the east. Jake knew that would all change in the afternoon when the winds would be out of the west. With no shovel or bucket or burlap bag he felt helpless to fight the fire. *Hell, even if I had something to work with*, said Jake to himself, *those red devils might knock me off just as soon as I show myself.* He snorted and quietly laughed as he whispered aloud, "Those sons ah bucks are purty clever thinking ta burn us out."

Jake started back up the canyon road at a jog, holding his rifle before him. He had but one thought, *we got ta save what we can.* By the time he reached the cabin he was breathing hard with profuse rivulets of sweat running down his reddened face. Once again he knocked on Ellie's door and shouted with urgency in his voice, "Ellie, it's me, open up."

She'd barely gotten the door open when her expression took on Jake's aura of alarm. "What is it, Jake? What's wrong?"

Jake's breathing was still somewhat labored and his chest heaved as he tried to steady himself. "The Indians set the canyon on fire. We got ta try and salvage what hay we can."

Ellie began to cry. "No, no, they're burning it. Why?"

"Revenge, Ellie. They're gitting even."

"But they started this."

"Ellie, we've got to go."

She shook her head as if she was close to becoming distraught. "To what end, Jake. I'll never be able to hang onto this place by myself. Maybe we should just let them have their way."

Jake acted as if he hadn't heard her and started towards the corral. He hollered over his shoulder. "I'm gonna git the horses hitched. You and Henry come along as soon as ya can. Bring yer guns, both of ya."

Ellie and Henry stood in the doorway of the cabin seemingly fearful to move from their sanctuary. Not until Jake reached the corral and looked back at them did they go inside and make ready for what awaited them at the hayfield.

It was close to mid-morning by the time they got to the meadow with the wagon and buck rake. The column of smoke was no longer timid and questionable as to its cause. It was thick and dark and billowy and rose up a thousand feet or more, but it still leaned to the west. "Keep yer guns handy and a sharp eye out," said Jake.

"Do you think they'll attack us?" asked Ellie.

"I don't know. They might be satisfied with lightin' off the canyon."

Ellie looked at the smoke. Her face was worried. "I don't care to be this close to the fire, Jake. You never know what it's gonna do."

"I'm of the belief we've got a few more hours before it might go against us. We need ta make the most ah that time."

Jake climbed on the buck rake and drove it to the far end of the field. The smell of smoke was strong but the horses seemed undeterred by it as they obediently took the machine wherever Jake directed them. In short order he had a load and headed back. He stopped the rake next to the wagon so Ellie and Henry could pitch part of the load directly onto it before spearing what was left on the forks and sliding it off. And then Jake was off to scoop up more while they pitched the rest of the hay onto the wagon. Things had gone well until about 1:30 in the afternoon when the wind not only finished its shift to the west, but increased its speed as well. The hayfield was now shrouded in smoke so dense it looked like ground fog. Jake had just come in with another load stopping right next to the wagon. He'd come to the conclusion some time ago that the Indians were not going to bushwhack them and instead were content to just burn them out. He took some solace in this and felt obliged to share it with Ellie and Henry. He hollered out to them, "I believe our neighbors have abandoned the idea of shootin' us."

Ellie paused in her pitching hay. "You're confident of that?"

"I'd probably bet ya ah sarsaparilla on it," replied Jake in a purposely jovial tone.

Ellie looked at him and smiled. It was the first time in a couple of days that he recalled her doing that. She said, "Well, that's a pretty serious wager so I reckon it must be a near certainty." And then her face became solemn again. "But what about the fire? We can't see from here exactly what it's doing."

"It has just reached the lower end of the field. I've already gathered the hay from there so there's not much for it to burn. Right now, it's just fingering out into the stubble here and there, kinda creepin' around. Outside the field, she's burnin' hot."

Ellie's concern ratcheted up again. "Well, won't it burn up the creek? It'll go straight to the cabin."

"I don't know. Depends on the wind and Henry's fishin' hole."

"The beaver pond, Ma," said Henry in response to his mother's vacant look. "It's pretty big."

"He's right," said Jake. "The beavers have flooded the bottom of the canyon just to the north of us." Jake paused and pointed to what he was talking about. "Ya see where them cattails snug up to the fence?"

Ellie nodded.

"They're standin' in about three inches ah water. I'm hopin' when the fire hits there it'll just skunk around in that bog and die out."

Ellie continued to stare at the greenness of the cattails trying to reassure herself that the picture Jake had painted of how the fire would go was plausible. When she finally convinced herself of this she turned back to Jake to tell him so, but her words were preempted.

"Looks like yer neighbors have come callin'," said Jake sarcastically.

Ellie followed Jake's gaze. Coming up the road through the smoke was George McDonald. "He looks to be angry, Jake. Be careful of what you say."

McDonald reined his horse in just short of them. His face was covered with ash and dirt and there were huge sweat stains on his shirt. He ignored Ellie and looked straight at Jake. "I'm of the belief this is your doing," he said tersely. "Is that true?"

"I don't know what yer talkin' about."

McDonald came back quickly in a loud voice. "I'm talkin' about them Indians you shot. We ran into 'em high-tailin' it outta the canyon with their dead friend."

"So they said it was me that shot 'em?"

"Said it was ah white man up the canyon. I reckon that'd be you."

"They musta left out the part where they rode up on us actin' all froggy wantin' us ta give 'em a cow right before they threw down on me. Yeah, I'll betcha they left that out."

"That may be your version of how it went, but the long and short of it is this fire they set came out of the canyon and got into my wheat. Me and my boys been workin' our asses off trying to save what we could. Somebody's got to pay for it."

"Well then, I would recommend you turn yer horse around and git after them Indians cuz ain't nobody here got any money or the inclination to be givin' it to you if we did have some."

McDonald rested his hands on his saddle horn and leaned forward slightly staring hard at Jake. The hate coming from his eyes was the equal of the sweat on his face. "You're a smart pup and pretty full of yourself, but make no mistake you're gonna get what's due you one day. And another thing, I know it was you that set the sheriff on me for killing that Ellsworth boy. I had nothing to do with that. So, I better not hear of you making any such accusations in the future or there will be hell to pay."

Jake felt bad for giving McDonald's name to the sheriff now that he knew his own father would be a strong suspect for Ben's killer. On the other hand, he felt no blame for the Indians setting fire to the canyon and McDonald's wheat as they'd come all liquored up making unreasonable demands. But then shame came to Jake when he recalled it was also his father who had sold them the whiskey that had likely made them do what they had. He came back, humbled as it were by his own thoughts, "I'm sorry for your losses, Mr. McDonald, but we're trying to avoid having any ourselves."

McDonald was caught off guard by Jake's apology. It seemed to stymy him to the point he could not speak. Instead, he tossed his head and scoffed before abruptly turning his horse around and spurring it back through the smoke and down the canyon.

It became apparent, after the sun went down and the air had begun to cool and the wind died away, that the sparsity of standing vegetation in the field and the beaver pond would beat the fire. Nonetheless, they continued to work taking the very last of the hay to the corral in the dark. There was a strong sense of pride amongst them. They smelled of smoke and sweat and their eyes were red and their noses had run, but they had worked well together. *It will*, Jake thought, *be hard to leave this.*

CHAPTER NINETEEN

It was close to noon on the second day after the fire when Bovill come riding up the road. He went right past where the dead vulture lay, unaware of its significance, and into the clearing where the gate was located. Seeing Jake and Henry down the meadow a ways, he reined in Jiggs and waited for them. After a time they came rumbling up in Ellie's wagon with two of the Percherons pulling it. Jake was not quite through the gate when Bovill hollered, "What the hell happened here?"

Jake cleared the opening before stopping the big horses. He then looked at Bovill with a degree of exasperation. "Indians."

"The hell you say."

"They came upon us all liquored up demanding our animals and, well, things just went downhill after that."

Bovill had a knowing, alarmed look on his face that had sprung up when Jake mentioned liquor. He glanced at Henry and then said cryptically to Jake, "I told you about that fella peddlalin' whiskey to 'em. Ain't no good ever gonna come ah that. It's just downright despicable a person that does such ah thing."

Jake looked at Bovill in a way that suggested he'd crossed the line, but then said, "Things got purty ugly."

"How so?"

"They pulled their guns on me. I didn't have no choice but ta shoot back."

"Did ya do 'em some damage?"

"Killed one, wounded another."

Mild shock registered on Bovill's face. "Ho-lee shit. I don't know who'll be comin' to see you first, the Army or the sheriff."

Jake sighed heavily. "I was thinkin' ah goin' and seeing them 'fore they git some version ah things that's all blowed outta shape."

"That might be wise." Bovill paused as a smug grin spread over his face, he added, "Yer gittin' ta be a real desperado, taking after yer old man." He then laughed as if it would make his sarcasm acceptable.

Jake shot Bovill an openly dirty look. "I take it you've come for yer hayin' equipment."

Bovill moved on, pretending he hadn't insulted Jake. "I have. We've actually got ah little spit ah meadow where we can cut some hay. It'll make those eastern boys that I work for feel like they ain't wasted their money on this equipment." And then Bovill laughed again, his voice filled with indifference.

In that instant it occurred to Jake that he was getting to where he didn't like Bovill. Nonetheless, he said, "C'mon up ta the house. I believe Ellie's fixin' sage chickens for dinner.

Ain't that right, Henry?"

Henry looked up at Jake from where he sat on the wagon seat beside him. "Yes sir, she's cookin' up those ones I got yesterday evenin'. They looked to be good eatin' birds."

Jake smiled knowing full well that he was projecting an image of him and Henry having bonded. It did not go unnoticed by Bovill. Jake said, as if to add to it, "Henry is death on sage chickens and trout. He keeps him and his ma and me well fed."

Bovill snorted and tossed his head slightly. "I'll bet he does."

Jake gathered the reins and rippled them over the backs of the Percherons. "Giddup, horses." The wagon, which was empty save for a couple of posts they hadn't used in repairing the fence that was burned, clattered off at a good clip. It wasn't a long drive to the house, but it was enough time for Jake to give more thought as to how he felt about Bovill. Until that day in the woods when Bovill had told him about knowing Pete Lafarge and what a scoundrel he was, Jake had generally been able, for the most part, to keep thoughts of his father at bay. He'd come to accept the fact that his father didn't want anything to do with him or his mother. But now, here was Bovill pointing out how despicable a whiskey peddler was. Unfortunately, it was a fact that Jake couldn't deny.

By the time dinner was over it was clear to Bovill that he'd lost ground to Jake in his quest to court Ellie, haying equipment or not. It wasn't so much what was said as he was still invited for dinner this Sunday next, but rather the way the three of them looked and talked to one another. There was something between them that no amount of dinners and slick talking would tear apart.

It was after Bovill had left with all of the Percherons and his equipment that an awkward air descended over the place. They were standing near the corral admiring all of the hay that had been harvested. The smell of it was sweet and nearly overpowered the pungent odor of the horse manure nearby. They were all aware that Jake had done the things he said he would do and it was time for him to go, or not. Neither he nor Ellie wanted to bring it up. And then out of the blue, Henry threw a rock into those still waters. "Are you leaving tomorrow, Jake?"

In a way the run-in with the Indians had made Jake's decision easy. "I got no choice. I've gotta account to the authorities as to why I killed Pale Bear and wounded his friend. They'll come ah lookin' for me if I don't."

Henry tilted his head back and peered out from beneath the brim of his tattered black slouch hat. He got a solid fix on Jake's eyes before asking, "But after that, are ya comin' back?"

"Probably someday I will."

"Well, when will that day be?"

"I ain't fer certain on that, Henry. I got ta talk to my boss first."

"Can't you just tell him that you don't want to work for him anymore and come right back?" Ellie rescued Jake from Henry's interrogation. "That's enough, Henry. Jake doesn't have to explain himself to you."

"But Ma, I know you want him to stay and you ain't said nuthin."

Ellie blushed. "Jake's aware of my offer."

Suddenly, a pulse of courage overtook the naysayer in Jake's mind. "I will be back. It'll probably be ah little while as, like I said, I've got some things ta tend to first."

"But are you gonna stay?" pleaded Henry.

Ellie said nothing but waited along with Henry for Jake's answer. He said, "I guess we'll see how things go."

CHAPTER TWENTY

In the morning, Jake's departure was not as painful as he had once conjured it up to be. To be sure, Ellie and Henry were teary eyed but it did not progress beyond that as he had promised to come back. It was a promise that, in Ellie's expectation, was made ironclad when in hugging Jake goodbye, she pressed her cheek to his.

On most days, Jake found the steady rhythmic pace of Rusty dutifully putting one hoof in front of the other to be soothing. Today, however, was not one of them. It was miserably hot, as had been the entire summer to this point, and the deer flies were ubiquitous. Before the events at Jawbone Springs Jake could, on a day like today, ease his discomfort by allowing his mind's eye to take him elsewhere, a cool mountain meadow, a good meal or a rip-roaring good time in town. But for a good while now his mind had been of no help in this regard. There were just too many unpleasant, disagreeable thoughts in it, the least of which was his father. In Bovill's eyes and likely most other people, Jake included, Pete Lafarge was despicable. *The old man is ah real snake in the grass*, said Jake to himself. *Takes a real sonovabuck to sell whiskey and guns to the Indians knowing damned good and well they're gonna make trouble for innocent folks.* Had he been able to accept his own argument at face value and simply write his father off as some stranger that he briefly knew a long time ago, Jake could've possibly found room in his mind for something pleasant and thereby countered, just a little, the heat and bite of the deer flies. But there was apparently some truth in the adage that a person always wants most in life what they can't have. *If anything, for Ma's sake, I've got ta call him on it. Why he would leave us without a cent. I know he won't have no good reason and then I'll tell him what a sonovabitch me and Ma think he is and then I'll just ride off.* For a moment Jake took some solace in playing this out in his mind, but it didn't last long before the nagging emptiness of not having a father who loved him took center stage. It caused him to sigh angrily as he rode on, periodically wiping the sweat out of his eyes and seemingly forever swatting deer flies.

It was late afternoon. He was just coming to where the road forked, to the right was the Rockin' C while straight ahead was the way to Miles City. On up the road a piece was a rider coming from town. Jake brought Rusty to a halt and waited, not because he was curious as to who was coming or just wanted to see what the latest news was from town, but rather he was pretty certain that it was the Sheriff. As he watched him get steadily closer, Jake wondered what Nye's take on his shooting the Indians was going to be. Some years back an affair such as what went on at the hayfield would have been akin to wolves getting into your livestock. Nobody would have given it a second thought, but things were more civilized now. At last, the Sheriff drew near enough to speak. He said loudly, "I hear you got yerself in another scrape."

Jake hollered back. "I didn't go lookin' for it Sheriff, it came to me."

Nye brought his horse to a stop across from Jake. "I didn't figure you'd shoot these boys for no good reason but their kin and friends are likely gonna see it differently, and you know what that could mean for you and your neighbors."

Jake spit a stream of tobacco juice off the far side of Rusty and then turned back to the Sheriff. "Lots ah ranchers, myself included, has gave 'em ah few beeves every now and again so as to avoid ah gunfight, but this was different. The widow English ain't got but one old milk cow and two saddle horses. She can't afford ta give 'em anything. These fellas was all liquored up and wouldn't take no for an answer. They went to their guns first. It was either shoot back or die."

"I don't doubt that, but those Army fellas over at Keogh are wantin' ta fix blame somewhere. I told 'em I'd come see ya, so for now they're content, I guess, to sit on their asses."

Jake snorted. "Maybe if those boys would show themselves ah little more outside their fort the Indians would not be so bold."

Nye shook his head. "They say there ain't enough of 'em to be everywhere that folks wants 'em to be."

It would be wrong, Jake knew, to let Nye go on without telling him about Ben's rifle and how the Indians said they come by it. The fact Pale Bear had gotten it from his father didn't prove he'd killed Ben, but for the Sheriff or the Army it'd be enough to arrest him or for Cyrus to kill him. It was an issue that had been fermenting in Jake's mind ever since Pale Bear had told him. Jake owed his father nothing. It bothered him that this sense of guilt, of betrayal, had taken hold of his conscience. Regardless, he'd run out of time to flip this coin. Right here, right now, whatever he told the Sheriff he would have to stick to it, Cyrus included. He said, "Sheriff, you should know the Indian I killed had Ben Ellsworth's rifle."

The Sheriff looked surprised. "You sure about that?"

"Got it here in my bedroll. I'd know that gun anywhere. It's got a sizeable nick in its stock."

Nye looked over at the rifle protruding from the bedroll tied on behind Jake's saddle. Part of the scar was visible. He snorted and tossed his head slightly. "Well, that's good to know as I was of the opinion this McDonald fella was to blame." The Sheriff paused briefly to allow the ramifications of what Jake had just told him to gel and then added, "Cyrus will be glad to hear this, especially when he finds out you got the fella that killed his boy. This oughta please the Army too, knowing they don't have to go on the reservation after this guy."

There was a part of Jake that wanted to tell Nye the rest of it but to do so would have been akin to tipping over a jar of marbles. The Sheriff, the Army and Cyrus would all be after Pete Lafarge. It would likely result in his being shot or hung. Images of Nate hanging, twisting slowly at the end of a rope quickly reminded Jake of what awaited his father. But then his mind went back to his childhood and all of the times that he'd seen his mother cry and the depravations they'd endured. Another part of him, the hateful part, challenged his conscience. *Why in the hell should I care what happens to him? He don't care about me or Ma.*

And then the Sheriff said, "I take it you're headed down to the Rockin' C."

"I am."

"You've saved me a trip out to the English place. Mind if I ride along to the Ellsworth's. I'd like ta git Cyrus' take on all this."

And just like that, Jake had told a half-truth to the law that he would soon have to pass on to the man who'd filled in for the scoundrel who had deserted him and his mother.

CHAPTER TWENTY-ONE

It had gone with Cyrus and the rest of the Ellsworth's pretty much as Jake had suspected it would. They quickly gravitated to the obvious conclusion that it was Pale Bear who had killed Ben. But from there it went to the why of it all and, once again, there was the reason just smacking them in the face. Cyrus was first to point to it, *Ben probably caught those red devils stealing cows and they just up and shot him.* And then Mrs. Ellsworth not wanting to resurrect her grief said, *at least they did not scalp him.* That night they had a big supper. Jake and the Sheriff were invited. They told stories about Ben and drank a toast to his memory. All the while Jake kept telling himself, *Pale Bear was probably lying. I'll bet he did kill Ben. He didn't git that rifle in no trade.* Jake tried real hard to convince his self of this, but the naysayer within him wouldn't have it. Nonetheless, he squelched that guilt and ate his steak and drank the wine. He even told the story of how Ben dinged up his new rifle in the rock slide. But it was after supper when his conscience nearly escaped. He and the Sheriff were leaving. Cyrus mistook his quiet demeanor for sadness and said, placing a hand on Jake's shoulder, *we'll all miss him but we got to move on.* It took everything that he had to remain quiet lest his conscience would take over his tongue. As he and Nye walked to the bunkhouse, he told himself, *yer ah despicable shit Jake Lafarge, just like yer old man*. He sighed quietly. He'd not said word one to Cyrus about quitting the outfit and taking the widow English up on her offer. For his conscience to bring it up now did not bode well for getting any sleep. He was not wrong about that.

There was just a sliver of light showing off to the east when Jake felt the call of nature. He considered just going barefoot in his Union Jack underwear outside and watering the weeds in back of the bunkhouse, but once he got out of bed he could see a light in the cook shack and decided to get dressed. He was tired, groggy tired. He'd not slept at all. *Gonna be a long damned day*, he said to himself as he tip-toed out of the bunkhouse. *Need ta git some coffee down me or I won't be worth ah pinch ah shit*. After relieving himself by the light of the stars, he began slowly walking, while yawning, across the expanse of bare dirt between the bunkhouse and the cook shack. He was just about to the door when through the window he could see Elmer moving about inside. Recalling how he'd startled Greta, he knocked on the door.

From inside, Elmer shouted in mock anger, "Go away. The damned chickens ain't even up yet."

Jake smiled and went inside. He feigned surprise. "Well, I'll be go ta hell. I didn't know they'd put you in charge ah the poison palace."

With a hint of a grin, Elmer came back, "Just keep waggin' yer tongue like you are and you'll see how well an empty plate eats."

"I'm sorry," said Jake continuing the good natured repartee, "it's just I didn't know you could cook."

"Well, accordin' ta all these ingrates that works here, I can't."

Jake broke out in laughter.

Elmer took it for granted that Jake had come for coffee. He took a rag from the counter near the stove and picked up the big gallon pot from the stove and filled a cup that went with one of the settings already on the table. Jake sat down next to it. "Much obliged."

"I was beginning ta think you wasn't ever comin' back," said Elmer as he returned the pot to the stove.

"There's been ah time or two I thought the same thing."

Elmer's look became serious as he cut to the gossip that he and the others had been deprived of last night by Jake and the Sheriff eating up at the main house. "Heard you had ah fracas with the Indians that killed Ben. Put the one under that done it is what I heard."

Jake took no pride in killing Pale Bear other than it allowed he and Ellie and Henry to survive. There was nothing to boast about as far as he was concerned, especially since he was perpetuating a half truth. He said simply, "Yeah, it was some nasty business." And then he reached for his cup and began to sip coffee for longer than a person might expect. At first Elmer waited for Jake to set the cup down and tell the story, but it quickly became apparent he wasn't going to do that. News from the outside was always a welcome diversion to the sameness and boredom of ranch life, but too often it came at somebody's expense. In this case, Jake was not willing to pay that price. He said, "So how do ya like cookin'?"

For an instant, disappointment paraded across Elmer's face and then it was gone. He came back, seemingly respectful of how Jake wanted it to be, "I'm too old and broke down ta do anything else."

Jake saw the sudden sadness in Elmer's eyes. He said, trying his best to sound sincere, "Naw, I'll bet you can still sit ah saddle daylight to dark."

Elmer snorted and laughed. "I might the first day but the next three I'd probably be down nursing my aching bones. I'll tell ya Jake, I'm damned glad Cyrus made a spot for me and didn't just turn me out to pasture."

Elmer's words caused a wash of emotion to flood over Jake. In a way Cyrus had done the same thing for him, taking him in years ago and giving him a home and a job. And now after he's just lost one of his son's, Jake was going to abandon him.

And then Elmer added to Jake's indecision. "Come this winter when it's twenty below and you boys is pushin' cattle outta the bottoms I'll be in here by this warm stove bakin' my biscuits." He paused and laughed in the gravelly tone of the old man that he was. He went on, "No sir, I don't think I'll miss punchin' cows, if I do it won't be for very damned long."

Elmer's words echoed in Jake's mind. Working cattle was all he'd ever known and he seriously questioned if he would be able to give it up for the life of a sodbuster, Ellie or not. But then he saw himself in Elmer thirty years down the road, alone in life, no blood kin, just working for wages and a place to sleep. And ranching, it was changing. The big outfits were getting broken up by all of the homesteaders laying claim to a parcel of government land. He said, as if to reassure Elmer, and maybe his self, that change was some-times ok. "I think ya done good takin' on the cookin'. There ain't no shame in it."

Elmer's demeanor brightened slightly before he turned back to the counter and began slicing strips of bacon off of a slab that was nearly a foot long. He said over his shoulder, "well, I ain't the equal ah Greta but I'm workin' on it."

Jake let Elmer's declaration stand as it was. In the silence that followed, he took out his Bull Durham and papers and began rolling a smoke when he noticed the wood box was almost empty. He said to Elmer's back, "Looks like yer 'bout ta run outta fire sticks. I'll go fetch an arm load or two."

"Yeah, I shudda filled it last night. It'll be worth a coupla extra pieces ah bacon if you was ta help me out."

Jake put a match to his cigarette and then waved it out before dropping it into an empty coffee can on the floor that served as an oversized ash tray. As he slid his chair back from the table he left a wake of blue smoke. "I'll be back in ah little bit."

"I ain't too sure," said Elmer in a sheepish tone, "but ya might haf ta split some."

Jake laughed. "Well, I guess that 'll teach me ta come prowlin' 'round the cook shack too early."

Elmer returned the laugh as he began laying thick slices of bacon into a big cast iron skillet. They instantly began to sizzle and pop as Jake closed the door behind him. The stars had mostly evaporated in deference to the approaching day. Still, the light was poor as the buildings, trees, corrals, everything was a dark outline that lacked definition. The wood shed next to the cook shack was no exception. Jake took a final drag off of his cigarette before grinding it out in the dirt with the toe of his boot. He then stepped through its open door frame and pulled the axe from the upended log segment that it was buried in. A large pile of similar chunks, none of them split, lay before him. Jake started in splitting the wood. He was on his third piece when a voice from behind him sounded, "You buckin' to be the chore boy?" It was followed by a laugh. Jake recognized the voice. It caused an immediate reluctance if not fear to turn around as he knew inevitably what it would lead to. "Mornin' Cyrus, just givin' Elmer a hand."

Cyrus snorted and tossed his head. "Likely he was pitchin' horseshoes last night when he should have been splitting wood. Lucky for him you're the obliging type."

"Oh, I don't mind."

"You're up a little early ain't ya?"

Jake shook his head. "Couldn't sleep."

"You're not alone in that regard."

A pang of guilt welled up in Jake as he was certain that Cyrus's insomnia had been due to Ben's murder while his, if he was honest with himself, was due to several things, the least of which was Ben. He thought to console Cyrus but his guilty conscience would not make room for it. He said, just wanting to get it over with, "I been thinkin', Cyrus, about movin' on."

"Movin' on, to what? Why?"

"That widow woman has made me ah tempting offer if I was ta partner with her on gittin' her place in shape. It would give me a stake in life."

"You don't think you've got that here?"

"I don't know. I guess not. I mean you've been good ta me, awful good, but –"

Cyrus laughed. "She been lettin' ya dip yer wick has she?"

Jake felt a sudden anger at Cyrus for referring to Ellie as he just had. He shot back quickly, maybe too quickly, as there was more edge in his voice than he had intended, "No, she's ah respectable woman. This is purely ah business arrangement."

The hard Cyrus, the cold Cyrus, the Cyrus that had shot Roy and hanged Nate surfaced in the shadows of the wood shed. He laughed again. "So says the old bull on the opposite side of the fence as the cows."

Jake was taken aback. He'd never envisioned his parting from Cyrus going this way. He came back like they were strangers and not almost like father and son, "I'd be obliged if I could collect my wages."

And like dominoes falling, Cyrus responded, "I'll have Walter bring it down to you." For a brief second he stared at Jake as if he'd been betrayed and then he walked out. And just like that, nine years of memories became tarnished.

CHAPTER TWENTY-TWO

It was a long ride back to Ellie's, not just in terms of the distance and intense summer heat and unrelenting insects but mostly due to the new emotional baggage that Jake had acquired. He'd not wanted to end things with Cyrus the way he had and it didn't help that Pete Lafarge had commandeered the stage before his mind's eye and would not leave. *All these years ah him bein' gone and now he shows up like this*, said Jake to his self. *It ain't right.* On he went through the burn, past the dead vulture and past the stain of Pale Bear's blood on the ground near the gate. For a while the images of that day pushed his father from the stage, but there was no comfort in that either. Finally, he came into Ellie's front yard. Bella was first to see him from beneath the bench in front of the cabin. She began barking and trotted out to greet him and Rusty. "Oh Bella, settle yerself down. You know me."

Henry appeared in the doorway of the cabin. He paused just long enough to shout back inside, "Ma, its Jake" and then he followed after Bella yelling excitedly, "You came back. Ma didn't think you would but I did. I knew it for sure."

Jake smiled at Henry. "Well, I guess that'll teach yer Ma to doubt what I say."

"Henry, what kind of tales are you telling?"

Jake looked over to see Ellie coming towards him and Henry. In that instant he could see the three of them and Bella too, together right there on Deer Creek. It was like his mind's eye had granted him a peek at the future as if it knew what was there. Ellie stopped just short of Rusty. "I wasn't certain if you would make it back tonight. I thought Mr. Ellsworth would try and convince you to stay or the Sheriff or the Army would detain you." She paused to laugh in a relieved sort of way and then added, "Land sakes, I had all kinds of reasons why you wouldn't be here tonight."

Jake shook his head. "I've no longer got ties to the Rockin' C and the Sheriff's got no hold on me either."

Ellie's look suggested that she had deciphered from Jake's tone that things weren't as settled as he would have her believe, but she did not go there. She said, "We finished eating a little while ago but there's still some fried spuds, biscuits and a trout that Henry caught. And there's wild plum cobbler too with fresh cream and sugar to go on it."

"Mercy sakes, woman," said Jake in a light hearted voice, "you sure know how to fire up ah man's appetite."

Ellie smiled broadly, something that Jake still took note of as a sign she was healing from the pain that he and Cyrus had caused her. She said, "Well, get yourself washed up. It'll be waiting on the table for you."

"Yes Ma'am," said Jake as he stepped down from his saddle. "I'll be along soon as I tend to Rusty."

"I'll take care of him," offered Henry.

Jake handed the reins off. "I'm much obliged, Henry. Give him ah little oats, won't ya?"

"Sure Jake, I'll do that."

From the corner of his eye Jake could see that Ellie had watched the exchange between him and Henry and the warmth that seemed to be there. And then she turned away, still smiling. It was clear she felt good about how things were going between the three of them. Jake wanted to share in this feeling. It was something that he had been wanting for a long time, but his conscience would not allow him to embrace it. He sighed deeply. *Dammit, I shoulda been more truthful about how it was Pale Bear come by Ben's rifle. I don't owe the old man ah thing, not a damned thing.* Jake watched as Ellie disappeared inside the cabin. *In the morning I'll tell her.*

Ellie had encouraged Jake to pitch his bedroll on the floor of the cabin, but he did not lest he give the appearance to a stranger that Cyrus' accusation was true. Instead, he again slept in his make shift tent along the creek. It was cooler there and the gurgling sounds of the water coupled with the crickets and his fatigue from having gotten no sleep the night before allowed his mind to shut down. And maybe, just maybe, being back at Ellie's had something to do with it too. He slept hard and vulnerable to anything that would do him harm. It was just getting light when he became aware of the birds singing. He sat up and tossed his blanket back. From what he could see it was going to be another cloudless, hot day. He yawned and stretched, reluctant to crawl out of his shelter, but as he sat there the angst from the day before began to pour into his mind. It soon destroyed what little tranquility he had awakened to and pushed him outside.

Henry had already turned the horses out so that they could go to water at the creek and from there feed on up the canyon. He was now inside the shed milking Daisy. At first Jake thought to just go to the house as he could see that Henry had already tended to the horses, but his fondness for the boy caused him to veer towards the shed. He stepped through its open door. "Yer ah heckuva hand Henry. The sun ain't up and yer halfway through yer chores."

Henry sat on his short wooden T stool nestled in against the cow's side with his back to Jake. Bella lay with her head resting on her front paws a short distance away, patiently waiting for him to finish. He did not break stride pulling and squeezing the cow's teats causing a rhythmic forceful splash of milk in the bucket beneath them. He said without looking around, "It ain't no big deal. It's just what needs to be done, I reckon."

"Well, I'm sure yer Ma is proud of ya."

Henry went quiet not knowing how to respond to the additional praise. The pelting sound of the two milk streams echoed inside the shed. Morning and night they were left – right, left- right, left-right hundreds of times over until Daisy had been relieved of her burden.

Jake broke the silence between them. "Do ya like it here?"

Without hesitation, Henry came back, "It's worrisome. It ain't like town living."

"So you don't wanna be here?"

"I don't know. I like the huntin' an' fishin' part of it, but not so much the other stuff that goes on. There ain't no kids close by either."

Jake nodded. "That's right, it's ah good ways to any school and other kids."

"Ma could teach it, if there ever was one."

"I'll bet she could."

"I reckon it don't matter cuz there's plenty to do around here. Ma says we got to get a wheat crop planted or we won't have anything to sell next summer."

Jake briefly considered not telling Henry the reality of their situation but, at the same time, it came to him that Henry was smarter than his years, so he went on, "That's gonna be ah tall order with no plow or harrow. I reckon if we had that equipment we could use the saddle horses to pull it, but we don't."

"I know. Me and Ma have talked on it some, but when it gets to this part she just gets upset."

"Maybe we can figure a way to git it done."

"I hope so. It'd make Ma happy."

And then the naysayer in Jake's mind shouted out to him, *Ya damned fool, whaddya tellin' him such ah thing when here ya are intent on going to find yer old man. It ain't right ta lead the boy on like that.* Jake said aloud, "I'm gonna leave ya to yer work, Henry."

"Alright, I'll be along shortly."

Jake started toward the house knowing that his conscience would never allow him to tell Ellie that he was leaving again. *Damn him*, said Jake to his self, *I don't know why he couldn't just stay gone.* And then the naysayer got in on it, *whaddaya gonna do if he admits ta killin' Ben? You gonna go tell Cyrus or the Sheriff that ya knew all along that Pale Bear likely wasn't guilty? You gonna shoot 'im yerself?* The naysayer was still badgering Jake when he stepped through Ellie's open door. She was standing near the stove tending some bacon that was frying. Her long dark hair was woven into a French braid that caressed the area between her shoulder blades. She looked over at Jake and smiled. "Good morning. How did you sleep?"

"Like ah bear in January."

Ellie laughed and picked up a cup from the table and filled it with coffee. She set it in front of him. "As soon as Henry comes in from milking we'll eat."

"He's about done."

"You talked to him."

"I did."

"He's come to respect you. It's obvious, don't you think?"

"He's ah good boy."

"He is."

"We were talkin'. He said you want to git ah wheat crop sowed down the canyon."

Ellie frowned. "I do, but without equipment or money for seed I don't know how we'll do it." Jake reached in his shirt pocket and took out a wad of bills. "I drew all of my back wages. Got ah hundert an' nine dollars here."

Ellie's eyes widened before saying, "but that's your money."

"I'd be willin' to invest it for a suitable return."

"And what might that be?"

"I don't know. It won't be anything you can't live with."

"This is very generous of you, Jake, to offer both your time and money. You've done so much already. I don't know what Henry and I would do without you."

Jake paused briefly before renewing the fix he had on Ellie's eyes, as if to make certain she would feel his contrition. He said, "It was me that put you in the situation yer in now, so I reckon I should be the one to git you out of it."

"It isn't all your fault. Like I've told you, there were cracks in this foundation long before you came into the picture."

"That might be, but I didn't do anything to mend 'em."

Ellie's eyes had gotten teary, such that the light from the lantern on the table reflected off of them. It was clear that she was trying to keep from crying. She said as she turned back to the stove, "I've got some plum syrup warming. Do you like plum syrup, Jake?"

CHAPTER TWENTY-THREE

For the time being Jake tried his best to bury all of his guilt and frustrations in hard work. They had agreed that part of the burn down below the hay meadow would be a good place to plant wheat but before they could do that it needed to be fenced, otherwise cattle from the Rockin C or Bovill's place would just grub it out. It would be a fair sized field, *right at 40 acres*, Jake reckoned. To protect it would require about a mile of fence entailing well over 300 post holes and the cutting of posts to go in them. August, as it turned out, was no less hot or dry than July had been. It had been a grueling process for the three of them, but by the end of the month the would-be wheat field was enclosed behind four strands of barbed wire. The wire and staples being paid for by Jake but purchased by a new Granger neighbor in the next canyon over who had made a trip to Miles City for supplies. His name was Zeke Willet. He was in his mid-thirties, married with four kids, and until about six weeks ago he had worked in a Chicago slaughter house.

It was early, not yet eight o'clock in the morning as Jake neared the Willet place which consisted of a wall tent, corral for their milk cow, and a half-finished cabin. His purpose in coming was to help Zeke with building his cabin. In return he would loan Jake a couple of mules and a plow and a harrow. Jake was still a hundred yards out when it became apparent to him that something had upset the Willet clan. There was too much arm waving, pointing and shouting for things to be normal. Instinctively, he nudged Rusty into a trot. He'd not gone far when Zeke noticed him coming up the faint wagon tracks and began jogging toward him shouting, "They stole my mules, Jake. The damned thieves just took 'em."

Momentarily, they drew close to one another and Jake brought Rusty to a halt. "Who took 'em? Did ya see 'em?"

Zeke was of medium build with a droopy black walrus moustache. He was dressed in a long sleeved blue flannel shirt and dark cotton pants with a gray wide brimmed felt hat. He looked to be the typical homesteader who was suffering a problem common to their kind, that being having their animals stolen. "I saw 'em right up there just a little bit ago," he shouted excitedly while pointing to some dark timber on the ridge to the east of them.

Jake looked to where Zeke was gesturing but could see no movement, only trees. "How many of 'em was there?"

"Just two is what I saw, but they got all six ah my mules."

"They Indians or white men?"

"They're white fellas. One of 'em is ridin' ah paint horse and the other a bay. I went up the canyon to check on my mules this morning and I saw these boys makin' off with 'em. They was purty far off and before I could git a shot at 'em they got into the timber."

Jake's heart was thumping hard. He called out to Zeke, "I'll see what I can do." He then spurred Rusty to a gallop in the direction of the dark timber. It was, however, a pace that he could sustain for only a short distance as the bottom of the canyon was populated with scattered ponderosa pine and a variety of shrubs such that he was darting left and then right until finally he was at a fast walk. Nonetheless, Jake was confident he would catch up to the thieves as their trail was, in his mind, *as obvious as swamp mud on a white picket fence.* It went on this way, the ground all churned up by the hooves of six mules and two horses moving at a good clip until, abruptly, they peeled off to the right and up the side of the canyon towards a saddle at the top of the ridge. The terrain was steep and the trees thick causing the animals to spread out some and each seek an easier way. Rusty was no exception. He was breathing hard. Jake allowed him to maneuver around trees and over deadfall until suddenly, it occurred to him that he would be a prime candidate to get bushwhacked going as he was. He brought Rusty to a halt and studied the situation for a moment. *They'll surely be watchin' their back trail*, he said to his self. *Ain't no point ridin' into ah bullet.* And with that, he started Rusty across the slope but down the canyon. He went about a hundred yards before turning toward the top of the ridge. In his mind Jake visualized the trees opening up on the south side of the saddle. "*I'll catch up to 'em there. It'll be a fair gunfight if it comes to that.*

As mules are wont to do, they are often reluctant to go where a person would like them to; such was the case with Zeke's animals. Jake could hear two different voices shouting and cursing the mules to, *git up the mountain.* They were close by. To Jake it sounded like a slow moving mob of angry chaos. Suddenly, he caught flashes of black amongst the pines directly in front of him as one of the mules burst into the open. Seconds later, the thief riding the bay horse emerged. He yelled, "C'mon mule, ya damned jug head. Hold up there." The last of his words had barely exited his mouth when he became aware of Jake sitting on Rusty across the little clearing into which the mule had run. First came the terror and shock in his eyes and next the reflex like he was swatting a deer fly, not a hint of hesitation to consider if going for his gun was the right thing to do. In this particular situation, it was the wrong decision as Jake had un-holstered his pistol some time ago. To his credit, the thief managed to get his Army Colt out a split second before Jake's bullet augered into his right shoulder. The man, being of slight build, recoiled backward from the heavy slug, dropping his revolver but managing to stay seated on his horse. Had Jake chosen to he could have shot the guy again, but the consequences of doing that were all too familiar to him so he allowed the man to ride off. His benevolence, however, ended there. The mules were critical to not only Zeke being able to make a living, but he and Ellie as well. He spurred Rusty going past the big black mule that had escaped the others and into the trees where the thief had gone. No sooner had he penetrated the thick woods than he spotted two more mules. Jake started toward them, thinking that he would push them out into the clearing with the black one. And then he heard the wounded thief shout, "Pete, I'm hurt bad. Let's leave these damned mules."

Jake's body became painfully rigid as his senses heightened. He strained to listen, telling himself that maybe he hadn't heard right or maybe it was a different Pete. In his gut, he knew better.

Again, the injured man hollered, "I'm quittin' ya, Pete."

From Jake's left, a voice came back, "Shut up, ya damned fool."

Jake tightened the grip on his pistol. The irony of doing so while waiting to see if the voice in the trees, this thief, was his father was not lost on him. *I reckon it would fit with everything else he's done if it was him*, said Jake to his self. Suddenly, like an apparition, there stood the paint horse about forty yards away. Not all of it was visible. Its head and most of its front shoulders and rear legs were hidden behind tree branches but its rider, a middle-aged man with short dark hair and a bushy moustache was in sight. He was wearing a gray Stetson with a wide, flat brim that was dimpled twice. It had been over twenty years since Jake had seen his father. He was peering through the trees studying the man's features when, all of a sudden, this stranger named Pete spotted him and instantly raised the pistol that he had been resting on his leg and fired at Jake. The bullet went wide of Jake's head but just barely as he could hear the popping, crackling noise that it made as it went past his ear. The hammer was back on Jake's Colt and had he not felt that he was looking at his father he would have instantly fired back, instead of hesitating like he did. And then the paint horse was gone. Towards the saddle he could hear horses running and garbled voices. Jake was about to take after them when he began to see the rest of the mules floating in and out of the trees in front of him. He was torn as to what he should do. It was a strange and angry, but sad, feeling he had knowing that most likely his father had just tried to kill him. For a moment, he just sat there on Rusty in the tall timber listening to his heart beat against his ear drum. It would not settle down. It was as if it had to keep pace with a pine squirrel, disturbed by all of the activity, that was chattering incessantly overhead or a Steller's jay in a neighboring tree that had begun screeching again and again. They were the forest sentinels, certain to provide a warning to all who would listen that something was amiss in the woods. Buried deep within Jake was the impulse to go after the thieves, after his father, to confront him now and make him explain his self. But then as that urge gained traction in his mind the rational side of him shouted out, *there'd be gun play if ya do that. Sure as shit, somebody 'll get killed.* Abruptly, an awareness of his surroundings and the good life he was about to embark upon came to Jake. He said to his self, *Damn him, I don't know why he couldn't have just stayed gone.*

CHAPTER TWENTY-FOUR

By the time they finished Zeke's cabin and got his crops planted it was near the end of October. It took both Zeke and Jake working six days a week to accomplish this, as they had to fence the cropland and that required going to the woods and cutting more posts. There was no getting around building the fence, as even more of Bovill's cattle had drifted into the area. The drought of the summer had continued into the fall, a fact that worried the big ranchers as they were wont to say, *the grass is already slicked off and here's winter comin' on.* The cowboys pushed the cattle here and there, chasing what grass that remained. They even, as was their custom, rounded all of them up during October and cut out this year's calves so they could be shipped out on the train, but it made little difference in the feed situation. In spite of how it looked for the ranchers Jake's melancholy grew from not being involved in the roundup and the weaning of the calves even though the end process of separating the calves from their mothers was a cacophony of bawling and bellowing that, in the past, persisted in his mind for several days after it was over. None of this, however, was of any consequence to Ellie as she had hay stored for her animals. All that mattered to her, at this point, was getting her wheat planted. That would be her crop to harvest next summer, assuming it rained but didn't hail and grasshoppers didn't come and their fence held out the cows.

The leaves of the cottonwood trees had turned yellow as had the grass a good month ago. The air had a bite to it leaving no doubt that fall was upon them and it was imperative they finish planting the wheat. For a time, Zeke had helped Jake but seeing how they were near the end of it, he had gone home yesterday for good. So now it was the three of them, Jake, Ellie and Henry. Jake walking behind the mule and the little five foot wide drag, covering the seed after Ellie and Henry scattered it over the soil that had already been worked. It was the middle of the afternoon. Ellie was the first to see him. She called out to Jake who was about a half dozen harrow widths over from her but going in the opposite direction, "Mr. Bovill is coming up the road."

Jake glanced over his shoulder but did not stop. The Indian's fire had burned most of the trees and shrubs in the bottom of the canyon making it difficult for anyone to approach the wheat field undetected, Bovill was no exception. Jake hollered back, "I'll talk to him on my way back."

Ellie nodded, "Ok," and kept on, parallel to Henry, taking handfuls of seed from a canvas bag suspended from her neck and flinging it in a hundred and eighty degree arc in front of her as she slowly walked along.

It had been a good while ago that Bovill had come to Ellie's for Sunday dinner, the intent on her part being a gesture of appreciation for the loan of the haying equipment and horses, but on his it was an imagined visit as a suitor. However, in the absence of any further encouragement by Ellie and Jake having moved his bedroll to the floor inside the cabin, Bovill seldom came around anymore. It was, therefore, a bit of a mystery to Jake as to why he should be there today.

After tying his horse to a fence post, Bovill pushed the top wire down and climbed over. He then set a course across the field's soft dirt that would intercept Jake on his return pass. Ellie had waved but continued on toward the other end of the field knowing that Bovill was likely there to see Jake, a fact that she preferred. For a time Bovill stood there in the midst of the bare soil wanting to stare at Ellie's backside as she walked away from him, dressed as a man in her dark cotton pants and red flannel shirt, but he did not for as crass and brazen as he was, he knew that he'd lost out in that competition. Therefore, he watched as Jake got closer until finally he hollered out in a cordial tone, "Looks like this farmin' business suits ya."

Jake pulled gently on the mule's reins. "Whoa Toby." The big sorrel mule was eager to comply and stopped next to Bovill. "Well, I might just be in this for fun if it don't rain one of these days," said Jake continuing the polite social banter.

"You damned sure could be. I'm scared that when we do get some moisture it'll be that white stuff and it'll be belly deep on one ah them Percherons that I got. We'll be in ah real shit pot then, I'll tell you what."

Jake dropped the reins and his gloves on the ground in front of him and pulled out his tobacco and papers. As he plucked a paper from the tiny packet he said with a laugh, "so, you lookin' for work or are ya just gaddin' about the country?"

The grin that had been on Bovill's face suddenly went away. He said in a serious tone, "I ran into yer pa a few days ago."

Jake's heart jumped up like it was in a foot race, nonetheless, he continued pouring tobacco into the paper trough that he had formed. He'd not told anyone but Ellie that one of the mule thieves that had shot at him was likely his father. He said, trying to sound not overly interested, "You purty sure ah that?"

"I'm sure it's the same Pete Lafarge I knew down in Wyoming, beyond that I reckon it'd be up to you to say if he's yer pa or not."

Jake struck a match on his belt buckle and lit his cigarette. After several deep puffs he removed it from his mouth flicking a bit of excess tobacco from the end of his tongue. "So, where was it you saw this fella."

"Ashland. He was playin' poker in a bar down there."

"Did ya talk to him?"

"I did, after he got up from the game I followed him outside. I told him that I knew him from what he'd been up to in Wyoming. He denied ever being in that part of the country and started to walk away and then I told him I knew his son and that you was bustin' sod up on Deer Creek. He just kinda snorted and said he didn't have no son. So, I asked him, Jake Lafarge ain't yer boy?"

"What'd he say?"

"I could tell it caught him off guard. It took him a second ta git his wits about him and then he claimed again to not have a son. After that he got mad and told me ta mind my own business and walked off."

It was hurtful to Jake that his father would deny he even existed. *Maybe that's how he lives with being ah scoundrel*, he said to himself. To Bovill he said, "I 'ppreciate yer lettin' me know his whereabouts, but I don't see that it would do me any good ta look him up."

Bovill was standing with his hands on his hips squarely in front of Jake. He turned his head slightly to the side and spit a stream of tobacco juice that splattered in the soft dry dirt. He came back, "You may be right on that count, but you should be aware that folks are wise to his doin's. My take on it is they ain't gonna tolerate it much longer."

Jake took a slow, methodical drag from his cigarette and blew the smoke out in an exasperated breath. His mind was spinning as to how he should be in this regard. Was he supposed to be concerned? He said, knowing that it would sound as if he didn't care, "He got his self into this jackpot so I reckon he can git his self out."

Bovill appeared a little surprised, but he had no use for Pete Lafarge so he moved on. "I got ah business proposition for ya."

"How's that?"

"I had a coupla hands quit and I'm out close to a hundert head ah cattle. I think they could be somewhere up in this part of the country. If yer willin', I'll give ya a dollar ah head for every critter that you can find and drive over to my neck ah the woods."

Jake scoffed. "Hell, they're probably lookin' fer feed. Ya got any grass over yer way?"

"Damned little."

"Going from one bad place to another don't ya reckon?"

Bovill ignored Jake's sarcasm. "So, are ya interested?"

Jake took a thoughtful draw on his cigarette, he said through the smoke, "Yeah, I'll go hunt up yer cows. Just gimme one more day ta finish this plantin'."

Bovill nodded. "I'm obliged to ya."

"I ain't found yer cattle yet."

"You will. I'd bet ah sarsaparilla on it."

Jake moved on. "So, where ya headed to now?"

"George McDonald's. Heard he might have some oats for sale."

"He probably does."

Bovill grinned and tossed his head slightly. "Gotta feed them Percherons."

The good old boys back east with more money than sense came to Jake's mind. "Must be nice to have access to that kind ah money."

Bovill laughed. "I'll be seein' ya with my cows." And with that he started back across the field towards his horse and a meeting with the McDonald clan.

CHAPTER TWENTY-FIVE

Since leaving the Rockin' C things had gone well for Jake. He and Ellie and Henry had accomplished a lot, even more they had bonded. It gave him a good feeling knowing that he had a stake in life. The one thing, however, that didn't put him at ease was how things were with his father. It was a rejection that nagged at him constantly since his father had, so to speak, come back into his life. He had written to his mother, who was now remarried, to tell her that he'd crossed paths with his father and that he was going to find him and make him explain why he'd done what he had. But now, after talking to Bovill, he wasn't certain that this would be the right thing to do. Regardless, he couldn't pass up an opportunity to make money as he'd spent most of his wages on fencing materials, oats for Daisy and the horses, wheat seed and food items such as sugar, coffee, flour and the like.

The sun was just a sliver above the mountain at the head of Deer Creek. It made for deep shadows in the bottom of the canyon, Ellie's cabin being no exception. Jake and Henry had done the chores together before saddling Rusty. The morning was unusually cold, even for the first day of November. Ellie's breath rhythmically puffed in front of her face as she walked from the house to where Jake and Henry were standing near the shed. As she came to them, her eyes settled on Jake. She pulled her dark green shawl together more tightly, clutching the two sides of it in her right hand. There was a faint shiver in her voice, "How long do you think you will be gone?"

For some time now they had been more affectionate with one another, not in an overtly obvious way but rather subtle smiles, touches and playful words. Jake sensed the cumulative effects of those actions coming from Ellie now. He said, "I aim to be back as quick as I can. Two or three days with any luck.'

"I hope so. We'll miss you."

Jake knew if they were *just* business partners he should get on Rusty now and ride off, but they had become more than that, despite the fact neither had spoken it. He thought to say as he stood there looking into her eyes, *I'll miss you too*, but he said aloud, "I wouldn't be doin' this if it weren't for the money Bovill has offered."

"I know. I appreciate your taking on this work."

Jake continued to hesitate. "I'll be back as soon as I can. Winter's comin'. Me and Henry has got lots of firewood to cut and we got ta git a shed of some sort built to keep it dry. There's plenty ah reasons why I need ta git back."

Ellie smiled broadly as she stepped close to Jake. "Here's one more reason," she said as she leaned up and kissed him lightly on the lips. "Be careful."

A warm tingling feeling consumed Jake in a way that he could never recall having ever felt. Emboldened, he drew her to him, kissing her again before hugging her tightly for a long time until finally he drew back. "I better be on my way."

Ellie's eyes had become moist and vulnerable. "Please be safe."

Jake reached out and squeezed her shoulder before turning to Henry and Bella. "Keep a sharp eye and remember the things we talked about if there's trouble. You can always git more critters but people are hard ta come by."

"I know Jake. I'll keep a watch out."

Jake gathered his reins and stepped up onto Rusty. He looked down. Ellie was standing next to Henry and Bella. Although he knew it wasn't so, Jake felt a sense of responsibility to take care of them. It was a perceived obligation that he welcomed. He felt like he really belonged here. For a moment he looked at them as if he had something more to say that was important until finally, he allowed his eyes to penetrate Ellie's one last time. He said, "Be seein' ya." And with that he rode off down the canyon in search of Bovill's stray cattle.

It wasn't until he had gotten to the mouth of Deer Creek and started south that Jake was able to tuck Ellie and Henry away in his mind and bring his wits to bear on the problem of finding the wayward cows, or as he had come to think of them, *those dollar bills walkin' around out in the hills.* It occurred to him that cattle might not be welcome in the next two canyons to the south of Deer Creek on account of the homesteaders that had moved in and went to breaking out the ground, Zeke being one of them. *A smart cow, if there is such ah thing,* said Jake to his self, *would cross over the Pumpkin.* And so that's where he went, Rusty barely making a splash as he slowly picked his way over the slick rocks beneath the trickle of water that Pumpkin Creek had become. As he looked down at the meager flow, Jake said aloud, "Rusty, I believe that ole boy up above has forgot about us, at least for this year he has."

By early afternoon, it became apparent to Jake that he had misjudged how bad the range actually was. Unbeknownst to him, a Granger had moved in about five miles west of the Pumpkin and brought a band of several thousand sheep with him. He too, just like Bovill's employers, was going to take advantage of all this free government grass which, at some time in the past had actually existed, but not now. The ground was littered with sheep manure and thousands of tracks that had pulverized the soil. Here and there bits of wool clung to the sagebrush. Jake shook his head as he looked at how things were. "I'll tell ya, Rusty, if ah cow was ta come ta this country, she better bring her damned dinner sack."

Jake turned north. Before the massive influx of homesteaders, sheep men and wannabe cattle ranchers this country had been considered Rockin' C range, but not anymore. There was no keeping the outsiders at bay, the latecomers who were now here courtesy of the fact that the early ranchers, those men tough enough to tame this country, had made it relatively safe for them. In spite of the poor range condition, Jake was seeing cattle scattered about because they had no place else to go. Some wore the Rockin' C brand and some had brands he was unfamiliar with, but none with Bovill's /3. The slash three brand supposedly represented the three easterners with more money than sense who were bankrolling Bovill's outfit.

When he made the decision to search what used to be Rockin' C country, Jake had it in his mind that he would go to a meandering drainage called Beaver Creek. In its present state, the name Beaver Creek was a misnomer as all of the beavers had been trapped out years ago, but it had typically produced good grass. Jake was less than a quarter mile from the shallow coulee where the creek was located when he saw his first dollar bill laying on grass stubble that used to be belly high to a horse. She was a young Hereford cow, apparently content to chew her cud and let Jake ride on by. *I'll just let her be while I check the crik out*, said Jake to his self. He rode on a short ways before picking up a cow trail and dropping down into the creek bottom. He'd no sooner got there than he started seeing /3 cows and this year's calves that had been missed in the roundup that had just ended. Two of the calves were slicks, meaning they hadn't been branded during the spring roundup and as such they would be targets for thieves looking to put their own brand on them. Jake nudged Rusty. "Let's just take ourselves ah little gander up the crik here and see what we got." And so they began weaving in and out amongst the willows and box elder as Jake counted /3 cattle. The vegetation had been used hard. There was virtually no grass left and the willows hadn't fared much better. Jake shook his head. He said aloud to Rusty, "It's a damned good thing I brought along some oats for yer supper as these thousand pound beavers have purty well slicked this up, willows and all. After about a half mile the willows petered out, as did the cows. Jake had counted 41 mother cows and 11 of this year's calves. As he looked back down along the creek a plan came to mind, he shared it with Rusty, "These cows has been here for some time. I reckon they ain't gonna go anywhere so we'll allow them one more night. Come morning we'll gather 'em up and start 'em home."

Jake made camp where he was, so as to stay above the concentration of cows that had crossed the creek back and forth so many times the water appeared foul. After unsaddling Rusty and giving him a liberal amount of oats he picketed him near the creek. He then found a sheltered spot near a couple of boxelder trees and threw out his bedroll. At a few minutes past six o'clock Jake watched, as he sat by the fire, the very last of the sun sink below the western horizon. In that instant it seemed to suddenly get more lonely and cold. In his mind he could see Ellie and Henry sitting down to supper inside a warm cabin. He recalled too, kissing Ellie before leaving and imagining what that might lead to when he got back. With his eyes he followed the Roman numerals on his pocket watch to where he would see the sun again. He sighed and said to his self, *fourteen hours*. It occurred to him that before he had Ellie and Henry, time, vacant empty time, was easier to deal with. Soon it was dark and colder. The stars had come out. He added a couple of pieces of wood to the fire waiting for his coffee to boil. Off in the distance a wolf howled. Jake took note of it. *There's one the wolfers missed.* He didn't have much use for wolves and the way a pack of them would set upon a cow hamstringing her and then ripping her apart. But on the other hand, he had little regard for wolfers and their indiscriminate use of strychnine laced meat. Too many dogs got into it and died. Some ranch dogs, but mostly Indian dogs and that got them riled up. And then these images piled up in his mind to where he couldn't abide them. He shook his head. *Sometimes there just ain't no good in ah thing.* He tried to push these thoughts out as he reached into the flour sack that Ellie had sent and took from it several biscuits, a jar of chokecherry jam and some cheese. He began to eat while watching the reflection of the fire on the surface of the coffee water in his little open pot. Suddenly, a bubble rolled up and disrupted the fire and then another until finally the image of the flames was imperceptible in the boiling coffee. After a few minutes, Jake put a leather glove on his right hand and removed the pot from the fire. He poured himself a cup of the steaming coffee and immediately took a noisy but shallow sip. The hot liquid felt good, seemingly warming his entire body. And so went the night, until about nine-thirty, eating and drinking and thinking about Ellie in carnal ways as a deterrent to the cold and loneliness. He'd not wanted to but he got into his blankets and allowed the fire to die down some as he was running low on wood. It seemed that the fire going out all together and him getting cold and his father walking into his camp happened at the same time. He awoke with a painful surge of adrenalin expecting, hoping to see his father standing there, but it was quiet and dark save for the cherry red embers of the fire. Jake opened the cover of his watch and held it close to the light of the coals. *Shit, quarter past twelve.* He lay back, pulling his blankets up under his chin and stared up at the stars. He was cold, not to the point of shivering but just enough to be uncomfortable.

At a few minutes before seven it was teeth chattering cold outside his blankets but Jake deemed it to be light enough to search for more firewood, so he got up. There was a heavy frost on the ground and much of the wood as well. Had it not been for the fact he had camped in these conditions many times before, he might not have had the foresight to cache some twigs and dry leaves under his saddle blanket which made starting a fire relatively easy. By eight-thirty he was done with breakfast and broke camp. The sun was not yet fully exposed, but it showed promise of warming the day as there wasn't a cloud in the sky or any wind. As he started down into the willows he wished that Henry and Bella were there to help. The /3 cows either stood and stared at him or took off crossing to the other side of the creek. Jake felt bad for Rusty having to out maneuver this many uncooperative cows. But to his credit, Rusty prevailed and by ten o'clock he and Jake were pushing 52 dollar bills back towards Antelope Creek and /3 country.

For all of their initial resistance to being removed from Beaver Creek the Slash 3 cattle soon accepted their fate and moved along at a steady pace. By mid-afternoon Jake's confidence was high. He said aloud, "Hells fire, Rusty. We'll be ta Pumpkin Creek 'fore the sun goes down." He then smiled broadly as if Rusty could appreciate the fact that he was happy. He went on, "When we collect our money Rusty, we're gonna go ta town. All of us, you, me, Ellie, Henry and the Bell dog. We're gonna treat ourselves to some town chuck and I'm gonna buy Ellie a new dress and maybe some books for this winter. She's ah schoolmarm ya know. And Henry, I'm gonna git him some fishing stuff and maybe some candy. And we'll stock up for winter with the goods we need. We'll git plenty ah oats too. It'll be grand Rusty, come tomorrow when we deliver these critters and collect our fifty-two dollars. Yes sir, it's gonna be downright grand."

Suddenly, gunshots erupted causing Jake's euphoria to vanish. They started with a single shot, a rifle he thought. This was followed by two quick pistol shots and then it was as if a dam had burst with four or five people firing all at once. For the next minute or so Jake sat there on Rusty, motionless, looking off in the direction of the gunfight. It was a lively ruckus that sounded as if it was taking place in a wooded canyon about a half mile to the south of him. There had been 25 or 30 rounds fired, their echoes colliding with one another in the choppy hills and coulees when abruptly they died away surrendering the silence to a lone raven cawing in the sky overhead. Jake sighed, knowing that his moral compass obligated him to investigate the shooting to see if someone needed help, but to do so would come at a price, he would have to leave the cattle unattended. He was hesitant to get involved, to risk what he had waiting for him at home and the 52 head of cattle and then his conscience goaded him one more time, it *could be some helpless sodbusters that Indians have set upon.* And then recollections of Greta and the horror she had experienced flooded his mind. Interspersed in this were images of Ellie and Henry. *What if it was them? You'd want somebody to help 'em.* Suddenly, he found himself pulling his rifle from its scabbard. Clutching it in his right hand, he touched his spurs to Rusty's sides urging him into a gallop. The sage covered bench that they were on sloped gently up to the mouth of the canyon where the gunshots had come from. Jake felt a queasiness, a burning in his stomach that intensified the closer he got until finally he brought Rusty to a halt just short of the ponderosa pines that filled the bottom of the canyon. He strained to see through the wall of green and what awaited him lest he ride into a bullet, but the trees were big and old and not giving up their secrets. On the other hand, the pine squirrels and Steller's jays were not as discreet. They were pitching a fit about three hundred yards on up the canyon. Jake got down from Rusty and tied him to a small pine. He patted the horse's neck and looking him in the eyes whispered, "It'll be all right." In reality, Jake was far from certain that it would be.

It was a challenge to move quietly as the drought had made everything crunchy dry. Nonetheless, Jake went on briefly analyzing the location of every step before he put his boot down. He did his best to not land on any pine cones or twigs, but there was no avoiding the carpet of needles that crackled under his weight. The sound of the needles being crushed caused him to cringe. Still, he continued slowly and methodically, hoping that whatever hostilities had precipitated the gunfight had been resolved. And then he heard it, a voice at about the same time a pine squirrel let out its staccato chatter. Jake froze in place and strained to hear. For a time, the only sounds were the squirrels and birds and the gentle moan of the wind as it coursed through the tops of the trees. Suddenly, the voice came again, louder and with a terrifying familiarity. "How is it you come by my son's watch?"

A feeling of humiliation and fear that Cyrus had discovered his deception swept over Jake. He wanted more than anything to back away and get on with his new life but his conscience wouldn't allow it.

A second voice came back, surly and insolent, "I told you I won it in a card game."

Time and being away had diluted his Cajun accent but Jake picked up on it. The angst, the frustration and anger, the indecision, it all hit him like a huge avalanche.

And then Cyrus came again. "A man this close to meeting his maker might want to tell the truth for a change. That ain't ta say it would be enough ta git someone of your caliber through the pearly gates but you never know."

Jake began walking then running towards the voices uncertain of what he would or could do once he got there. Abruptly the trees gave way to a small clearing. On the far side of it was a paint horse, seated on it with his hands tied behind his back and a noose around his neck was Pete Lafarge. He spit at Cyrus. "Yer ah big shot cow man. Yer gonna do whatever pleases ya so you can just wonder who killed yer damned kid."

It was in those few seconds that the man on the horse was spewing his vile epithets towards Cyrus that Jake made eye contact with the person he suspected was his father. He was certain of it, but his father looked away not knowing who Jake was.

And then Silas saw what had caught Pete Lafarge's eye. He hollered out, "Cyrus, we ain't alone. Jake's over yonder."

In that instant, both Cyrus and Pete's heads turned in the direction of Jake. Their expressions, however, were decidedly different. Cyrus showed annoyance, even anger, and in Pete, there was a sudden awareness and hope that he would be rescued. He called out, "Jake, it's me, yer pa."

Jake said nothing but began walking slowly towards where his father sat on his horse at the end of a rope.

Cyrus scowled at Jake before turning away. He said to Pete, "Last chance, Mister."

Pete came back. In the absence of any show of concern by Jake, fear had taken hold of his voice, "That's my boy. You can't hang me in front of him. It wouldn't be right. Jake, tell him who you are."

Jake remained silent as he walked past Silas and the other cowboys until finally he was standing next to Cyrus and the paint horse upon which his father sat.

Pete broke into a hopeful smile. "Tell him, Jake. Tell him I'm ah good man."

Jake looked up at his father. He stared into his eyes as if the reason, the justification for him having deserted Jake and his mother and for being so evil and wicked would be apparent, but it was not there. He thought to berate his father but he could not muster the words for such a pathetic person. And then he felt Cyrus' eyes upon him.

"You lied to me, Jake."

The enormity of his shame hit Jake like he'd been kicked in the chest by a mule. He made no attempt to explain away his behavior; he said simply, "I'm sorry."

"I'll not be denied my revenge. The good book allows for it."

Tears had come to Pete's eyes. "Don't listen to him, son. He's not the law."

Over the years Jake had gone over in his mind so many times the things he would say to his father if they ever met, but now it all seemed so pointless.

"Leave us, Jake. There'll be no good of you staying."

Jake turned to Cyrus. "Yer set on doing this?"

"I am, it ain't just the rustling he's got Ben's watch, but I imagine that comes as no surprise to you."

The indifference in Cyrus' voice told Jake that whatever bond they once had was now totally gone. He shook his head. "No, it doesn't"

Cyrus looked away to Pete. He said as if Jake's presence made no difference to him, "You gonna confess to killin' my son or go to yer grave a liar too?"

Pete looked at Jake and scoffed, "How can you just stand there and do nothing? This man aims to kill me. For hell sakes son, we're of the same blood."

Once again, Jake looked at his father hoping to see some hint of redemption in his demeanor but he saw only a desperate stranger trying to save his self. Jake shook his head. "I don't know you."

And then Cyrus' voice boomed, "Enough of yer sniveling, Mister. Either make yer peace with the creator or take yer chances in hell."

Pete glared at Cyrus. He was haughty and smug and cavalier, using his last breaths of life to impart a contemptuous image, he said, with a cruel smile on his face, "I believe we're going to the same place, me and you. I'll just be there ah little ahead ah you." And then he laughed.

"Yes you will," said Cyrus as he slapped the paint horse on the butt.

Jake turned away, but not before he saw his father hit the end of the rope and begin to do a dead man's mid-air jig. He pushed past the Rockin' C cowboys and began running back down the canyon, stopping twice to throw up and then he came to Rusty, mounted quickly and rode away from his past, or so he hoped.

EPILOGUE

The winter of 1886-87 was extremely bad with record snow and cold temperatures. Many ranchers who never planned for such contingencies by cutting hay in the summer to feed in the winter were nearly wiped out. Cyrus Ellsworth and the owners of the /3 were among these people. The range was littered with thousands of dead cattle, rotting in the summer sun. It was not pleasant to ride through the country. On those days when Jake's conscience badgered him about not checking to see that his father had been given a proper burial, he fell back on this depressing sight that caused the air to be filled with the smell of death and despair as his excuse for not going. He thought of the turkey vultures and ravens and what they had done to Nate and Roy and Pale Bear. His inner self shouted out to him, *Yer ah real shit heel, Jake Lafarge.* But then he wondered if his father would have done the same for him and his conscience backed off. Truth be told, he was more saddened by the fact he had lost his relationship with the only man who had ever been anything like a father to him. These thoughts, however, he generally kept at bay knowing that he and his new wife, Ellie, were expecting a child. He was excited about the prospect of becoming a father. It was a role that he was confident he could fulfill.

CPSIA information can be obtained
at www.ICGtesting.com
Printed in the USA
FSHW012133230619
59353FS